EMERGENCE

THE VALMORAN CHRONICLES

BOOK 1

POPPY ORION

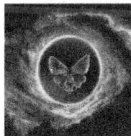

To those with the audacity to hope.

The world needs you.

Never stop.

ACKNOWLEDGMENTS

First, I absolutely must thank my daughter, Lucina, for being a sounding board and a critical, passionate alpha reader. This book would never exist without you.

To my parents and brother: Thank you for supporting my dream, even when it made very little sense to do so.

To the TVC Discord members: Thank you for being encouraging, engaged, and awesome. You often served as my muses, as I imagined how you might react to each new episode. (There may have been creepy cackling involved as I hunched over my laptop in the wee hours like a gremlin.)

To my author friends: How can I ever thank you enough for your guidance and support? The community we've built is one I never want to live without.

To my doggos, Link and Zelda: Thank you for loving me even when I'm an utterly grouchy, writers-blocked mess with bad hair. You're fuzzy, cuddly, and loyal enough that I'll overlook the fact that you lick my fingers when I'm trying to type.

And to you, dear reader: Thank you for reading TVC. It means the universe to me to share this with you. I hope you love it.

CONTENTS

THE VALMORAN CHRONICLES

PROLOGUE

[DON'T SKIP THIS. OR DO, I GUESS, IF YOU WANT TO SKIP SOMETHING AWESOME]

KATHERINE MILLER, FROM THE DISTANT FUTURE

UNKNOWN LOCATION

-AND-

PLANET KRONAI, THE NIGHT BEFORE MATTHAI VALTRELLIN'S ORDINATION CEREMONY

~

KAT'S BODY screamed with pain, muscles trembling from exhaustion. She shivered violently, wishing she could curl in on herself for warmth. But she was shit-out-of-luck thanks to the sadistic—but ingenious—mechanism her captors had devised for trapping a chronojumper.

The metallic tang of blood hung in the air. Her blood.

She could feel it oozing down her left arm, and drip, drip, dripping into the pool she couldn't see but could hear was

1

there.

The goons had left her alone, squinting against the harsh white lights above the cold metal table they'd strapped her to. She had long since given up trying to get out of her cuffs, which only had a few inches of give.

Instead, she tried to conserve her energy. And think.

The stupid restraints. Whoever these people were, they understood she could only sustain a jump through time and space for a brief period before she snapped back to her origin, naked.

The jerks rigged a table with a high-tech blanket-thing hovering over it. It slammed down over Kat's torso like saran wrap whenever she returned from a jump. Then it held her ruthlessly in place until they could re-attach these god-awful restraints to her wrists and ankles.

She never even had time to wriggle out of the way.

Then, they reset the trap, lifting the wrap off her so they could resume their 'work.'

Her captors also apparently understood they could force a chronojump by inflicting sufficient stress. So time had long since lost all meaning in this endless cycle of torture. They pushed her to the brink.

Over.

And over.

They could force her to jump, but she refused to jump to where and when they wanted. She'd die first.

Not that they'd allow it. They seemed pretty intent on keeping Kat alive.

The sound of the cursed door sliding open behind her sent a shock of reflexive panic down her entire body. She needed to stay calm, but she lost a little more of her will to fight every time they came. After all, they were only going to torture her until she jumped, anyway. And then she'd get a brief respite in the freezing lab to recover.

Panic clawed at her guts, but she remained perfectly still, watching out of the corners of her eyes. The cronies in the black full-body suits filed back into the room, each carrying their favorite torture devices like macabre toys.

They were either Valmorans or humans with access to Valmoran technology—their armor and Billy's neurowhip made that obvious.

And despite the tireless efforts of Matthai and the others, scouring the universe for any hint of her whereabouts, the few clues she'd been able to share during her jumps to them had led nowhere. Not even Vi's supernatural insight or Callum's vast network had made any headway.

Her friends still had no clue who was holding her or where in the universe she was.

She'd been spending most of her jumps at the apartment she and her sister had once shared. No need to torture Matthai and the others by forcing them to see just how often these assholes were making her jump.

Her sister, Beth, *hadn't* eaten all the cookies all those years ago.

Back then, Kat would have told anyone who tried to explain the truth—that she was traveling through time and space from the future and eating all their snacks—that the notion was insane and broke the laws of physics. But it was true, and her torturers still hadn't caught on.

You can't starve a chronojumper, dimwits.

As she braced for 'the voice,' she surveyed the four torturers who now surrounded the table.

"Hey, Edward!" she said. "Where's Boris? On break?" She nicknamed each of them, keeping track of their body language and preferred torture implements. Edward was into cutting. Boris liked to use his fists.

She was reasonably sure there were seven of them, but with their full-body zylon suits, it was hard to be sure.

They never responded—only the voice ever spoke to her. But playing this game gave her mind something to do. Plus, she didn't want to give the voice the satisfaction of seeing her broken.

She leaned towards the left, as far as her restraints would allow. "Come, now, Edward—you can tell me. We're friends, right?"

The electronic disembodied voice she'd grown to loathe rang out from the ceiling, speaking in the same clinical tone as always. "Hello, Kat. I see you've recovered nicely."

She hadn't been able to glean a damn thing from the voice. They must be using a scrambler, because she couldn't tell if it was a man, woman, or even multiple people on the other side of those speakers.

"Now, Kat. Let's try this again."

As Indiana stalked toward the table carrying the neurowhip, she had to focus on not betraying her terror. The whip, she had discovered, delivered a special kind of pain, lighting all her nerve endings on fire at once. She hadn't been able to conceal how effective it was, so they'd been using it more and more.

However, there must be some sort of safety limit, since they still relied on other, more traditional, torture.

Waterboarding, fun stuff like that.

She braced herself, focusing on the details of her old apartment, the phantom scent of Beth's vanilla candles, and the soft give of the microfiber couch. But at the last moment, she faltered and wished for ... Matthai.

Pain exploded through her as the whip made contact, incandescent agony consuming her. The world blurred and tilted, and the whine of the neurowhip deepened in pitch as her body jumped.

∼

As THE CLINICAL smells and sounds of the torture chamber faded away, the cool press of stone beneath her bare skin replaced them.

The scent of plants wafted through the air, but beneath it ran an earthy musk she would recognize anywhere in the universe.

Her heart raced. Joy and relief surged through her, momentarily eclipsing the pain. She struggled to her feet, but her tortured body refused to comply. A broken whimper tore from her throat.

The rustle of fabric and a groggy, familiar groan filled the air, a dim light illuminating the room.

"Matthai?" she said, her voice thin and trembling. It was one thing to fake strength in front of her captors. But seeing Matthai made her want to shatter into a miserable mess and let him pick up the pieces.

Her lip trembled, and she blinked, choking back the tears that threatened to break free.

It killed him to see her in pain, and it killed her to watch him agonize over her suffering.

But he only stared at her, eyes wide and jaw slack, frozen in place. She felt simultaneously relieved and guilty—jumping to him meant tormenting him with the effects of her torture ... and his inability to do a damn thing about it.

Even so, comfort surged through her at the mere sight of him.

"Matthai?" she repeated.

Gritting her teeth against the searing pain, Kat hauled herself upright, her legs trembling with the effort. Each step was agony, but she staggered forward, one excruciating foot in front of the other, until, at last, she fell into his lap.

He curled his arms around her, almost reflexively, but his expression was dazed.

"What's wrong? Where are we? Matthai?" The questions fell from her lips, but his lack of response sent a chill down her spine.

Where was the desperate embrace?

She studied Matthai's familiar yet strangely youthful face, noting the subtle differences—the sleep-mussed cobalt hair tumbling around the points of his ears, his unfamiliar sleep clothes.

His sculpted features held a wide-eyed innocence and deep sadness she hadn't seen in a long time.

Then her breath caught in her throat. This was not her Matthai.

Her power hadn't latched on to the Matthai she knew. Instead, she jumped to the innocent man he'd once been.

Of course, they had always known this would happen because, for her Matthai, it already had.

This moment had loomed over their lives like a guillotine.

This was the day he first met her, the day he learned his mate would one day be tortured, and the day his life became exquisitely complicated.

She cupped his face in trembling hands. This beautiful, lonely man. He'd been so starved for affection his whole life.

Someday soon, he would come for her, but the things that were about to happen in his life would devastate him. She ached to wrap him in her arms, to shield him from what was coming—even to warn him.

But even if she had the strength to fight the pull of this strange loop, she wouldn't.

Everything that was about to happen to him needed to happen. The next part of his life was the crucible that forged him into the man he needed to become.

His arms tightened around her with a tenderness that threatened to break her resolve.

"Matthai," she breathed, her voice breaking on his name. "By all the Gods, I love you. Even after everything, I wouldn't change a thing. Do you hear me? None of this is your fault. You're going to get through this. Come find me. I'm waiting for you."

His brow furrowed in confusion. He gently turned Kat's face to the side, fingers ghosting over the skin behind her ear.

Realization crashed through her. Those jerks had removed her Hix implant. No wonder Matthai couldn't understand her. His Hix implant didn't know English yet.

His fingers drifted to her other ear, finding only smooth skin, before tapping the Hix implant behind his ear. She remembered this part of the story—he was running a diagnostic, checking to see if the problem was on his end.

His hand skimmed the rounded shell of her ear, so different from his own, and he startled at the unfamiliar shape. A ghost of a smile tugged at Kat's lips.

Yep. Kat was indeed *not* a pointy-eared, blue-haired Valmoran. Instead, she was a non-Kronai chronojumper who defied everything Matthai understood about the universe. A human with dirty blond hair.

And right now, it was literally dirty. Not the way you hope to meet your future mate, with hair caked in ... she didn't even want to know what.

She angled her face to meet his gaze and mustered a tender smile. The way he looked at her, you'd think she was wearing a gown rather than rivulets of her own dried blood.

With shaking fingers, she pressed her palm to his chest, right above his heart. The absence of his mate mark, so vivid and precious in her memories, struck her like a physical blow. She splayed her hand and said, "Matthai."

Then she took his hand and guided it to her own mark above her heart. "Katherine," she said, though she already knew he would get it wrong.

It would take him months to break the habit of calling her 'Kat-a-reen.'

Then she pressed their joined hands more firmly against one another's hearts, knowing the next word she uttered would blow his mind and shatter his world.

"Amara." Soul of my soul. My mate.

Matthai went utterly still, wide-eyed and reverent. He grasped her hand a bit too tightly, but she ignored the stab of pain. He would remember this moment for the rest of his life.

"Amara?" he whispered, sounding almost like a question.

Or a prayer.

He wrapped his arms around her again, cradling her against his chest as if she were the most precious thing in the universe. In that moment, she watched as the truth dawned in his eyes—she would become his everything, just as he was hers.

Matthai pressed his forehead to hers, his breath warm as it ghosted over her skin.

Sorrow welled up inside her, fierce and sharp. The path stretching before him was so dark, so fraught with pain and doubt. It would be a long, arduous journey before he found his way back to her.

Matthai drew back, cradling her face in his hands. Cherishing her.

Even in this moment of shock, he was still the sweetest man she'd ever known.

He spoke to her then, his voice low and fervent. She couldn't understand his words, but knew their meaning by heart from all the times he'd recounted the story to her.

"It's going to be okay. I promise I'll find you, that I'll never stop looking."

"Kat-a-reen, my Amara," he murmured, brushing a reverent kiss against her forehead. Those words, at least, she understood. It was a ritual, one his future self maintained in their life together.

A sickening lurch in her stomach sent dread coursing through her. The end of the chronojump.

If she weren't so weak, she might have been able to extend the moment. But that would also mean altering this strange loop, and that was not something she would ever do, even if she could.

Besides, with an event so intimately tied to her life, it would be almost impossible for her to change it.

She could feel the time stream tugging her back to her origin. That cold, clinical hell. And there was nothing she could do to stop it.

"I'm sorry," she whispered, a smile tugging at her lips. "I'm sorry for how difficult I'll make it when you come to Earth to find me."

With the last of her strength, she surged forward and captured his lips with her own.

His first kiss, she knew, and perhaps her last.

She clung to him, memorizing the feel of being in his arms for what could be the last time. And then, with a sickening wrench, the time stream tore her away, ripping her out of his arms.

Hurling her back to the voice, enraged by her defiance, her refusal to bend to their will.

~

BUT EVEN AS she appeared back on the metal table and the wrap slammed down over her body, she clung to that perfect, shining moment.

As they shackled her wrists and ankles to the table, she savored the taste of Matthai on her lips.

The Matthai she had just left would cross galaxies, risk everything to find her.

Her Matthai could do it again. They just had to keep fighting.

Their story couldn't be over—they still had so much work to do.

And both of their galaxies were depending on them.

[PART 1]
PRIESTS AND POLITICIANS

THE VALMORAN CHRONICLES

DESTINY APPROACHES

VALMORAN REPUBLIC, PLANET KRONAI, TEMPLE OF THE SEVEN

MATTHAI VALTRELLIN, FUTURE HIGH PRIEST

~

MATTHAI VALTRELLIN SLAMMED into the ground, the impact driving the air from his lungs. He stared at the bright afternoon sky, struggling to catch his breath.

For a fleeting moment, he imagined lounging in the East Garden with his sister, watching the clouds and whispering secrets, the phantom scent of flowers permeating the air.

If he just glanced over, he almost believed she'd be there, grinning at him, her blue hair dancing around the gentle points of her ears in the breeze.

Reality shattered his reverie as another VIP shuttle roared overhead, casting an ominous shadow as it passed, destined for the gleaming spaceport atop Valtrellin Tower.

Another cruel reminder that he would be taking sacred vows tomorrow ... not Liyara.

It had been almost five years, but her absence still haunted him like a phantom limb.

The rustle of fabric alerted him to a figure leaning over, backlit by the blinding sun, hand outstretched. "You alright, Scion?" Priest Jarron asked, his usual stoicism replaced by a flicker of concern.

Matthai nodded and clasped his trainer's calloused hand, letting the man haul him to his feet.

"It's been a while since I landed a hit on you. Distracted?"

Matthai coughed, sweeping the dust off his blue robes while glancing around at the other adepts, searching for an appropriate response. The air crackled with excitement, strikes meeting blocks and bodies colliding with the ground. Laughter, teasing, smiles ...

Envy twisted in his gut, bitter and ugly. He forced it down. These were his people—he wouldn't begrudge their happiness.

But he wanted to run. To scream.

Then it started—a tingle at the back of his skull. An electric zing, irritating and foreboding.

His stomach dropped.

"Yeah, distracted," he said. "I'm gonna go grab a drink." Turning away, he strode toward the ancient stone wall of the training yard, praying it looked more like an athletic jog than an escape.

He was losing control of his powers.

Stress triggered his chronojumping. If he couldn't control his roiling emotions, he'd end up naked in the East Garden.

Bracing his arms against the cool bricks, Matthai commanded himself to be as steadfast as the weathered stones.

His heart raced like it was determined to flee without him, surroundings fading in and out. In and out.

Shit.

Chronojumping always took jumpers to a place and time associated with safety. For Matthai, that was the East Garden, where he and his sister used to whisper about their hopes and dreams.

His view of the wall distorted, dimensions warping out of alignment. The sounds from the training yard grew muffled, slowing and deepening in pitch.

No, no, no.

Chronojumping was instinctual—his only hope was to prevent the jump by remaining calm.

Which he was not doing.

His ears began to ring. His body quivered, losing its hold on the here and now.

Just breathe.

He refused to lose control today, of all days.

The High Priests had to present the pinnacle of poise. If he jumped now, he'd reappear naked in front of his entire training cohort. Even his parents couldn't keep that sordid story from flooding the galactic web.

"I am here. I am now. I will not jump away," Matthai whispered, reciting the mantra from his chronotraining.

He crouched down to grab his flask, then took a deep swig, the tang of metal hitting his lips.

The sleeve of his robe rasped against his skin as he wiped stray droplets away.

Chronojumping was such a useless power. A status symbol to be revered and never used.

An endless font of humiliation.

Gradually, the world refocused, the sounds of the training yard returning to normal.

"Scion."

Matthai flinched. He hadn't heard Jarron's approach.

His trainer's tone held an edge, as if he had called out several times and was growing concerned.

Matthai took a deep breath and turned to face Jarron. He leaned himself against the wall, hoping his unsteadiness wasn't noticeable.

Jarron's brow furrowed, grizzled features etched with worry. "Training you too hard, Scion? With the ceremony tomorrow, perhaps we should stop for the day."

"I'm fine—just needed a moment."

He couldn't give the priests any more reason to doubt him. Besides, maybe a decent spar would ease his tension.

But Jarron slumped against the wall and sat, snatching his own water. "You may have the right idea—you're wearing this old man out today."

Matthai huffed a laugh. "You're taking pity on me, don't think I can't tell that."

His trainer responded with a nonchalant shrug, hints of a nostalgic twinkle in his eyes.

"Big day tomorrow," Jarron said.

Matthai didn't know how to respond. The other priests knew he wasn't ready for this—he saw it on their faces every day.

The concern.

"Yes, it certainly is." Tomorrow, he would be formally recognized as the Ordained Scion, future High Priest of the Temple of the Seven. He was just a man, no different from anyone else, but the people of the galaxy would revere him as an emissary of the Gods.

The thought of being even more set apart from others filled him with dread.

Jarron's voice turned wistful. "You can almost feel the excitement in the air, you know? Everyone getting their career assignments, mating season about to begin ..."

He tilted his head towards Matthai, one side of his mouth quirked up.

"I mean, I know the next cycle doesn't begin until the babies start coming, but we're on the cusp. A new beginning is just around the corner."

Matthai flung a pebble into the dirt. "Sure. A new beginning," he echoed, forcing a smile.

For others, it was the start of their adult lives, the end of the Phase of Completion, the true mark of adulthood in the eyes of society. Their excitement was understandable.

Oblivious to Matthai's meandering thoughts, Jarron said, "I can still remember the end of my first cycle like it was yesterday ... checking out the other adepts, wondering who I'd be matched with, praying to the Gods I wouldn't get some wretched administrative duty ..."

Jarron grinned. "Can you imagine? Me, stuck in some fancy office in Valtrellin Tower?"

"I can absolutely imagine you barking orders at the poor priests in the Order of Finance," Matthai said, grinning despite himself. "I'm sure they thank the Gods you're out here, not in there."

The older man laughed. "There's a role for each of us, just a matter of matching the right priest to the right job."

There would be no matching for Matthai. No chance he would join the Order of Protection or the Order of Service. His path had been set in stone since Liyara's death five years ago: to serve as High Priest in her stead.

Finally, Jarron spoke. "Scion ... it isn't my place to ask this, but—propriety be damned, I'm asking. Are you okay?"

He had to be. As the future spiritual leader of the Valmorans, Matthai had to inspire and guide them, just as his parents and their parents before them.

"As you said, it's about matching the right person to the right duty," Matthai said, tossing another pebble into the dirt. "I'm the only one left for this role, so we're all going to have to live with it."

The bite in his tone sent a wave of shame running through him. Jarron didn't deserve his ire—he was only trying to help.

His trainer opened his mouth as if to speak, then closed it again, frowning.

"I was never suited for this," Matthai said, his sigh almost a sob. "Not like Liyara was."

Jarron's expression turned to one Matthai had grown to loathe: that helpless look everyone wore when Liyara was mentioned, the one that said, 'Your grief makes me uncomfortable, but I can't say that, so I'll just stand here awkwardly.'

He couldn't blame them, not really. It had been five years. Everyone else had moved on, and perhaps he should have, too. But letting go of his grief felt like letting go of Liyara herself, as if she'd never existed.

Jarron's face softened. "Matthai ..." He lifted a hand as if to clasp Matthai's shoulder, then hesitated.

No one touches the heir.

The hand hovered between them, a tentative question. Matthai held his breath, afraid to shatter the fragile moment.

With Liyara gone, ensuring he mated with a God-touched Kronai female to continue their bloodline was more critical than ever. Jarron and his guardians were exempt, permitted to touch him, but only for instruction and protection, never comfort. It would set a dangerous precedent.

Finally, he clasped Matthai's shoulder, giving it a reassuring squeeze.

Emotion swelled, but Matthai swallowed, clearing his throat to mask it.

Jarron withdrew his hand as if burned.

"You're a good man, Matthai—you'll find your way," Jarron said, his voice gruff as he nodded toward the other adepts. "Best get back to it. Wouldn't do for the future High Priest to go soft, now would it?"

A heavy weight settled in Matthai's chest as his trainer spun on his heel and strode back to the yard, barking, "Kreslin! Elbows in, watch your stance!"

He started after Jarron, only for an urgent notification to pop up on his Hix interface.

Matthai squeezed his eyes shut. He should have been used to this by now—it wasn't as if he had control over his time. And after tomorrow, it would only get worse. A flick of his eyes opened the message.

Please report to the Office of the High Priestess and
Priest at your earliest convenience.

His stomach sank. 'Earliest convenience' meant now.

His seven guardians were already approaching, making their way around the training yard's perimeter.

From birth, Valtrellins were assigned a dedicated guardian. For him and Liyara, it had been Talia and Janna, a mated Vraxai pair.

All Vraxai had four arms, but Talia and Janna were God-touched, so they also possessed enhanced intuition. This gave them an uncanny ability to read situations and anticipate outcomes, making them formidable bodyguards. Talia had been his shadow since birth.

After Liyara's death, his parents also assigned Janna and five more God-touched guardians to him. They were wonderful people, but having seven people dedicated to keeping him safe and untouched felt excessive, oppressive even.

"You're early," Matthai grumbled.

"Apologies, Scion." Talia handed him a heavy blue robe. "We thought you'd want to bathe before your meeting."

Matthai slipped it on over his training robe.

He wasn't ready for his last day as a normal adept to be over. Wasn't prepared for the fate that drew closer with every step, every moment.

He paused, then strode back to the center of the training yard, where Jarron stood instructing his fellow adepts. Before he could second-guess himself, he cleared his throat.

When Jarron faced him, Matthai's chest felt tight. He hadn't planned this out, but had to do something. Swallowing, he gave a slight bow. "Priest Jarron ... it's been an honor."

Before the man could respond, Matthai turned and strode away. It wasn't appropriate for the Scion to bow to a trainer, to defer to anyone. But the thought of leaving things on such a miserable note, after everything Jarron had taught him ... had felt wrong.

Talia fell into step beside him, matching his stride. "Was that wise?"

"It's fine."

She snorted, one eyebrow arched. "If you say so." Her tone added, 'We both know that's a load of dung.'

"Scion, perhaps we should take the inner path today, given the crowds and security—"

"No," he cut in. "We take the long way, as always."

She pressed her lips together but said nothing. Matthai tried to ignore the other adepts, who averted their gazes as they left the yard. They knew why he went this way.

Everyone knew.

His GUARDIANS FORMED a protective circle around Matthai, obscuring him from view as they stepped onto the wide pedestrian road that encircled the Temple's inner sanctum.

His heart raced at the massive crowds filling the usually tranquil space. The courtyard path was 200 paces wide, paved with intricate mosaics depicting Valmoran Temple history, and peppered with small flower gardens.

Today, the dense crowds almost completely obscured those details.

Anxiety and unworthiness surged as he gazed at the ocean of pilgrims.

"Do you understand now, Scion?" Talia leaned in, her voice brusque. "The crowds are unprecedented, almost twice as large as they were for your mother's Ordination. We still have time to turn back—"

"No," Matthai interrupted, voice firm. "I need this. Besides, it's good for me to see the full spectrum of my people. Nearly every subspecies is here today. Remarkable."

He stepped into the throng, his guardians 'encouraging' the eager crowd to part before them.

Matthai couldn't help but feel like an imposter, unfit for the role thrust upon him. His gaze drifted to the outer wall, its inviting arches offering glimpses of the lush gardens and winding paths beyond.

He tore his gaze from the horizon toward the seven inner towers, each signifying a critical phase in the Valmoran life cycle. They loomed above, connected to the inner wall like silent sentinels, watching over the inner sanctum. Valtrellin Tower rose from the center of the citadel, modern and sleek, standing resolutely over everything.

As he neared the Tower of Becoming, his pulse thrummed in his ears.

His guardians closed ranks around him, facing outward in a standard defensive formation, projecting the appearance of simply doing their duty.

Matthai knew better. This was the only privacy they could offer him in the bustling Temple courtyards.

Beneath his robes, he clenched his trembling fists. The scents of food and incense, the chatter and excitement, were a stark contrast to his memories of that night.

Crisp night air. Murmurs of disbelief, his gulping sobs as he collapsed onto the unyielding tiles.

If only Liyara were still here.

He could have handled this if she were still here.

But if Liyara were here, he would be her advisor as she ascended. As it should be.

"You would have been a perfect High Priestess, Li," Matthai whispered, imagining her in the High Priestess's formal robes and Zanchion, resplendent and joyful.

She would have inspired the galaxy. But that future had shattered right along with these tiles.

His eyes stung, tears threatening to break free. The urge to chronojump away, to escape, surged through him, his skin practically vibrating with it.

"I am here. I am now. I will not jump away," Matthai whispered, blinking rapidly.

His gaze again strayed to the outer wall of the citadel.

The Temple gates were wide open. He could put up his hood, walk through one of those open archways, and take a magcar into Kronai City.

Republic citizens could claim basic living expenses and free education. He could train as a botanist, gardener, maybe even a poet—and live a blissfully ordinary life.

But no—everyone knew his face. No matter how far he ran, he could never escape his birthright.

Besides, he wasn't a citizen of the Republic—he was a citizen of the Temple of the Seven. Unlike Liyara, he had never even left the grounds.

Matthai forced himself to face the last place he'd ever seen his sister.

He'd made the Order of Maintenance leave the cracked tiles un-mended, a visceral reminder. He needed the evidence, still couldn't face what had happened here. Couldn't accept it.

He couldn't let her go.

"I'm so scared, Li," he whispered. "I don't think I can do this."

His pulse quickened, cold sweat beading on his brow. He swallowed reflexively as nausea churned in his gut.

The world tilted around him, edges blurring, colors bleeding together. A too-familiar tingle began at the base of his skull, electric sparks skittering across his skin. The timbre of the sounds shifted, the pitch deepening as the world slowed.

"I am here. I am now. I will not jump away." Matthai whispered, praying that he could stave it off.

But the East Garden beckoned him, trying to wrench him away.

He would not jump. He refused—

"Scion Valtrellin!" a voice called out, the sudden distraction jolting him back.

His guardians flowed around him like water, effortlessly assuming a defensive formation. He peered through their ranks at the unfamiliar Kronai man approaching, his accent marking him as foreign.

"Halt," his first guardian commanded. "None may approach the Scion."

"Please, I must speak with him," the man implored, stepping forward again.

"Another step, and you will be restrained."

His Vultrai unfurled their ruddy wings and inclined their horns in the man's direction, a not-so-subtle reminder of the pain the God-touched of their subspecies could inflict.

The man continued forward, undeterred. Matthai's guards moved as one. Talia and Janna were a whirlwind, eight arms restraining him with practiced ease.

His Elodai guardian—gifted with empathy, said, "He means the Scion no harm, but he is agitated."

"I am not agitated!" the man said, struggling against his captors. "Scion, please! The Gods sent me a dream—I am your Amara!"

Matthai froze, his heart sinking with compassion. Another desperate soul deluded by dreams of ascending to the High Priesthood through a mating bond.

It was impossible, of course.

The man continued to struggle against Talia and Janna, heedless of the scene he was causing, the watching crowd.

His Anokai guardian approached the restrained man.

"Please, you must understand! The Gods chose me for him!" The man struggled, likely imagining she had some other, more sinister power. Anokai, Elodai, and Adorai—over a hundred Valmoran subspecies—had no distinguishing physical traits.

But his Anokai guardian only influenced emotions through touch.

She reached out and laid a gentle hand on the man's shoulder. "Calm," she said. "Be at peace, my friend."

This was the playbook. The two Vultrai stood ready to unleash pain should the man turn violent. But they often resolved such incidents peacefully—restrain, assess, influence, and remove.

Matthai felt a sudden urge to do ... something. "A moment," he said, holding up a hand.

His first guardian threw him a disapproving glare but didn't challenge him. Not publicly, never where others could see.

"Let him stand," Matthai said, stepping closer.

Talia's jaw tightened, but she and Janna hauled the man upright, keeping him firmly in their grasp. Matthai approached, staying out of reach but near enough to talk privately.

This close, he recognized the man's clothing and violet eyes as marks of a Zeltai monk. They followed a false prophecy of the Jubilant One, who would mate into the Valtrellin High Priesthood and become the Herald of the 4th Epoch.

Matthai's heart ached for the man. Powerful faith and fierce devotion drove him to this delusion.

"Your name?"

"Kiran of Zeltix, Scion," the man replied, reverence and wonder shining in his eyes.

"Kiran, you know the Gods must choose a God-touched Kronai female for me during the Season of Debauchery. They have a different path for you. Trust in their wisdom."

The words almost stuck in his throat. Mates were forged by skin contact. Creating a list of 'approved' mates for Matthai—and ensuring he touched no one else—had always felt like trying to control the will of the Gods, almost an unspoken blasphemy.

Kiran's shoulders sagged, eyes downcast. "But the dream, Scion ... it was so vivid."

Matthai's heart ached. Kiran's people were probably back on Zeltix, celebrating the fulfillment of their ill-fated prophecy.

He reached out, hovering his hand over the man's head, ignoring his guardians' sharp inhales at Matthai's proximity to the pilgrim. "Kiran, child of the Gods, may your upcoming Season of Debauchery be fruitful and joyous. May the Gods gift you with companionship and love."

The words felt hollow, a script he had memorized, recited a thousand times. What right did he have to bestow blessings on anyone? He was no God, just a man.

"Thank you, Scion," Kiran whispered, tears brightening his eyes. "I will strive to trust in your wisdom."

At Matthai's nod, his Adorai guardian led Kiran away. He watched them go, a weary shame settling over him. This would be his future.

An impostor pretending to be a spokesperson for the Gods. A fraud.

Liyara had been the one who shone, the one most beloved by their people. The Bright Scion, they'd called her, not knowing her inner sadness, since she hid it so well. She'd always been able to cope, as long as she had Matthai to confide in, and could sneak out into the city.

The people had adored her.

He forced himself to face the mosaic tiles and crouched to trace his fingers over the fractured pattern. Liyara was gone. Truly gone.

When he stood, his features had smoothed into a mask of perfect composure. He betrayed no hint of the macabre memory that was forever seared into his mind's eye.

Liyara's blood on the mosaic tiles, blooming around her head like a terrible flower.

~

AFTER A QUICK RINSE in his private bathing pool, Matthai went to the High Priests' wing of the administration tower. Since the inner priests' sanctum was so well secured, it was just him and Talia.

The floors beneath his feet were smooth and cold, their polished surface reflecting the bright overhead lights. The crisp, clean scent of modern architecture filled his nostrils, so different from the earthy aromas in the more ancient parts of the Temple complex.

He missed the pungent scent of life—flowers, dust, even decay. He realized he was imagining the East Garden and caught himself. His body had been threatening to jump away all day, and he couldn't allow himself to imagine the peacefulness of the garden.

His footsteps echoed in the empty halls, bouncing off the sleek walls and high ceilings.

The High Priests' floor of Valtrellin Tower was mostly empty. His parents' rooms were just down the hall, as were the rooms he would soon be forced to take. The thought made his stomach twist.

He hesitated when they reached the sliding door to his parents' private receiving rooms. What could they want with him now, so close to the ceremony?

His hands shook, cold sweat beading on his temples. His nerves were flayed, exposed.

"Matthai ..." Talia whispered. "Maybe you should just let it happen."

His heart sank. Even Talia doubted him.

He shook his head, frustration mounting. "And have the entire galaxy whisper about it?"

"People will understand," she insisted, eyes darting along the corridor. "Your parents will ensure it never reaches the media."

He followed her gaze to a shadowed alcove. Perhaps he should allow it. It could be handled discreetly, with no witnesses here and only the gardeners and guards in the privacy of the East Garden.

"No, It's bad enough that everyone thinks I don't have what it takes," he said, his voice strained. "I won't prove them right."

"Scion, a chronojump is hardly proof that you're unfit to lead," Talia said. "Let me inform them of a delay."

Perfect. Now Talia was offering to lie to his parents to cover for him. He was already shaping up to be an outstanding future High Priest.

"No." Jumping was proof he wasn't in control. His parents' concern over him was constant and had been since Liyara's death. He was their only choice, but hadn't been their first choice. "I'll be fine."

She pursed her lips, but nodded. "I'll wait for you here, then."

Matthai took a deep breath, then straightened his posture, squaring his shoulders as if he could physically prepare himself for what was on the other side of that door.

With a sense of trepidation, he authenticated his identity via Hix. The doors slid open silently. Matthai steeled himself, then stepped inside, his footsteps echoing in the stillness of the room as he fought the urge to fidget.

His parents rose to greet him, their expressions a mix of solemnity and concern. They ushered him towards the sitting room overlooking the Temple grounds. Silence stretched between them as they walked, unspoken words hanging heavy in the air.

Their formal robes and the ceremonial tea felt like an ill omen.

Matthai's anxiety intensified with every step, stomach twisting into knots as he tried to guess the purpose of this unusual meeting.

High Priest Soren Valtrellin was commanding, as always, his cobalt hair pulled into a low knot and angular brows lending an air of harshness. But his appearance belied the fact that he was the gentler parent.

In contrast, High Priestess Phina Valtrellin was almost ethereal, her deep blue hair in looping braids that framed the delicate points of her ears. A deceptive softness. She wasn't unkind, just unyielding in her role as High Priestess.

They settled into their seats, the rustling of fabric and clink of teacups the only sounds in the room. Matthai's heart pounded as he prayed for someone to break the oppressive silence.

"Your schedule for tomorrow's ceremonies," his mother said. "You have reviewed it?"

Matthai nodded. "I will accompany Father to meet Representative Torion in the late morning. Then, I will dress for the ceremony in my chambers. Following that, my procession to the cathedral, the vows before the Obelisk, then before the galaxy. Finally, the ceremonial feast."

Phina nodded, her expression unreadable. She exchanged a glance with Soren, a silent communication passing between them that set Matthai's nerves on edge.

After a pause that felt like an eternity, Soren cleared his throat, his expression grave. "Matthai, the High Priests of the First Temple have served as faithful guardians of the Obelisks for 217 generations, a sacred duty passed down through the Valtrellin line. We guide the High Priests of every Temple and serve as the aspirational ideal of poise and morality for all Valmorans."

His father, so empathetic, was often the bearer of bad news. That he was delivering this rigid and ominous preamble was far from comforting.

Matthai braced himself, curling his fingers into the sides of his robe.

Soren paused, setting aside his teacup with a deliberate clink. "We also protect them from knowledge that would do them harm."

A chill zipped down Matthai's spine, the fine hairs on the back of his neck standing up.

"What ..." Matthai began, his voice wavering. "What does that even mean?"

Soren sighed with a depth of weariness he had never heard from his father.

"Son, I won't lie to you—our secrets are a tremendous burden, sometimes almost a prison, but ..."

That telltale tingle at the back of his skull returned. *No.*

"You are our sole heir. If circumstances were different, if you had a sibling ..." His father blinked his eyes rapidly and cleared his throat.

"Now that you know that the Valtrellin High Priesthood carries secrets—some of which you will find shocking, unbelievable, and excruciating ..." he trailed off, then looked at his mate. "When your mother showed them to me, I might have run myself if not for our bond."

Phina Valtrellin reached out to squeeze Soren's hand, guilt and sadness written across her face. "But as you will learn, our unspoken duties are essential to the survival of all Valmorans."

Matthai couldn't help the perverse curiosity that rose. What could be so terrible, so essential?

"Selfish as it may be, we refuse to lose our only remaining child." His mother said, voice brimming with emotion. "You are more precious to us, Matthai, than you could ever comprehend."

To Matthai's astonishment, a tear slipped down her cheek.

"These loathsome secrets will not steal you from us. I won't allow it. So, if you believe you cannot bear this," Phina said. "We will find another way."

They were giving him an escape. They knew how much he struggled—

—no. He was the sole remaining heir, the last in an unbroken line. His parents could hope for another child in the next fertile season, but it was unlikely.

Breaking the line of succession would defy generations of sacred tradition. The scandal would rock the foundations of their faith, and the blame would fall squarely on his shoulders.

He couldn't fail them, couldn't put them in such an impossible situation.

The tingle at the back of his skull became incessant.

Clawing, demanding.

He didn't want this—would never deserve or desire such a lofty role.

But this wasn't about what he wanted. It was about the Valmoran people.

The weight of his future—the near-worship he would forever endure, the responsibility for leading trillions of Valmorans, these ominous secrets—threatened to crush him. To swallow him whole.

The ringing in Matthai's ears thrummed, the world tilting around him.

I am here. I am now. I will not jump away.

It was his duty to ascend as the next High Priest, 217th in an unbroken line.

His fate.

He had to do this, for the people, for his family, for the Gods.

Matthai parted his lips, determined to pledge himself to that sacred duty—

～

—AND INSTEAD FELT the world splinter around him as the chronojump finally claimed him.

Cool air caressed his bare skin as he appeared in the East Garden.

Just a man, feet planted firmly against the ground, rich soil sifting between his toes. A creature amid the beauty of flourishing plants and life.

Here, he was safe.

If not for his shame, he might have collapsed in relief.

"Oh, my sweet boy! Did it happen again?" Miral, their venerable gardener, hurried over to him, carrying an all-too-familiar robe.

"It's a bit musty, but I still keep it here, just in case." She wrapped it around him as she spoke. "Do you want to talk for a few minutes before you jump back?"

Humiliation burned through Matthai, icy and searing. Minutes from now, he would snap back—naked, head pounding—to face his parents' disappointment.

He knew what they must be saying to one another. What if he lost control tomorrow, with the entire galaxy watching?

THE VALMORAN CHRONICLES

2

THE IMPOSSIBLE MEETING

VALMORAN REPUBLIC, PLANET KRONAI, TEMPLE OF THE SEVEN

MATTHAI VALTRELLIN, FUTURE HIGH PRIEST

~

MATTHAI'S private chambers felt smaller than usual when he stepped through the door that evening. He slipped off his adept's robes and hung them in the wardrobe next to the ceremonial robes he would wear tomorrow, his gut twisting at the sight of them.

A familiar sense of relief washed over him as the cool air hit his naked body.

Stripped of his robes, he was no longer Scion Matthai Valtrellin, 217th generation in an unbroken line of High Priests, sole heir to an entire religion.

He was just Matthai.

The day's events weighed on his mind. He frowned, remembering how disastrously it had ended, but pushed thoughts of his accidental chronojump out of his mind. Unfortunately, there weren't many positive things to focus on instead.

Tomorrow, he would become even more of an outsider than he already was, his new role as the Ordained Scion setting him apart from his peers. People would give him a wide berth, not because of some rule his parents had made, but out of reverence for the High Priest of the First Temple.

The galaxy would treat him like a precious relic to be admired from a distance.

Thoughts of tomorrow—donning the ceremonial robes, attendants weaving the heavy silver Zanchion into his hair, the long, lonely procession to the cathedral—pressed at the edges of his mind.

Crossing the room to enter his private bathing room, he used his Hix to fill the tub with water at his preferred temperature. Before he reached the edge, he undid the low knot that had secured his hair, shaking it out and releasing a deep breath as it fell over his shoulders.

He descended the stairs into the small bathing pool and sighed, his tense muscles easing as he sank into the warm water. Crossing to sit on an underwater bench, he reached for the soap, dispensing the cool cream into his hands and working it to a silky lather before massaging it into his long tresses.

As Matthai leaned back in the heptagonal bathtub, his gaze drifted over the intricate mosaics adorning the seven walls, each depicting one of the seven phases of Valmoran life in vivid color.

This bathing room, the entire Temple, and all of Valmoran society were reflections of that seven-phase rhythm.

He reached out and ran his fingers over the tiles along the tub's edge, tracing their eternal cycle—Fertility, Beginnings, Discovery, Stability, Becoming, Completion, and Debauchery. The pattern repeated along the entire rim of the bathtub, just as the phases repeated with each generation of Valmorans.

His fingers traced over the red and orange tiles of Fertility and Beginnings, the two phases that made up the season of birth. Matthai remembered very little of those early cycles. He hadn't been born until the middle of the season of Fertility, and Liyara hadn't come until the start of Beginnings.

Lingering over the yellow tile of Discovery, he recalled the most carefree and innocent part of his life. Matthai hadn't yet understood how different he was, and he and Liyara still had time to play before their studies consumed all their time.

He walked his fingers forward to the green tile of Stability, the phase when the truth of his birthright had sunk in. They had begun to prepare him in earnest to become Liyara's future advisor. It was also when her spark had started to fade.

When he got to the sky blue tile, representing Becoming, he hesitated, as always. Liyara had grown melancholy and rebellious during the Phase of Becoming, sneaking into the city and getting Matthai to cover for her.

Until that night, at the end of the phase during their Ceremony of Becoming, when she had fallen from the Tower of Becoming.

If it weren't so terrible, it might have been poetic.

Next was the indigo tile for Completion, the phase now coming to a close, one shadowed by ever-present grief and endless studies as they readied him for his new role as heir.

Finally, the violet tile of Debauchery—also known as mating season—the time when mate bonds were forged. He'd never lived through a mating season. His parents intended to make a spectacle of it by bringing the Kronai females from his list of potential mates to the Temple, and inviting the media to observe the proceedings.

But that was a problem for the future, since it wouldn't occur until the middle of the next phase.

He continued to trace over the patterns, endless cycles composed of the seven phases of life.

Valmorans lived by the cycles, worshipped by the cycles—an infinite sequence of phases, each flowing into the next, creating a never-ending whole.

They were born together, found their vocations and mates, and began a new generation together, a synchronized society across the hundreds of Valmoran worlds.

But while the others fit seamlessly into the grand design, Matthai felt ... broken. Separate. Alone.

He felt a twinge of guilt at his own self-pity. The out-cyclers had it so much worse than he did. Those poor souls were, for unknown reasons, born outside of the season of birth.

And he would meet with one of the most famous out-cyclers tomorrow before his ceremony.

Callum Torion.

You would have to live on an edge planet to not know who Representative Torion was. Most representatives kept a low profile, reporting to their ansibles and waiting for the AI Council to pull them into various debates. Representative Torion was more vocal and created a loyal following with his incisive series of vids on injustice.

Callum wasn't just born out-of-cycle—he was born radically out-of-cycle. When he was born, everyone else was already a teen.

Like most out-cyclers, his family had shipped him to the out-cycler ward in Kronai City as a baby. While everyone else was preparing for their first mating season, Callum was still a youth.

A radical out-cycler like Callum would have been painfully 'other' everywhere he went. He was between generations, forever set apart.

He would understand what it felt like to walk through crowds, surrounded by people, and still be lonesome.

Born into the Valtrellin dynasty, Matthai had always been set apart from his peers—both revered and isolated simply because of the blood that ran through his veins.

Many people still reviled out-cyclers like Callum. He was, to many, untouchable, because of *when* he was born.

In a way, they were both outsiders by circumstances of birth.

Perhaps Callum would prove to be a kindred spirit.

Matthai hoped they would at least find common ground, since Callum Torion would be his lifelong advisor on matters of Temple and State.

~

After his bath, Matthai donned a soft pair of sleep trousers and a lightweight sleeping robe. They were silky and cool against his skin, refreshing after his hot bath.

His stomach growled, reminding him he had skipped dinner. After convincing his parents he would not be chronojumping away during tomorrow's ceremony, he hadn't had much appetite.

It was going to be a long night on an empty stomach.

As he debated whether to call the kitchen to see if they had leftovers, there was a knock at the door.

He knew who it would be, since Talia would have sent anyone else away. At this time of night, Talia and his parents were the only ones who would dare knock on his door, and he knew his parents were busy entertaining foreign dignitaries.

The savory scent of fried draffla and mashed gon root struck him when he opened the door.

"You didn't," Matthai said.

"I did," Talia said, grinning at him.

Now that they were out of earshot of others, they could speak plainly. Well, somewhat. She still worked for his parents, so he had to watch what he shared with her.

"You have to eat. We've been worried about you. Anyway, Janna's busy tonight, and I could use some company. Mind if I come in?"

"Sure," he said, spirits lifting. His favorite food and a conversation with Talia sounded like a welcome distraction.

"I'm fine, by the way," he said, leading her into the room.

Talia entered after him, but stopped before she'd made it two paces in. "Gods and Obelisks, that's a lot of plants," she muttered before returning her attention to Matthai. "You're obviously not fine, since you ..."

"Jumped?" Matthai cut in. He buried his face in his hands, shaking his head. "Ugh, don't remind me."

She laughed good-naturedly. "Hey, at least you got it out of your system, right? Okay if I set this on your desk? *Literally* every other surface is covered with plants."

He murmured his assent before lifting his head. "Sometimes I wish my power was more useful, like yours." Bitterness seeped into his tone as he continued, "My superpower is accidentally showing up naked in the East Garden, then snapping back with a crushing headache."

She shot him a stern look. "Don't let anyone hear you talking like that. That's a gift from the Gods."

He sighed, feeling a twinge of shame at his outburst. "You're right. It's just been a struggle."

"I know," Talia said, her face drawn into a pained smile. "We miss her, too."

"Thanks, that means a lot. I just can't stop thinking ..." he shook his head. "I wasn't suited for this, not like Liyara."

Talia furrowed her brows. "Liyara was ... special to many of us, but ..." she looked up at the ceiling and heaved a breath. "And it's not that I'm speaking ill of the dead, but ..."

Matthai took pity on her. "It's okay, Talia, I know you cared about her. What are you trying to say?"

Talia lowered her gaze and looked him in the eyes. "It's just that ... you seem to have this idea that she was perfect, that you're somehow inferior. Liyara was many things—joyful, infectious, willful, a complete pain in the ass ... you know it was Janna who had to run after her all those times, right?"

Matthai chuckled. "Yeah."

"And remember the times you got in trouble for covering for her?"

Matthai nodded. "But still ..."

"But nothing," Talia said. "We miss her, too, but you're not some poor replacement for a mythical perfect Scion. You're going to make a wonderful High Priest in your own right.

And you might not like to hear it, but I think you're more suited for the role than Liyara ever was."

He opened his mouth to protest, but Talia held up a hand to stop him. "I've said my piece. Now, let's eat." She smiled, "And then I thought we could watch that new Legends adaptation to get your mind off things."

The tips of Matthai's ears twitched with interest. "Which one? The one with the Feralix or the one about the lost homeworld?"

"Well, we could watch whichever one you want, but I was thinking of the one with the Feralix."

Of course, Talia would go for the thriller. But it would be an effective distraction. "That's fine with me." He crossed the room to his small table, which was almost entirely covered with potted cloria blooms and horticulture texts, as Talia had so mockingly pointed out.

He hadn't been prepared to entertain, since he'd been in the middle of a new batch of cross-breeds. This breed of luminescent blue cloria flowers grew but refused to blossom in their climate.

Once, he and Liyara had dreamed of visiting the garden at night, illuminated by the intricate blue flowers. He hoped one of these varieties would finally work out.

"You're still at it?" Talia said, reaching out as if to stroke the petals of one. "You'll need to get these packed up soon."

Matthai swatted her hand away, then picked the plant up to move to his desk so they could eat. "I'm not letting anyone but Miral or me touch these. They're delicate."

"I see how it is," she teased. "Well, Scion, can I at least help you move these books to the desk?"

He chuckled. "Of course, but don't close the ones I left open unless they have a bookmark, and don't stack the open ones on top of one another."

"Got it," she said, and they moved everything from the table to the desk. Matthai headed for his bathing chamber to grab a cleansing rag to wipe off the table.

Talia shouted from the other room, "I'm looking forward to the move."

"Don't remind me. I like it here. It's simple," Matthai called back, re-entering the main room and moving to clean the plant detritus from the small table.

He finished wiping it clean and retrieved the food containers from his desk. His stomach gave an involuntary rumble as he sat down and opened his food.

Talia sat and grabbed the second container, dragging it in front of her and opening it. "Janna's already got everything packed. I had to pull my work shoes out of a box this morning."

Matthai knew the mashed gon root was likely the better place to start, since it would be cool enough to eat. But the crispy draffla smelled too delicious to ignore. He took a tentative bite, recoiling and blowing on it when he learned it was, in fact, far too hot.

"Where is Janna?" he asked.

"Oh, she's helping your parents with foreign dignitaries." She heaved a breath. "She got stuck with Vargus Trix's delegation."

"My parents invited *him*? Why?" Vargus Trix, mob boss and de facto leader of the pleasure planet, was not exactly the pious sort.

"Beats me. But I know Janna will be thrilled to see him go. He's ... fond of his gladiators."

Talia hung her head, suddenly intent on her dinner. Her subspecies, the Vraxai, were prized not only as bodyguards, but as gladiators. There was a long and wretched history of Vraxai children being snatched by slavers and sold on Ioria Prime to be trained as gladiator slaves. After a near miss, her mate Janna's parents brought their daughter to the Temple for sanctuary.

The practice was barbaric.

Slavery was ancient history in the Republic and had been abolished even in the Federation generations ago.

Ioria Prime was another matter.

He shook his head. "Seriously, why would we invite someone like him?"

She snorted. "Politics, I'm sure."

"Yeah ... probably." He wasn't privy to that sort of thing yet. Scions lived with the other adepts, getting the same training, eating the same simple food, and living in the basic stone dormitories. The only difference was some of his classes.

Matthai had a much heavier course load than most adepts.

"Ready to watch the vid?" Talia piped up, clearly wanting to change the subject.

Matthai nodded and pulled some cushions out from under his bed, giving each a firm smack and kicking up small puffs of dust.

Poor Janna, having to serve a monster like Vargus Trix.

A wry smile tugged at his lips as he arranged the cushions in front of the bed, remembering Janna's sharp tongue. She was probably literally biting it to keep from giving Vargus a tongue-lashing.

"Ready for the Feralix vid?" she asked. "We can watch the gooey romantic one, if you'd rather."

Matthai shook his head, a soft chuckle escaping his lips. "The creepy Feralix one is fine."

"You won't get too scared?" she teased, poking him in the side like she had when he was a child.

Matthai rolled his eyes at her.

As Matthai and Talia synced their Hix devices, firing up simultaneous 3D displays, Matthai had a sudden realization.

His parents wouldn't have put his personal guardians on duty with dignitaries, which meant Janna had volunteered. She may have had her reasons, but he was almost certain that part of it was to give Talia an excuse to spend the evening with him.

His heart warmed with affection for Talia and Janna. Sometimes, it felt like they knew him better than his own parents.

Matthai used his Hix to dim the lights, grabbed a blanket off his bed, and wrapped it around himself. He released a deep breath as he and his first guardian settled in to watch a creepy vid about a space monster who tortured adventurers on an expedition to find a secret homeworld.

He almost felt like an ordinary man, watching a vid with a companion, spooking at the scary parts. As the vid ended, Matthai savored the fleeting sense of normalcy that had settled over the evening. Talia excused herself for the night, explaining that Janna had just gotten off her shift and was fixing to vent about Vargus Trix.

It was so gloriously mundane that he wished he could freeze time and prevent the sun from creeping around the planet. As he crawled into bed, his heart sank into the mattress.

The next day, Matthai would become holy in the eyes of the galaxy and lonelier than ever.

This was his last night before the galaxy put him on a pedestal he had neither earned nor desired, and one from which he could never step down, only fall.

Sleep eluded him, his mind racing with thoughts of the impending ceremony and the weight of his new responsibilities. He tossed and turned, the luxurious bedding offering little comfort as he grappled with the reality that his life would never be the same.

∾

MATTHAI JOLTED AWAKE, his heart pounding as his eyes snapped open.

A muffled sound pulled him from his slumber, and he blinked, trying to orient himself in the darkened room.

As his eyes adjusted to the dim light, he made out a small, huddled figure in the corner of his room, shaking and whimpering.

Matthai's mind raced, trying to make sense of the situation. No one should have been able to enter his chambers, especially not undetected.

A sudden, impossible thought struck him. The figure had to be a chronojumper—it was the only explanation for their presence in his heavily guarded room.

Chronojumpers only ever jumped to their past or future self, or to a place they had been before that felt safe. There was only one exception: they could jump to their mates, another place of safety. But that was impossible. This jumper couldn't be ...

The figure let out a whimper of pain.

Driven by a sudden sense of urgency, Matthai used his Hix to raise the lights, illuminating the room in a soft glow.

It was ... a woman. She was wounded, with bloody gashes and bruises all over her. She looked too thin to be healthy, and her hair was tangled and dirty.

Matthai's heart clenched at the sight of her battered form, a wave of compassion and protectiveness surging through him.

And she was mated—the mark above her left breast made that clear.

Instead of silvery skin and bluish hair, her skin was a shade of tan, and her hair looked like pale gold, though right now, it was caked in blood, so it was hard to be sure.

Matthai furrowed his brows.

The woman's appearance raised more questions than answers. She was unlike any Kronai he had ever seen, yet she possessed the ability to chronojump—an ability exclusive to his subspecies.

"Matthai?" She whispered, though it sounded like she didn't trust the word even as she said his name.

Shock rippled through him at the sound of his name on her lips.

His mind raced, trying to make sense of the impossible. How could she know his name? Why did she seem so familiar with him, when he was sure he had never seen her before?

He watched as a wave of emotions crossed her lovely face. Confusion, recognition, hope, relief, and finally, resolve.

Matthai barely had time to ponder the situation before she scrambled across the room and straight into his arms. She slid into his lap, her knees straddling his thighs.

Her sudden actions left Matthai breathless, his senses over-whelmed. The heat of her skin, the weight of her body against his—it was all too much and not enough at the same time.

His heart raced, his skin tingling where her body pressed against him. Every nerve seemed to come alive, electrified by her touch.

She felt ... familiar. No, it was more than that—she felt *essential*.

Every rational thought urged him to push her away, maintaining the distance befitting his station. But as he gazed into her eyes, Matthai found himself powerless to resist the pull he felt toward this mysterious woman.

Instead, his arms wrapped around her delicate frame. She fit perfectly, as if she belonged there.

Her eyes were red and glossy, like she had been crying. She started speaking to him, her voice imploring and urgent, but in a language he didn't understand.

Matthai couldn't make out a word she was saying, apart from his name, which she kept repeating as if invoking it could somehow force his mind to understand her words.

Frustration gripped him as he struggled to comprehend her foreign tongue. He should have understood her—his Hix was programmed for all Valmoran languages.

She was desperate to tell him something.

A troubling thought occurred to him, and he reached out to check behind her right ear, searching for the telltale bump of a Hix implant. His fingers met only smooth skin, marred by a jagged scar. Matthai's eyebrows shot up in surprise.

He checked behind her other ear. Maybe they had implanted it on the other side? But there was nothing there, either, not even a scar.

The absence of a Hix implant only deepened the mystery surrounding the woman. Who was she, and where had she come from?

Then, Matthai noticed her ears—hers were cute and rounded, whereas those of a Kronai were long and delicately pointed.

The woman turned her head back to him, a sad smile on her lips. She stopped speaking and caught his gaze. Then she took his hand in hers, pressed it to his chest, and said, "Matthai."

Lost in her gaze, he nodded.

She moved his hand to her chest and said, "Kat-a-reen."

That must be her name. He attempted to repeat it, clumsily, and she smiled.

Kat-a-reen pressed his palm harder into her chest, right above her heart, right over her mate mark. Then she spoke a single word, one that filled Matthai with joy and terror.

One word that shattered the perfect future everyone had planned for him.

The word that changed everything.

"Amara."

Amara. Soul of my soul. My mate.

This woman, Kat-a-reen, was his mate—he could feel it. His skin warmed and sparked, as if he was standing too close to a ceremonial fire.

She took his hand from her chest and moved to press it above his heart, but for a moment, she stared at him in apparent confusion. It looked like she was searching for a mate mark, but of course, it wasn't there.

Of course, he didn't have a mate mark.

Although Kat-a-reen acted like she knew him intimately, and had known him well enough to jump to him, this was the first time that Matthai was meeting her.

Oddly, Kat-a-reen didn't appear surprised. She had composed herself.

If she knew him well enough to jump to him, but he didn't know her, there was only one explanation. It was an impossible explanation, but it was the only thing that made any sense.

This girl, who was not a Kronai Valmoran and did not speak any known Valmoran language—somehow could jump through time and space, but her ability far exceeded any Kronai in recorded history.

Somehow, in her panic, his mate had jumped to him from the distant future.

Matthai would never have believed it if it hadn't been happening before his eyes. Even now, it felt more like a dream than reality.

And yet, Kat-a-reen rested her hand above his heart and stared into his eyes.

Matthai grasped her hand. "Amara?" he asked, his voice breaking.

She nodded. Kat-a-reen gave him a wan smile, but tears shone in her eyes.

The sorrow in her expression tore at Matthai's heart. He ached to take away her suffering, to shelter her from whatever horrors had driven her to seek solace in his arms. His mind raced with questions, with the desperate need to understand, to help, to protect.

Matthai pressed his forehead to hers and curled his arms around her. She was his mate, the most important thing in the universe.

And he was failing her. Just like he had failed Liyara.

And like Liyara, Kat-a-reen was broken and bloodied. But she was still alive, he reminded himself. He still had time to figure out how to save her—a lot of time, if he had to guess.

A sickening realization settled in his gut. Kat-a-reen had sought him out in her time of need, but he was not the man she had hoped to find. Not yet.

The Matthai he was right now ... he was utterly useless to her.

Soon, she would snap back to the time and place she had come from, where someone was hurting her, but Matthai wasn't sure he could help her. He didn't even know where to look, let alone save her from whatever this was. The least he could do was offer her some comfort before she returned to that horror.

It was the only thing he could do.

He pulled back and cupped her cheeks with his hands. She wouldn't understand his words, but he wanted to reassure her somehow, so he spoke to her, hoping the look in his eyes, the tone of his voice would mean something to her.

"Kat-a-reen, my Amara," He kissed her forehead.

Matthai's heart ached with a fierce protectiveness he had never known before. This woman, his mate, had endured unimaginable horrors, and he was powerless to stop it. A swell of emotions surged through him—desperation, fear, longing, and above all, an overwhelming need to shelter her, to take away her pain.

He cradled her face in his hands, his thumbs sweeping away the tears that spilled down her cheeks. In that moment, nothing else mattered—not his impending Ordination, not the expectations of his family and his people, not the scandal that would surely follow.

All that mattered was the woman in his arms, the other half of his soul.

Her desperate expression told him they didn't have long—like him, she must have felt when her jumps were about to end.

Matthai needed to reassure her. "It's going to be okay. I promise I'll find you, that I'll never stop looking. I—"

Suddenly, she leaned in to press her lips to his, and, for a heartbeat, there was softness and warmth. Connection. He grasped her tighter, as if he could keep her there by sheer force of will.

And for a fleeting instant, everything was right in the universe.

In that moment, Matthai understood with startling clarity that his life was forever changed. This woman, Kat-a-reen, was his destiny, his future. He would tear the universe apart to find her if that was what it took to keep her safe.

And then—nothing.

His arms collapsed in on themselves. Kat-a-reen was gone, the warmth of her skin replaced by cold, empty space.

Matthai choked back tears. For a moment, it had felt like he knew who Matthai Valtrellin was supposed to be, that he knew his true purpose in life, before it had been ripped away.

Kat-a-reen had returned to some terrible place, wherever and whenever she was, and he had no way of finding her.

Despair threatened to engulf him, but he refused to let it consume him. He had to be strong, for Kat-a-reen's sake. Matthai had to save her, no matter the cost.

Bloody smears painted his skin. But the most remarkable, astounding thing was the mate mark forming on his chest, right above his heart.

Right where Kat-a-reen had expected it to be.

His chest tightened with a newfound sense of purpose. He would find her, no matter what it took. But how in the galaxy was he going to explain this?

Kat-a-reen wasn't Kronai; worse, this was an out-of-cycle mating. A thousand Kronai females were on his list of potential matches, waiting until the Phase of Debauchery to see who would become the next High Priestess.

It would be none of them.

Matthai's High Priestess was a beautiful, terrifying enigma— and she needed him.

Scandals, expectations, and politics aside, his mate was a chronojumper from the future. Future Kat-a-reen was being tortured, and he had no clue where to find the present version of her.

The entire galaxy would watch him take his vows tomorrow, and all he wanted was to find someone, anyone, with a ship, answers ... something. He had only just met Kat-a-reen, and already, her absence was tangible.

Matthai had never yearned to abandon his duties more.

THE VALMORAN CHRONICLES

[3]
THE OUTSIDER, LOOKING IN

VALMORAN REPUBLIC, PLANET KRONAI, VALMAR CITY

CALLUM TORION, REPRESENTATIVE ARBITER FOR THE VALMORAN REPUBLIC

~

CALLUM SAT STOICALLY in the conference room where he had been tucked away.

Inside, he seethed.

The Central Director of Occupation and Education was late. It had taken forever for his AI to hound her into this meeting. All that time and two cancellations later, she was late.

Quite late.

He was beginning to suspect the woman had something to hide.

This visit should have been routine. As the Director of OccEd for the entire Valmoran Republic, the woman should have ordered a root cause analysis as soon as her office delivered the report on Occupational Participation.

After all, they didn't have forever to address any systemic issues they uncovered—mating season was just around the corner. Afterward, the whole grand circle of Valmoran life would begin again.

It meant they had only about five Kronai years before the first children of the next generation—those born at the 'proper' time—began to join their society. If they hadn't addressed any gross inequalities by then, those inherent in the system would persist and fail this upcoming generation, too.

Callum shook his head, willing his fury to dissipate as the door to the conference room slid open. He stood when the Director entered, and she took a reflexive step back.

"No need to stand on ceremony. I apologize for my tardiness." She gave him a wide berth as she skirted the room's edge and sat on the opposite side of the table.

He didn't have to use his empathic senses to know what she was feeling—disgust.

And now he knew what sort of despicable he was dealing with.

It was a myth that being born out-of-cycle was contagious, as if touching him would cause her body to revolt against the natural order of things. It wouldn't—she clearly hadn't watched the vid where Callum interviewed one of the Republic's foremost specialists on Valmoran reproduction.

Ironically, the only difference between out-cycle and in-cycle Valmorans was a higher chance of being God-touched for out-cyclers.

Either Director Avros was ignorant of the truth, or her prejudice ran too deep for it to matter.

He also couldn't call her out on her bigotry. He didn't want to risk giving away his secret—no one but his ward-sister Zalila knew Callum had been born God-touched.

His undisclosed ability to sense the emotions of others was quite a boon for a politician, and he concealed his God-touched status like a precious jewel.

"Representative Arbiter Torion ..." she began, then flicked her eyes to read something on her Hix.

Her use of the most formal version of his title and name did not surprise him. The woman was being technically respectful while distancing herself from the taint—*him*—as much as she could.

It didn't bother him anymore—he had been dealing with people like her his whole life.

"... I see you have requested additional investigation. We at OccEd believe you should consider the results in another way. Rather than focusing on isolated pockets of minor inequality which could theoretically still exist in the Republic, we should focus on the overall cycle-over-cycle improvement, which, you may note, was six percent."

Her face was blank, but her emotions were loud and clear—superiority, pride, and annoyance.

Callum wanted to smile in victory.

He could work with pride.

"Director Avros, you misunderstand my purpose. I do not mean to diminish your department's impressive accomplishments over the past cycle. A six percent improvement within a single generation is commendable indeed.

"My purpose is to *partner* with your office by providing a platform for amplifying your past and future successes. As I'm sure you are aware, OccEd's mission aligns seamlessly with my political platform—to strive for a world where the circumstances of one's birth do not limit the Educational and Occupational opportunities and participation in our Republic. "

She nodded, leaning closer in her seat.

"As such, I believe we have an opportunity here. I propose an episode in which I interview you as my guest. We can inform the citizens of the Republic about the successes over the past cycle and your office's determination to make the next cycle a bigger triumph. We can also cover the actionable steps our citizens can propose to the AI Council to further our mission."

At this, Director Avros' emotions shifted to something akin to greed.

Callum had learned those driven by pride and ego were often the easiest to work with.

Director Avros found him distasteful. She resented him for asking her to do additional work.

But she wanted her moment of fame.

Callum found her rather horrid, but he wasn't above using her ego to serve the good of the people.

Time to wrap this up. "Do you think it would be possible for your people to perform the root cause analysis within the next three spans? I would like to work on the script for our interview then."

And from Director Avros—excitement.

"Well, I suppose it shouldn't be a problem. Is there anything else you need, Representative Torion? Perhaps some refreshment?" Decorum dictated she should have offered this when he first arrived, and she damn well knew it.

"No, I need to cut our meeting short, I'm afraid. I have an afternoon appointment with High Priest Valtrellin at the Temple."

Callum didn't need to read her emotions to register her shock. Her brain must be struggling to understand why one of the two most influential religious figures in the Republic would deign to meet with someone like him.

He was surprised she had retained such a prominent position, given her disgust for out-cyclers. She must mask her prejudice well.

Callum had half a mind to prepare a petition for Director Avros' position to be put back on the job market. While it wouldn't cause her to be removed from the role outright, she would need to reapply alongside all other qualified individuals.

But he wasn't there yet—as long as she did her job, she could be a secret bigot to her heart's content.

He excused himself, keeping his distance from the odious woman, and hurried for the elevators to take him to the street level.

∼

WHEN HE EXITED the front doors of the building, Callum realized with irritation that he had forgotten to request a magcar.

He used his Hix to find the nearest single-passenger vehicle. It was a few blocks away, so he followed the indicators his Hix projected across his field of view to head in that direction.

As he stepped onto the street, he was struck by the early morning bustle. Vendors were already setting up stalls, their wares spilling onto the sidewalks. Indigo banners fluttered overhead, being hoisted into place by workers on ladders.

The preparations for the Festival of Completion were well underway, despite the early hour.

Callum felt a twinge of annoyance. This was his second Phase of Completion, though he'd been a child during the first one. Now, as an adult, he felt out of step with the fuss and pageantry. Every festival was a stark reminder of his out-cycler status, even though he now blended in with the current generation.

Honestly, he felt far too old for this.

Most of the new generation eagerly anticipated the seventh phase, the mating season, and tonight was the last hurrah before it began.

For Callum, it was an unpleasant reminder that he would be expected to take part in this cycle's mating nonsense.

As he navigated the growing crowd, a first-generation Valmoran dressed in cybermod fashion bumped into him. The youth's distinctive full-eye replacement whirred as it adjusted to the real world beyond his Hix overlay.

"Whoa, your Glitz meter just broke the scale!" the kid exclaimed, his cybernetic eye focusing on Callum. "The stars are totally aligned for you, my friend!"

Callum managed a polite smile, even as he suppressed a sigh. "That's an interesting app you've got there," he said, his tone carefully neutral.

Callum's thoughts drifted as the young man beamed and launched into a detailed explanation of his AR game.

It never ceased to amaze him how people had forgotten the true purpose of the Hix implant. Invented six generations ago, it revolutionized communication across the Valmoran Republic by providing seamless, real-time written and spoken language translation.

It was the cornerstone that unified their diverse society, allowing everyone to communicate even without knowing Standard.

Yet this kid used this miraculous technology for nothing more than frivolous AR games.

With a few pleasantries, Callum extricated himself from the conversation and continued.

Foot traffic was busy, as always, on the ground level of Valmar City, and Callum barely noticed the buildings looming overhead on all sides. The entire city was crisscrossed from ground to sky with intricate footbridges and mag tubes for the AI-powered public magcars.

Everything flowing, like the city itself was a living organism composed of billions of people.

Unlike some Valmoran homeworlds, where most of the population belonged to a single native subspecies, Planet Kronai was only about half Kronai Valmorans. And in Valmar City, it was more like a third.

The result was that walking through Valmar City was like walking through a parade, showcasing the wondrous variety of Valmorans. Winged or horned, bulky or lithe, some with four arms—so many fascinating forms.

With skin tones from basic silver, tan, or deep brown to shades of red, blue, or green, Callum often thought it was like walking through a rainbow of people. He moved through it, though he never felt like part of it.

He noticed the absence of children. Most Valmorans wouldn't even see it—this was all a natural part of the cycle of life. As they neared the end of the Phase of Completion, all the children were grown, ready to enter the next phase of Debauchery.

But Callum noticed. He always noticed.

Because he had been one of those strange out-cycler children, moving through a sea of adults who looked at him with surprise. Or, worse, with open disgust. But even when they stayed silent, Callum's empathy meant he felt their reactions to him.

He was other to them, less.

Though he now blended in with the current generation and could be just another part of the crowd, Callum could never shake the feeling that he was outside, watching the world rather than living in it.

His Hix led him to a busy stairwell, and he descended into the illuminated transport loading zone before being guided to one of many short queues. The woman in front of him was elderly, maybe in her fifth cycle, so when her transport arrived, Callum offered his hand for support as she climbed into the vehicle.

"Thank you, Representative Torion," she said as the door slid shut, emotions warm and friendly.

Not everyone was like Director Avros. In fact, discrimination against out-cyclers was less of a problem with each passing phase.

But the woman's kindness wasn't what surprised him—it was that she had recognized him at all. Sometimes, he forgot how popular his vids had become. He wasn't used to strangers on the street knowing who he was.

Then again, she might have been using one of those Celeb-Tracker AR overlays, though it was strange to think of an old woman with a silly app like that.

It was a shame. The Hix implant was arguably the most vital component of their intergalactic civilization, with the Ansible —which allowed for instantaneous communication across their vast Republic—as a close second.

Yet, people thought it was for playing music, watching vids, and fanciful AR overlays.

After Callum's transport glided into place on the platform, the door slid open, and he stepped inside. Since he had provided his destination—the Temple of the Seven—when he ordered the ride, the autonomous vehicle began navigating the network of mag tubes as soon as the door shut.

Callum made this trip every month, so he knew he had a few minutes to catch up on work during the ride. He used his Hix to set the side panels to opaque. Watching the vehicle worm through the network, negotiating the shortest path with the rest of the system, was distracting and made him queasy.

"Transport, let me know when we're approaching Temple grounds," he told the vehicle AI.

A solicitous feminine voice replied, "Certainly, Representative Torion. Is there anything else you require?"

Callum despised AIs with simulated personalities. It was a tool, not a person. There was a reason sophont-level AIs were a thing of the past. "No, just make the windows transparent when we leave the city. That will be all."

He sat back and then checked in with his own AI assistant. "AI, report."

Unlike most people, Callum's AI assistant didn't have a name or personality patch. Instead, it spoke into his mind with a synthetic tone and didn't inject any pesky opinions into the conversation.

"Representative Torion, your only remaining appointment today is at the Temple of the Seven. Besides your monthly meeting, you have accepted an invitation to attend the investiture of Matthai Valtrellin this evening. You have 432 new messages, four of which require your attention."

"Send me the ones I need to address personally and a summary of the others. Reply to the others as needed.

"Send a thank you to Director Avros for meeting with me today, telling her I'm anticipating her root cause analysis. Add a reminder to check for her response—three spans from now." Not that Callum was worried she wouldn't follow through—he had her sights set on an interview now, and he'd probably have it within days. "AI, do you have any other updates for me?"

"I have reports for you on the Valmoran Defense Force, the Peacekeepers, Foreign Trade Agreements, and your public image."

"Public image—what's changed?" Managing his image was one of Callum's least favorite parts of the job, but it had to be done.

"A local gossip personality named you among the most eligible unmated males in the capital. This has led to speculation about your apparent lack of participation in the upcoming mating season."

Ugh. Callum supposed it was progress that he, an out-cycler, was considered a desirable mate—it was a testament to the progress they had made as a society. But he despised the current state of Valmoran mating rituals almost as much as he hated the bias against out-cyclers.

"Elaborate."

"Some speculate that your lack of participation is a political statement on social hierarchy."

True.

"Others speculate you medically cannot take part since you were born out-of-cycle."

False and grossly misinformed.

"Still others interpret your lack of participation as a rejection of sacred Valmoran tradition."

That was somewhat true, but politically problematic.

Huh. Who knew not wanting to throw a fancy party to find a mate would cause a political uproar? Ridiculous.

But however pointless and backward Callum found the mating festivities of the Valmoran elite, he also couldn't afford to let the speculation continue unchecked. He just wasn't sure how to navigate this particular issue. He'd spent years walking a tightrope with his public image, and would need to do so with this, as well.

The transport came to a halt, but the windows were still opaque, so they must not have reached the grounds of the Temple. "Transport, why have we stopped?"

The AI answered in a cheerful voice. "Heavy traffic, sir."

That wasn't something to be cheerful about. "AI—set windows to transparent." Everywhere Callum looked, he saw vehicles queued up as far as the eye could see.

"Transport queues began forming yesterday around the Temple grounds in anticipation of the investiture ceremony," the AI chirped.

"But they're huge! Transport, how long is this line?" Callum imagined what the Temple must look like today—a massive swarm of vehicles closing in from all sides on a perfect green circle.

"Estimated time to the front of the traffic queue—two hours and fifteen minutes."

At this moment, he again wished he had somehow gotten out of today's meeting. Still, the Vatrellins had extended him a personal invitation to the ordination, which would begin shortly after.

He looked out at the congested traffic and groaned.

In the end, his AI delivered a solution.

"Your invitation to the ceremony today came with approval to use the priority gate. I will direct the vehicle to take us there."

Good. He wasn't above waiting in a line like everyone else, but also hadn't planned on it today, so he might have missed his meeting with the High Priest. Of course, this problem could have been avoided if he allowed his AI more autonomy, but Callum would never be comfortable with that. It was crazy how much other people allowed a mere thing to control their lives.

Fortunately, he always left early, or he would never have made it on time.

And to think, he might have shown up late for a private intro-duction to the esteemed Matthai Valtrellin, the fancy man at the center of all the fuss. That would not have been an auspi-cious start to their working relationship.

He reminded himself he needed to be diplomatic today. Just because he thought Matthai was an elitist and an incredible hypocrite for enforcing the 'no touching' rule on everyone around him didn't mean he could afford to let him know.

If he could work with a bigot like Director Avros, he could handle a snob like Matthai Valtrellin.

As the transport worked its way to the front of the queue, Callum marveled again at the stark contrast between the Temple grounds and the rest of the world.

Most of Kronai was consumed with trying to squeeze in more people; the Temple's open lands seemed vast and wasteful, with meandering paths through open fields, beds of flowers, and patches of fresh fruits and vegetables.

Emerging into this from the city left one feeling vertigo at the sudden expanse.

Callum looked out over the inviting grounds, unusually populated with throngs of revelers. So lush, so welcoming. There were smiling priests everywhere he looked, ready to guide pilgrims to where they needed to go.

But he knew the truth—the hospitable display was yet another component of the stronghold that was the Temple of the Seven.

Every Temple was the same, on every Valmoran homeworld —a shining, walled monstrosity with seven gleaming towers surrounded by expansive gardens.

But few knew, or even cared, that in contrast to what was above ground, a network of defensive tunnels—accessible only to the guardians of the Temple—wove through the ground underneath. It was no coincidence there were no tall trees, no buildings to use as cover.

And those smiling priests? Each could disarm and incapacitate a person before they had time to blink.

Anyone approaching would be known to the Temple guardians well before they reached the walls, and if they were not welcome, they would never reach the gates. No one was privy to this or cared, because no one ever attacked the precious Temples. Who would want to? Who would dare?

The Temple may have looked like a paradise, but Callum could see the terrifying fortress behind its beauty.

A fortress designed not only to protect the sacred Obelisk but also to conceal its secrets.

THE
VALMORAN
CHRONICLES

[4]
PEOPLE ARE ALMOST INVARIABLY
INTOLERABLE

VALMORAN REPUBLIC, PLANET KRONAI, TEMPLE OF THE SEVEN

CALLUM TORION, REPRESENTATIVE ARBITER FOR THE VALMORAN REPUBLIC

～

AFTER A BRIEF WAIT in the priority transport queue and a quick identity verification and security scan at the edge of the grounds of the First Temple, Callum was dropped off near the main gate and found himself plunged into a sea of people.

The festive atmosphere was in full swing, the Temple grounds transformed into an overwhelming tapestry of color and life.

Banners in the Valtrellin cobalt and silver rippled in the breeze. The air was thick with a miasma of scents—exotic delicacies, the heady scent of incense, the perfume of the expansive flower beds.

The vivid pavilions and finery of the attendees, along with the cacophony of celebration and odors of festival food, would have been nearly overwhelming on their own. For Callum, adding the massive crowd's heightened emotions made it an assault on his senses.

At least the emotions that bombarded him were primarily positive, a small mercy.

He waded through the throngs of people and priests, a veritable maze of pavilions, before joining a short line waiting to enter the Temple courtyard.

Callum wished he had anticipated just how busy the grounds would be today. He'd never seen the Temple so overrun in all the time he'd worked with the Valtrellins.

A group of lavishly dressed young Kronai females chattered in front of him, draped in the frippery and finery that was the fashion. Their blue hair was braided in complex styles that must have taken their servants all morning.

Their laughter rang out, irritating and brash, as they speculated about the handsome Scion and his impending mating ceremony. Callum couldn't help but overhear their conversation, as they seemed determined to ensure the entire crowd could listen in.

Their age and the style of their clothing made it obvious that they belonged to the new generation. Callum's generation, although he never felt like one of them. His half-cycle age difference felt like an unbridgeable chasm when faced with the young and frivolous.

"Isn't this exciting? I came to First Temple once and saw Matthai sitting behind his father. He's very handsome." the shortest young woman said to her companions.

Callum felt her desperation to be accepted so acutely that he wanted to take a step away as the sensation oozed through him. He glanced around, trying and failing to ignore the women's mindless chatter.

Valmorans from all walks of life were in a jovial mood, enjoying food and drinks from the pavilions while Temple musicians played jaunty festival tunes. Everywhere he looked, priests in the blue and silver colors of the Valtrellins stood, smiling and offering assistance to the partygoers.

"Oh, I know—that deep blue hair—"

Callum couldn't help but note the dense crowds and wonder if it was safe to cram so many people into the area. Then again, the place was also crawling with priests—each one trained in defensive combat.

And from how their watchful eyes roamed the crowds, Callum was sure their Hix implants must have sophisticated surveillance overlays.

Gods, they probably had color-coded threat assessments for every attendee, access to their identification, job history, homeworld, everything.

Nosy bastards.

"—and he looks like he will grow into his father's powerful jaw—"

Typically, the level of military sophistication exhibited by the Temple unnerved Callum. Still, crammed between thousands upon thousands of people, he had to admit that he felt safer knowing the priests were on top of security.

"—but those lovely long ears ... just like his mother's."

"I wonder who he will match with?"

The women let out a chorus of sighs, and Callum barely resisted the urge to roll his eyes. He peered at the line and wondered if he should call ahead to High Priest Valtrellin to see if there was another entrance he could use. But then, the line started moving forward again, and he figured it was best to wait his turn.

Despite his better judgment, he found himself listening to the girls' insipid conversation.

"Well, that won't be for a while still—the Valtrellins always have the matching ceremony at the very height of mating season. No one can even go near Matthai before then—everyone knows that." the tall one said, her voice dripping with superiority.

Callum shuddered when he reflexively reached out to read her emotions—ego with a side order of cruelty towards her own companions. Gods, people were such assholes.

"I heard they picked his potentials when he was still in his first phase."

"Oh, yeah—as soon as Kronai girls started showing as God-touched, their parents started putting in applications. The list was finalized ages ago. And now that he's the heir, one of them will get to be High Priestess. Can you imagine?"

"But what if he doesn't match with anyone on the list?"

The girl with the upturned nose and the rotten soul snorted. "Don't be stupid—just look at him—the Valtrellin bloodline is so pure, they always get a mate."

The short girl sounded wistful. "Must be nice. No one has been God-touched in my family for four generations. I'm not even sure if I want to have a matching party. What if I don't match? I would just die."

Callum had to pull back from the sudden wave of despair he felt emanating from the girl.

He clenched his jaw. This was precisely the sort of nonsense he wished their society could move past.

So what if you didn't end up with a mate bond? It wasn't like you couldn't find another unmated person at the tail end of the season and decide to pair up for the next cycle.

Most people never had a mate bond, and their lives turned out fine. And this girl would just die if she didn't match? What in the world were Valmorans teaching their children?

Eventually, they neared the gate, and Callum could see the reason for the hold-up. Security was much tighter than usual today. On a typical visit, he could walk up to one of a hundred wide-open archways, scan his Hix, and walk inside the inner courtyard.

Today, however, most gates had been closed, and a veritable wall of priests stood in formation just inside this archway.

Not in a threatening way—no, they were smiling and looked for all the world like they were thrilled to be part of the celebration—but Callum wasn't fooled. Those smiles would vanish in a heartbeat if they sensed a threat.

A glance upward revealed yet another hidden gem. He wondered what that nasty girl would think if she knew that the large, welcoming gateway she was standing under hid a thick metal door that could cut a person in two.

The gleaming architecture of the Temple always revealed its secrets if you knew where to look.

Nothing in the design was accidental.

The entire citadel could lock down in mere heartbeats, and the seven gleaming towers that encircled the inner Temple also secretly housed the most advanced defensive laser array that money could buy.

Callum's mind could never figure out why the Temple required such extensive, advanced security. Sure, the Temple technically couldn't depend on the Valmoran Republic for defense. But no Republic decision pool would ever fail to rise to the Temple's aid.

Even after years spent working on the politics of Temple and state, Callum found it surreal that the small tract of land that housed each of the Temples wasn't part of the Republic but a sovereign theocracy unto itself, one distributed across hundreds of planets throughout the galaxy.

It was suspicious, though, how the ancient priests had gone to the trouble of constructing a massive fortress to house every Obelisk in the galaxy.

Every last one.

Were they genuinely protecting and honoring the Obelisks, or were they hiding them?

Perhaps his cynicism was harsh, a product of his mistrust of the Temple. After all, for countless Valmorans, the Obelisks represented a tangible connection to the divine, a source of guidance in a chaotic galaxy.

After all, the Temple did allow pilgrims to request an audience with an Obelisk and even touch it to receive wisdom from the Gods. Callum had done it himself, in fact, and found the experience to be rather underwhelming.

It was normal, mundane even, to want to protect your sacred artifacts. He might be spinning a conspiracy out of nothing.

Raised voices and heated emotions drew his attention back to the girls in front of him, who appeared to be in some sort of dispute with the priest running identity checks.

"But my mother is the Assistant Director of CommTech—I'm here to get footage of the ceremony." the cruel one whined.

The Temple guard's voice was warm and neutral when he responded. "I'm sorry—I don't have you on the approved media list. Your invitation is for the outer Temple grounds only."

"But we've been traveling all day!"

Callum suppressed a groan of irritation. He really couldn't stand people.

Sure, he cared about 'people' in the abstract—about justice and fairness and the good of the people. But Callum had found that individual people were almost invariably intolerable. There was only so much spite, envy, and dishonesty Callum could stomach.

Entire crowds of people were enough to make him want to hide in his Ansible chamber for days.

"We appreciate your support for the Scion, but unfortunately, entrance into the Temple proper is by invitation only today. We apologize for the inconvenience and would be delighted to receive you again soon. If you please follow Priest Doren, he will escort you to one of the outer guest pavilions."

The spoiled young woman and her friends huffed and trailed after their guide. Apparently, being invited to one of the most exclusive events in the galaxy wasn't good enough for her.

Callum approached the priest with the security scanner, which he used to scan his Hix ID.

"Welcome to the First Temple." The man smiled warmly, then moved his eyes, reading something projected via his Hix device. "Representative Arbiter Torion, we're honored you could join us today. I see that you have been formally invited to attend the investiture ceremony."

"Yes, that's correct."

"Scion Valtrellin has requested that we escort you to the Second Tower when you arrive. If you will, please follow Priest Jexil." Then, a young priest stepped forward and gestured for Callum to follow.

After a short walk through the less crowded ornate Temple courtyards, his escort ushered Callum through a security door, down a short hallway, and into an opulent sitting room. Matthai Valtrellin was already seated on a luxurious chair, an expensive-looking tea set on a low table before him.

Matthai stood when Callum entered. The young man's emotions were a maelstrom, and Callum had to take a moment to adjust to the sensation.

The tumultuous swirl of feelings emanating from Matthai caught Callum off guard. It was a potent mix of anticipation, trepidation, excitement, fear, and guilt—more emotions than Callum could keep up with.

A stark contrast to the composed, almost serene exterior the young Scion presented.

The Scion was probably just worried about whether he would look pretty enough when they broadcast his face all over the galaxy. It was always the same with these elites.

Callum stepped into the room and heard the door slide shut behind him. He kept his distance—he knew better than to get too close to Matthai, since his family had taken the 'no touching' rule to unprecedented levels of absurdity. Such hypocrisy.

"Scion Valtrellin, it is an honor to finally meet you," Callum said, maintaining a respectable distance.

Matthai's complex emotions calmed, and he graced Callum with a generous smile. "Please, just call me Matthai. I must confess I am a huge fan of your work, Representative Torion. It's great to finally meet you." His emotions showed his sincerity and his warm welcome felt like a psychic hug.

Huh. This was not what Callum had expected from the future High Priest of the First Temple.

"Just Callum is fine."

Matthai gestured to the chair across from his own. "Please, sit. My father has been wearing himself out attending foreign dignitaries, so I told him I'd be thrilled to receive you on my own today. I hope you didn't have anything critical to discuss with him."

"No, I believe the agenda for today was for the two of us to become acquainted—we can manage that on our own."

Callum was surprised to find that the smile he tried to summon was already on his face, without his permission. They took their seats, and Callum smoothed out his slacks while he puzzled over his positive reaction to the young priest.

"Can I fix you a cup of tea?" Matthai offered, gesturing to the etched silver tea service.

Callum couldn't help comparing Matthai's hospitality to that of the bigoted OccEd director he had met in the morning. It could not have been more different.

"Yes, thank you," Callum responded, unsure of where to take the conversation next.

This wasn't at all how he had expected this meeting to go, and he realized he was utterly unprepared. He had expected to make awkward pleasantries with High Priest Valtrellin and his son—maybe feel out Matthai's true feelings about equality.

He had expected this entire day to be nothing but a tedious obligation necessary to maintain his partnership with the Valtrellins.

Matthai Valtrellin, by all rights, ought to be full of himself and consider himself as extraordinary as everyone else did. But so far, the young priest had been inexplicably kind and humble.

As Callum watched Matthai gracefully prepare two cups of tea, the pleasant silence gave him time to notice something … refreshing about the young Scion's emotions.

He wasn't a ray of sunshine or anything like that. In fact, a deep undercurrent of sadness hummed beneath him like a low drone.

That alone gave Callum pause—no one carried that level of grief without enduring terrible hardship. He wondered what could have caused such heartache in Matthai's pampered life.

Matthai set a cup of tea on the table before Callum, then sat back in his seat, feeling ... resolved.

The Scion seemed to have his own agenda for the day, and Callum was surprised to find himself intrigued to hear it.

As he reached forward to accept Matthai's offering of tea, Callum heard the young priest's voice tear through the silence, calm and patient, yet almost painfully direct.

"Representative Torion, are you a man of your word?"

BARTERING IN SECRETS

VALMORAN REPUBLIC, PLANET KRONAI, TEMPLE OF THE SEVEN

CALLUM TORION, REPRESENTATIVE ARBITER FOR THE VALMORAN REPUBLIC

~

"REPRESENTATIVE TORION, are you a man of your word?" Callum gave Matthai an appraising look. The young priest's gentle directness was both unexpected and refreshing—a pleasant change from what he usually encountered in his line of work.

Life as an empath—and a politician at that—had accustomed Callum to the art of verbal sparring, where both parties invariably attempted to glean as much information from the other as possible without divulging their own secrets.

He sensed no deceit or cunning from Matthai, who remained seated across from him in the opulent receiving room, calmly awaiting an answer.

Callum took a moment to measure his words before answering. "I'm not entirely sure how to answer that question, Matthai. For politicians, circumspection comes with the territory."

His eyes locked with Matthai's as he made his concluding statement. "But I *can* assure you that if I explicitly make a promise to someone, I keep it."

Matthai's shoulders relaxed almost imperceptibly, and Callum felt a hint of hope emanating from the young priest. For some reason, Matthai needed to believe he could trust Callum.

Urgently.

And Callum's interest was further piqued.

"I thought as much. My father has spoken highly of you, and I've admired your work for years. I'd like to believe that we could start our relationship from a position of honesty and trust, without the need to guard our words."

"That would certainly make things simpler." It was a struggle for Callum to suppress a smile, much to his surprise.

He couldn't help but respect the young man for his forthright approach, although he was concerned Matthai wouldn't be able to navigate the deceitful world of politics outside the Temple.

Callum made a mental note to guide Matthai in navigating the treacherous waters of politics. While *he* appreciated the young man's guilelessness, others would almost certainly take advantage of it.

He watched with interest as Matthai studied the intricate carvings on his silver teacup.

Finally, the Scion cleared his throat and looked up. "I fully expect that you will become one of my closest advisors over time, but I find myself in more immediate need of your guidance."

Callum set his cup back on the table, focusing on Matthai.

Matthai continued. "You've been navigating Temple politics for almost a phase, if memory serves. I'm not sure if you know this, but Scions of the Temple go through the same training as any other adept." He swirled the tea in his cup before taking a sip.

Callum quirked an eyebrow. "I was *not* aware. I assumed you spent your life training to be a High Priest."

"No, I didn't. In fact, it wasn't until ..." After swallowing, the boy stopped and took a breath.

Callum was hit with a sudden wave of grief that nearly took his breath away, and it was then that he remembered that Matthai's sister had died—how could he have forgotten?

It had been a long time ago—before Callum had begun working with the Valtrellins—but he should have remembered.

Matthai's emotions were potent, more intense than most people, and churning right below the surface, as if the slightest remembrance could call forth their full fury.

Callum realized he needed to watch himself, or he'd end up giving away the fact that he was an empath.

"... I wasn't always the heir. I spent most of my life as the Second Scion and was prepared to serve as an advisor to my sister."

The Scion's pain and deep reluctance were balanced only by the strength of his resolve.

Callum realized with a shock that Matthai Valtrellin did not hunger for the power of being High Priest—he did not even *want* it.

Oblivious to Callum's surprise, Matthai continued, "Training with the other adepts teaches the Scions humility. The difference in our training comes after we take our vows—that's when priests begin training in our specialties. So, you see, on the political side of things, you have infinitely more experience than I do."

He looked up at Callum and gave a soft smile.

"I'm sure you know more than you give yourself credit for."
"Perhaps. But 'A wise man knows to seek guidance, and who best to provide it.'" Matthai said, and Callum recognized it as a line from *The Tome of the Obelisks*.

"But surely the current High Priest and Priestess—"

"—may not provide objective advice on this issue," Matthai said, sitting up straighter.

"I see."

Callum tried to imagine what could be an issue of political importance that the High Priest and Priestess couldn't be objective about. Perhaps Matthai didn't want to take his vows, or it might be about his future mate.

He couldn't think of anything else that it could be unless maybe Matthai was privy to deeper Temple secrets …

Now, that would be interesting.

Whatever it was, Callum suspected it was significant, and he fairly burned with curiosity.

Matthai looked intensely into Callum's eyes, as if staring into his soul. "Tell me, Representative Torion—how can I know you can be trusted with my secrets?"

There was an opportunity here.

One that he hadn't expected and might not get again. Matthai needed his help, was practically begging for it. And if Callum rose to the occasion today, the future High Priest of the First Temple might be forever in his debt.

And even if that didn't turn out to be the case, the prospect of an open and frank working relationship with Matthai Valtrellin was appealing in and of itself.

Callum knew one way he might instantly gain Matthai's trust. He had used similar tactics before—a secret for a secret. It would almost certainly work in this situation.

He could tell Matthai didn't mistrust him, and more than that
—Matthai wanted to trust him.

He just needed a push.

So the decision fell to Callum—he was almost certain, just
from Matthai's emotions, that he was trustworthy. But the
young man's emotional reaction to his next question would
settle the issue.

If Callum sensed even a whiff of deceit or greed, he would
not divulge a thing. Otherwise, he would trust Matthai.

At least with this.

"Just call me Callum—no need to be formal." He leaned
forward and rested his elbows on his knees.

"Perhaps, if I told you something only one other person
knows about me, something that I *never want anyone else to
know* ...?" He let the sentence trail off.

Matthai's emotions didn't disappoint—he was surprised at
the offer ... and honored.

"But why would you do that?" The boy sat back, looked at his
hands, then back to Callum's face.

"Of course, I would never break your confidence, Callum,
but how could you know you can trust me?" Matthai wasn't
suspicious of Callum, just baffled at his offer.

Callum had spent his life crawling through the ugliest under-
bellies of human emotion and had learned that very few
people are genuine, most are cruel, and many are lying most
of the time.

He rarely met a person whose emotions didn't cause him to think less of them.

Matthai was one of the kindest, most honest souls that Callum had ever felt. He decided the risk was minor compared to the potential gain.

Callum, a lowly out-cycler and ward of the state, had no distinguished family line that would cause others to suspect he was God-touched.

In fact, his subspecies, the Elodai, were one of the more physically nondescript, coming in a wide range of skin tones and hair colors, and with no particular traits such as the wings or blue hair of more distinctive subspecies.

Because of this, he might have belonged to any of a hundred subspecies, each with different God-touched specialties, ranging from heightened senses to enhanced cognition or physical speed. His own ability—empathy—was one of the more powerful, prized and feared in equal measure.

No one liked to know that another could peer into his heart, but many sought to spy on others' emotions.

Callum had never divulged his subspecies. His public statement was that he opposed bloodline discrimination, which was true.

But the real reason he had never claimed a bloodline was that no one would suspect someone as low-born as an out-cycler to be both God-touched and an Elodai.

Prejudice, it turned out, was beneficial when one had a secret such as his.

"Is this room secure?"

Callum might choose to trust Matthai, but that did not extend to complete trust in the Temple.

"Of course—these rooms are where priests receive the public for private audiences. They are maintained as unmonitored spaces, which is why I chose to receive you here."

"Good." Callum took a breath, then gave Matthai a pointed look. "My secret is the very reason I know you are telling the truth."

Matthai's eyebrows creased for a moment, then his eyes went wide, and Callum suppressed the urge to grin. The future High Priest had a keen intellect to have puzzled it out so quickly.

"Oh—but you—"

"—could never be God-touched because I am an out-cycler?" Callum felt a twinge of irritation and raised his eyebrows in censure.

Matthai's face fell.

"... I suppose some people might say that, but I was actually thinking how unusual it is for someone to keep it a secret. Most people would boast about such a formidable gift, but you—"

Callum felt a surge of guilt when he realized he had misjudged Matthai's meaning, so he softened his tone. "—kept it a secret. It's a valuable secret, Matthai. And you are now one of only three people who know it, including me."

He leaned back, then loosened his neckline.

Matthai gave Callum a bewildered smile. "Thank you, Callum, for trusting me. This information will never cross my lips."

He took a shaky breath, then continued. "I suppose that means it's my turn."

Matthai looked down, staring into his teacup as if it contained the secrets of the universe.

Apparently, he was going to need some convincing. Callum knew Matthai wanted to talk, and that the fastest way to get him there would be to make him think he might lose the opportunity.

"We can discuss it some other time—you probably need to get ready for the—"

"—no, I need your advice. Securing it was my goal when I came here today."

Matthai sat up straighter, then scrubbed a hand over his face.

It was strange to see the stoic priest's composure fail him.

"It's ..."

Matthai heaved a huge breath, and Callum felt a barrage of relief, worry, hope, longing, giddiness, and panic crash over him with the force of a tidal wave.

Matthai looked up at the ceiling, blinking, and Callum suppressed the urge to press his hand to his heart at the overwhelming emotions.

"That's … intense," Callum said.

"Sorry, I forgot—"

"—No need to apologize. Just … start at the beginning, and we'll work through it. I've never met a problem that didn't have a solution."

Matthai nodded soberly, and Callum sensed his tentative relief.

"Okay, but it's going to sound insane."

The young man then told Callum a tale so incredible that if he hadn't been able to read his emotions, Callum would never have believed a word of it. Even now, he wondered if the young man was insane, although Matthai's emotions made it clear he believed every word he said.

Then again, if he were delusional, his emotions would have read the same.

"—you don't believe me," Matthai said flatly.

Then Callum felt a fresh wave of resolve from the young man as Matthai pulled his robe to the side and exposed the mate mark beginning to form above his heart.

"See?"

"And you're sure it wasn't just that someone snuck into your room?"

Matthai shook his head, a hint of exasperation sneaking into his tone. "Callum, my guards didn't notice a thing. Plus, she already had a mate mark, knew my name, and then she literally disappeared from my arms."

"Okay, give me a minute to process."

Callum leaned back and tried to sort through everything he had just been told, while Matthai busied himself making them each a fresh cup of tea.

Matthai didn't seem insane—overwhelmed, yes—but not insane. Callum was inclined to believe that his story, however bizarre, must therefore be true.

After taking some time to order his thoughts, Callum nodded to himself, then spoke.

"Okay, our working theory is that your mate is a chrono-jumper—but far more powerful than any Kronai in recorded history. At some point in the future, you will meet her, she'll get her mate mark, and you'll fall in love. Right?"

"Right."

"Then sometime after that, she'll be in trouble—starved and bleeding. And then she will jump back in time to you, last night—in reflex."

Matthai nodded. "Yes, and I have no idea what to do about it. Should I go looking for her? Should I take my vows? Tell my parents? I'm tempted to take my vows as planned and work out the rest later, but it also feels wrong. What if I take my vows, but then the Temple, or the people, won't accept Kat-a-reen as their High Priestess—"

Matthai's face blanched, and Callum's gut twisted with the boy's horror.

"—what if that's the reason she ends up being tortured? What if it's my fault?"

Callum held his hands out in a placating gesture. "Hey ... calm down. We have no way of knowing any of that, right? So, let's just take this one step at a time. I think you're right to go ahead with the investiture. It will buy us time to figure out your next steps."

He leaned forward and gave his best reassuring smile. "Think of it this way—if what happened to you last night wasn't an act of the Gods, then I don't know what is. Maybe the Gods meant for Kat-a-reen to come here. Right?"

"I hadn't considered that," Matthai said.

"Right. The next thing to sort out is your priorities."

"Priorities?"

"Yes—does your loyalty lie with your mate, parents, the priesthood, or the people? We'll try to find the most optimal solution, but you need to prepare yourself for the likelihood that you won't be able to keep everyone happy."

"I won't abandon my mate." Matthai slumped down into his seat. "But I also don't want to upset my family. They would support me, I'm almost certain, as their son. Their primary concern would be the scandal of me mating outside the pre-selected potentials, and the fact that the future High Priestess is missing."

"And that she's not from any known Valmoran homeworld."

"—and that she's not Kronai," Matthai added.

"—and that it's out of cycle, but that could be mitigated by waiting to announce the match. So, if I understand you, we're looking for a plan that allows you to find and save your mate, and you'd like to do it without causing a scandal if possible."

"Yes."

"Good. Now that we're clear on our goal, here is my advice—go ahead with the investiture. Let's each take a few days to think through our options. Then how about you and I meet up for lunch or tea? Would that be suspicious to anyone?"

"No, my father would be happy to hear we were getting along."

"Good. Let's connect via Hix so our AIs can set something up. But Matthai—we shouldn't message about this over Hix or write anything down. Agreed?"

"That seems wise."

"In fact, tell no one else about this until we have a plan. As long as we control the information, we still have options. But if word gets out, rumors will spread and take on a life of their own."

"I agree. I had planned on telling no one, but knew I would need help. It's only a matter of time before someone spots the mate mark."

"Oh?"

"Yeah, if I weren't the heir, I wouldn't have any hope of hiding it—I have a private bathing chamber, so I don't have to use the Temple baths. But it will be difficult to keep my robes from ever falling open during training."

"Even the heir trains in combat?" The question poured out of him. Matthai was easy to talk to. Maybe too easy.

"Not combat—protection. The same as every other adept—I won't receive the advanced training that the priests in the Order of Protection get—but we all learn how to deflect and neutralize violence."

Callum leaned forward with interest. "I have to ask—don't you think it's strange for the priests of a religion to learn how to fight? I thought you were all about peace and harmony and such."

"We are—training to defuse the more negative aspects of our nature allows us to walk through life without fear of violence, so our judgment isn't clouded by it."

His words sounded genuine, but also like he was repeating something he had heard countless times.

Callum nodded. He was still wary of the Temple's military prowess, but if there was anything to suspect, at least Matthai seemed blissfully unaware.

"I suppose it's not much different from how I prepare and catalog evidence. Knowing that I have my arguments prepared on important issues means I'm never caught off guard if drafted for a vote."

Matthai's eyes lit up.

"Sometime, you'll have to tell me how that all works. I know there are thousands of Representatives, and the AI Council pulls you in to vote on things, but that's about it. Oh, and that you use the Ansible."

He paused. "It seems so complicated. We use Ansibles, too, of course, but we have the Council of High Priests to make decisions."

Callum nodded. "Sure—the Temple is ruled by a hierarchy, and the Republic is governed by democratic consensus."

"You sound like you think hierarchy is a negative thing."

"Well, it shouldn't come as a shock to you that I'm not a fan of arbitrary hierarchy—that's why I'm so vocally opposed to bloodline, subspecies, and class discrimination. A person has no control over the circumstances of their birth. But hierarchy formed based on achievement doesn't bother me as much, because it can be earned."

Matthai nodded. "So you must be particularly opposed to the High Priesthood. We choose our leaders based solely on circumstances of birth, with bloodline and subspecies discrimination inherent to the process."

Callum smiled. He was going to enjoy working with Matthai Valtrellin. The boy was sharp, didn't mince words, and didn't get defensive—only curious.

"I do find it *odd* ... that the Temple urges its followers to eschew discrimination while maintaining controlled mating among its leaders."

"It does seem odd, doesn't it? Honestly, Callum, I've questioned it myself, but have only been told it is necessary. For now, I think my role is to learn and understand things before I try to change anything. It may sound strange, but I am as bound by the circumstances of my birth as you are."

"More so, I would think."

"Perhaps. But our philosophies may not be so different, after all. Blood may have secured my role, but it is mine to earn the right to rule."

Callum chuckled. "Matthai, has anyone ever told you you have a way with words? In another life, I believe you might have been a poet."

The Scion's pale skin flushed at the compliment. "You flatter me. I like to think if things were different, I might have been a gardener. I've always had a great love for growing things." He smiled, and his eyes lit up for just a moment.

"But it sounds, if I understand you correctly, like you're not opposed to change?"

Matthai shook his head. "No, I am not. Of course, as a Valtrellin, and still only the heir, I'm not at liberty to publicly question the running of the Temple. But I have always admired your work, Callum, and have imagined how things might change."

He sighed. "And now, with Kat-a-reen, change will undoubtedly be necessary."

Matthai's emotions had calmed during their conversation, but the reminder of Kat-a-reen had brought a fresh surge of worry to the young priest.

Callum wasn't sure why, but he felt compelled to cheer him up. "Matthai?"

"Yeah?"

"What was it like, meeting your mate?"

Matthai's joy invaded Callum's heart, like a ray of pure sunshine piercing the clouds. A slow smile spread across the boy's handsome face.

"It was ... she was—I could feel she was my Amara, Callum. It was like standing too close to a fire, but one I wanted to step into."

Callum couldn't help but smile in response. "Focus on that, and get ready for your big day. We'll figure the rest out soon. But for today, we should wrap things up."

He stood and prepared to leave.

"Thank you, Callum. I prayed through the night for help with this situation, and eventually, my mind settled on you. It was right to ask you for help."

"Try not to worry, Matthai. We'll get it sorted. I promise."

∽

Lost in thought, Callum made his way to the reception hall where the honored guests would gather for the ceremony.

His steps faltered when he realized he was still seeing Matthai's stricken face, still feeling the boy's fear for his mate.

Still running through the entire conversation on a steady loop.

Searching for solutions to the Scion's problems.

Frustrated and amazed, he ran his hand over his jaw.

In just one conversation, Matthai Valtrellin earned not only his respect but something much more extraordinary—Callum had begun to care about him.

As a person.

Caring about people just wasn't something that Callum did. He cared about 'people' in the abstract, but not individuals. The vast majority of people had hearts so black that he could barely stand to be around them, let alone care about them.

But when they were children, his ward-sister Zalila had wormed her way into his heart, and now Matthai had joined her. His concern for them felt uncomfortably akin to weakness. It wasn't worth worrying over, though, because it was done—he hadn't cared about many people in his life, but he had discovered that once that boundary was broken …

Once again, Matthai's worried expression skipped across his mind.

Callum felt a wave of anger—his own, this time—as the full injustice of the situation struck him.

Matthai Valtrellin had done absolutely nothing wrong. In the dead of night, his future mate suddenly materialized in his bedroom.

From the future.

It was ... astonishing.

In a just world, it would be cause for celebration, extolled as a miracle.

But this wasn't a just world, and Callum worried that even his considerable skill and influence might not be enough to circumvent the biggest scandal the Temple had seen in generations.

[PART 2]
EARTH GOT … WEIRD

THE
VALMORAN
CHRONICLES

[6]
SOMETIMES A BASEMENT IS A METAPHOR

EARTH, OMAHA, NEBRASKA

KATHARINE MILLER, MEDICAL MICROBIOLOGIST

∼

THE SUDDEN BLARING of Kat's ringtone pierced the silent room, startling her out of sleep. Disoriented, she pawed at the cardboard box that served as her makeshift bedside table, trying to find her phone.

Thunk.

It was tempting to leave it on the floor, but whoever was calling wasn't hanging up. With a groan, Kat strained her body to the side and retrieved her cell by pulling on the charging cord.

As sore as she was, it was the only way that cell phone was ending up in her hand.

She mashed the power button in a bleary haze, intending to decline the call and go back to sleep.

Unfortunately, she must have bungled it and hit accept, because her best friend's voice shrieked through the small basement, brimming with worry and impatience. At least it wasn't her sister.

"Kat! Don't you dare hang up—I swear to god, if you do, I'm calling Beth Ann—"

Wincing, she lowered the volume to a less agonizing level.

Kat's head screamed in protest as she fumbled the phone to her ear.

A weird croaking sound emerged as she attempted to speak. She cleared her throat and tried again. "Oh, hey, Claire." The stale taste of sleep coated her tongue. Yuck.

"Don't 'Hey Claire,' me—where have you been? Never mind, it doesn't matter. You're meeting me today at Zen, eleven fifteen, and I'm not taking no for an answer."

As her brain took its sweet time coming online, Kat realized she was *freezing*.

Because she was naked on top of the comforter again. Lovely. Annoyed, she reached behind her, grasping the edge of the musty blanket and hauling it over, wrapping herself up burrito-style.

How did this keep happening? Was she sleepwalking or something?

"Claire—" she whined from within her cocoon. Her entire body ached, and the mere thought of coffee was revolting. Sleep sounded infinitely better than coffee.

"You'll be there, or I'm calling Beth."

Claire's voice took on a sweet yet firm tone, the one she reserved for unruly children and stubborn patients.

The stick.

As if on cue, Claire continued, "Also—I have a surprise for you."

The carrot.

Kat let out a dramatic groan, snuggling deeper into her blanket. "You know I hate surprises."

Her friend's voice brimmed with mischief and enthusiasm. "I do ... but I also know the curiosity will drive you absolutely bonkers."

It would. "That's playing dirty."

"Whatever it takes," Claire was far too chipper this morning.

"Fine." Kat rubbed the sleep from her eyes, resigned. "You win."

"Awesome! Eleven fifteen, don't be late." *Click.*

Kat's stomach twisted as she dismissed the text notifications from her sister Beth and tossed the phone onto the rumpled bed. She told herself it was merely a wave of nausea, not guilt, that churned within her.

Soft morning light filtered through the window in the walkout basement door, glowing gently over the devastatingly messy room. It looked like someone had moved in but never bothered to unpack any boxes.

She sat up gingerly, as she had every morning that week, to avoid the disorienting sensation of the room spinning. An epic groan slipped out as she stood, forcing a stretch as her joints protested every movement.

It felt like a migraine, the flu, arthritis, and the world's worst hangover all at once. Kat almost *wished* she'd been partying the night before—at least then, she'd have a simple excuse for why she felt so terrible. Well, other than Syndrome Q.

Kat was reluctant to accept it herself, let alone tell anyone else.

A nagging voice in her head chimed in, reminding her she also needed another explanation. Namely, why she woke up naked on top of a crumpled bedspread most mornings. Pajamas *under* the covers.

But Kat commanded that unhelpful voice to shut up and go away, because she had enough to deal with.

The garage door opening reverberated through the house, breaking the silence. It was weird.

Wasn't Danny supposed to be at work? It's not like he'd be home sick, she groused to herself. The rest of her family and most of humanity had dodged the Syndrome Q bullet.

The first order of business was scrounging up something to wear. Kat's suitcase was still sitting open on the floor, so she rummaged through it, finding a well-loved Radiohead tee and yoga pants to tug on.

Then she gave her favorite hoodie a sniff.

No detergent or perfumes, since Beth had always been sensitive to fragrances and chemicals. But it was taking on the delightful odor of *Eau de Basement*, along with everything else she'd brought to her brother's place.

It was fresh enough. Kat tugged it over her head, snuggling into the oversized sweatshirt, grateful for the warmth.

She'd need to ask Danny if she could use his washer and dryer soon. He wouldn't mind, but it was a cruel reminder that she'd been in his basement longer than planned.

Heavy footsteps thundering down the stairs were followed by a familiar rapping on the door.

"You decent?" her brother hollered.

"Yep. Aren't you supposed to be at work?"

"Eye doctor," Danny explained as he cracked open the door. He squeezed into the cramped walkout, which was cluttered with teetering piles of random boxes.

It was ... absurd. Kat had been tiptoeing around them for a week, trying to prevent an avalanche.

"It was the weirdest thing. My eyes sort of ... fixed themselves?" Danny said, voice a mix of surprise and wonder.

Her brother wore loafers, khakis, and a black T-shirt that said, 'Oh, joy ... another PEBKAC Error', whatever that meant.

Danny was a system administrator and had like a million of those geek shirts.

"Seriously?" she replied.

"Yeah—apparently, it's a thing now. The magical microbe can cure myopia."

Stupid Microbe X. Wrecker of lives, destroyer of careers.

"No shit?" she said, curious despite herself.

"It's a slow process, though. Doc said I'll need to come in every time my eyes start hurting."

"For a weaker prescription?"

"Yup."

Huh. First cancer, then the common cold. Now, poor eyesight was a thing of the past. Microbe X was a miracle ... for most people.

For her sister, for sure.

Her brother glanced around, then moved a couple of boxes off a beanbag chair and flopped onto it. The scraping they made as he rearranged them grated on Kat's sensitive ears. "Ugh, I need to take care of all this crap," he muttered.

"Yeah—I was wondering why this place looks like an episode of Hoarders."

"Oh, you know." He scrubbed at the back of his neck. "Just some housecleaning."

Kat burst out laughing as understanding hit her. She pictured her brother pacing around his entire house, tossing everything in boxes, frantic as he vacuumed and scrubbed the toilets. There was only one explanation for it.

"You threw all this crap down here the first time you had Brooke over, didn't you?"

"Guilty."

"It's been like, six months, Danny."

"I've had a lot going on," he said, "and it's actually been closer to seven and a half."

Her mouth fell open as she looked at him. "You're going to ask her to marry you."

Despite her crappy mood, a smile quirked at the corner of her lips.

He threw her an indignant look. "And exactly how did the brainiac come to that conclusion?"

"—you said seven and a *half* months. You sound like a little kid. 'It's *seven and a half, actually*,'" she mimicked, flopping back onto the bed.

He reached into the box next to him, rustling through the items, and before she knew it, a soccer ball was flying at her head. Her stiff arms failed her as she fumbled, and it bounced onto the mattress beside her.

"Watch it—I just woke up!" She whined, then snatched up the ball and flung it back at him, feeling the strain in her tender muscles after the throw.

He caught and juggled it a few times with practiced ease before returning it to the box. "So ... mom and dad asked about you last night."

"Ugh. Lemme guess, mom was like, 'Is she still moping about that job?', and dad was like, 'Maybe she can become a *real* doctor now.'"

Her brother snickered. "Pretty much. He suggested ortho-pedic surgery, but mom thought the ER would be cooler."

"Yeah, because that has *so* much in common with microbiol-ogy. I'd have to go back to school again. Never mind that I have zero interest."

His gaze filled with understanding, mouth tightening into a thin line. "Yeah ... it sucks. Did you ever hear back from that one place? You know, where doctors go to villages in third-world countries or whatever?"

"Doctors Without Borders?" She snorted. "Yeah. I actually got a really nice rejection letter."

He raised an eyebrow.

She raised her shoulders, then dropped them with a sigh. "They're full up, apparently. It's a good thing, it's just—"

"—it sucks for you," he interrupted, his face contorting in a genuine show of sympathy.

"It sucks for me," she agreed, though it was the understate-ment of a lifetime.

After Microbe X swept the globe, she'd spent seven months riding out the end of postdoc funding, documenting research that had become irrelevant. There wasn't a playbook for what to do when an entire field disappeared, and no one knew how to react.

Everyone in microbiology with the right connections had joined one of the new projects studying Microbe X.

Kat had always attested that brown-nosing was for people whose work didn't speak for itself, a sign of corruption in the system. So when the worldwide game of 'Microbe X Musical Chairs' ended, she found herself without a seat.

No one understood that it wasn't a 'disappointment.' Or a 'setback.' Or a 'perfect opportunity for a career change.'

It was a sucker punch.

Her research hadn't ever been just a job to her. It had been a purpose. An obsession—the good kind.

Losing her work had been at least an order of magnitude more painful than when things with Brian had ended. Not that she *told* people that losing her career was ten times more devastating than a failed engagement. That wasn't the sort of thing most people understood.

"I told Mom and Dad you're taking a mini vacay, and that seemed to satisfy them for now." Danny's voice broke into her musings. "But *Beth* ... you *really* need to talk to her, Kat. She thinks she did something to piss you off."

Beth didn't do *anything*. And Kat was the most wretched monster who ever lived, because she couldn't manage to be happy for her.

A surge of bitterness rolled through her, followed by overwhelming guilt, and she tried to shake it off.

It was ironic, almost tragic, that she had dedicated her entire life to studying chronic diseases, and now everyone in the entire world was healthy.

Everyone except her.

Okay, that was melodramatic. Kat wasn't the only person in the world who developed Syndrome Q from Microbe X. It was rare, but not *that* rare.

"Well, did she?" Danny asked.

"Did she what?"

"Did she piss you off? If she did, she's like ... ridiculously sorry."

Kat forgot to be gentle as she shook her head, and a stab of pain lanced through it. "She didn't do anything. This is all me."

He scrubbed a hand over his chin. "What's going on, Kat? This isn't like you."

The truth was unspeakable. Petty. Horrible.

She'd devoted her life to taking care of her twin sister, to finding a cure for her chronic fatigue syndrome. They were best friends, roommates. Inseparable. Beth was her favorite person in the entire world, and Kat had always wanted more for her.

But over the past eight months, while Beth had been getting healthier, Kat had hidden her growing sickness.

It felt like a cruel cosmic joke. Kat's reward for all her hard work was to switch places with her sister.

It was childish, but thoughts like 'Why me?' and 'It's not fair' repeated in her head like a perverse mantra. She felt an indescribable guilt for not being able to look her sister in the eyes, but Beth was so empathetic she would *know*.

And then Beth would feel guilty for being well, which wasn't fair, either.

So last week, Kat packed a suitcase and escaped to her brother's place to have her petty little meltdown in private.

Like a total coward.

"No, yeah. I mean, no—Beth didn't do anything. I'm just, you know," she waved her hands, grasping for the right words, "taking a minute to regroup."

"If you say so." He scrutinized her.

She squirmed as his gaze lingered on her tired eyes and unkempt hair, a testament to sleepless nights and the weight of her crumbling life.

"Hey—why do you look like shit?" he blurted out.

What could she say? That was the million-dollar question. How could she explain looking sick when she didn't want anyone to discover that she had the only illness left on Earth?

Kat refused to lie about it, but withholding was another matter entirely.

She mustered a weak smile. "Gee, thanks. I haven't been sleeping well, what with my entire life going up in flames."

"Man, if I didn't know you, I'd honestly think you were on drugs or something. You look awful. You feeling okay?" His eyes narrowed.

Okay—time to shut this down. "Of course. It's just ennui and shitty sleep," Kat replied, voice weary.

If he was going to come down before she had a chance to put on her makeup, she would have to sleep with it on. She wasn't prepared for them to find out about her illness. Her family had already gone through so much with Beth's illness that they deserved to believe that everyone was finally healthy.

Even if it wasn't true.

"Well, I'm here if you wanna talk, or whatever," he offered, his voice gentle but hesitant. He glanced at his watch. "I gotta get to work."

"Yeah, I gotta meet Claire for coffee in a few minutes." The fabric of her hoodie rustled in the quiet room as she adjusted it.

He scrunched his eyes at her. "You're going out like that?"

It took her a moment to realize what he meant. "What?"

"How many days has it been since you took a shower, little sis?"

She pursed her lips, fingers absentmindedly tugging at a loose strand of hair. "I'll wear a hat," she muttered.

In a display of feigned disgust, he shook his head and headed towards the door. At the entrance, he paused. "Oh, hey—Brooke's coming over on Friday."

"You two are *so* getting married," she teased.

He screwed up his mouth into what he likely intended to be a scowl, but he couldn't conceal the grin that spread over his face. "Dammit, Kat—you're too smart for your own good."

He maneuvered through the maze of boxes until he stood before her. Then he pulled a small black box out of his khakis, revealing a simple yet elegant silver ring with a square-cut diamond.

She peered down at it. "It's nice—for a diamond."

He play-punched her arm, but Kat had to suppress a yelp of pain. She masked it up by enveloping him in a bear hug. "I'm so happy for you. Even if your taste in gems is pedestrian."

See? She could still find happiness for other people. Now, if only she could find it for Beth.

"I'm *thinking* of asking her to marry me, but ... I'm not quite there yet. Like, not sure she'll say yes."

"Why wouldn't she?"

"Oh, you know—she's ... *her*, and I'm just a nerd who used to spend all his time playing computer games."

"Used to?"

"Not as much as before," he said, voice indignant. "Anyway, I was *gonna* ask you to have dinner with me and Brooke, but if you're going to be a pain—"

"I'll be good." She pulled back and mimed zipping her mouth shut. "And, of course, she'll say yes—you're a catch."

"You better. She's—" Danny paused, absentmindedly scrubbing at the back of his neck.

"Oh my god. Daniel Michael Miller—are you blushing?" She jostled him, wincing as her sore muscles protested.

He raised a shoulder, a dopey smile on his face. "I really like her. Beth does, too."

So Beth had already met Brooke. Kat felt a twinge of jealousy, but it made sense. Kat had missed a ton of family stuff during med school and her PhD program.

And the last eight months had been so hectic. She'd been ... preoccupied.

"That's not difficult," she quipped. "Beth likes everyone."

"Truth. But Brooke is awesome."

"What about mom and dad?" she asked. "Have *they* met her yet?"

He snorted. "Yeah ... not ready to go there."

She raised an eyebrow.

"Brooke's younger than me, and you know how mom and dad are."

"How young?"

"Like, 26?"

Kat gave a little whistle. Danny was 34. "Yeah, but they'll get over it. I'm sure they'll be happy at least one of their kids might give them grand-babies."

He shrugged.

Kat's jaw dropped. "Damn. You were supposed to wave that off or something. Who are you, and what have you done with my brother?"

"I mean ...?" He said, grinning like a fool. "I could get one of those T-shirt sets, like where I wear a CTRL-C shirt and dress the kid up in a CTRL-V," he stopped and cocked his head. "Um, what are those things the babies wear, the ones that look like swimsuits?"

"What, onesies?"

"Yeah, those."

"God, you're such a geek."

"Yeah? And you're a nerd." He started backing towards the door again. "So, Friday?"

"I'll be there."

He took off, and Kat walked over to the bed to check the time on her phone.

10:43.

A pullout couch had never looked so inviting.

It was so tempting to crawl back in—*under* the covers this time. If Kat texted Claire *right now*, she could catch her before she left the office ...

But the last thing she wanted was for Claire to call Beth. Besides, she was already up, and coffee sounded—not terrible. Enticing, even. She needed to face the world at some point, and today was as good as any.

But she needed to hustle.

She went to the small three-quarter bathroom to freshen up and fix her hair.

It was ... pretty gross. Her brother was right—she could use a shower. But there wasn't time, so she threw her long blond hair into a low ponytail. She was sure she'd packed her old Creighton ball cap.

It was impossible to miss the dark circles under her eyes, so she dug through her makeup kit to find some concealer.

Before getting sick, she seldom wore makeup, but felt exposed if she looked like this in public.

As if everyone who saw her would recognize that she had Syndrome Q.

Gazing at her reflection, she couldn't help but wonder aloud, "Why me?"

This was not a rhetorical question. Kat wanted—no, *needed*— to understand why this microbe affected her pathologically. What was different about her?

What *was* Syndrome Q?

It had started like everyone else's for her—the acute Microbe X infection felt like the flu: aches, fever, and overwhelming fatigue.

As people recovered from their 'Microbe X Flu,' they also found themselves free of cancer, diabetes, acne—everything, but it had taken a while to puzzle it out.

After all, no one was on the lookout for an epidemic that made everyone healthy.

But Kat never got better.

Her initial illness was far more severe than most people's, with a fever that almost had Beth rushing her to the emergency room. And when she'd recovered from the 'flu,' this strange cluster of symptoms had taken hold and never let go.

Fatigue, muscle and joint pain, headaches, sensitivity to light and sound, nausea. A brain that felt like something was crawling around, scratching inside her skull.

Irritability.

Depression, though she didn't know how much of that was Syndrome Q and how much was just ... losing her career and getting sick.

Shoot. Now, there were those weird yellow spots under her eyes.

She fished through the bag, hearing the tubes, compacts, and bottles clink and jostle. Then she spotted the fancy Sephora foundation her sister had convinced her to buy last summer.

Thoughts of Beth tugged at her heart, but she pushed them aside and focused on applying her makeup.

With a background in medical microbiology, she expected some sort of revelation, a moment of clarity from the universe. She needed to understand why this infuriating microbe—which appeared to function as a super-symbiote for everyone else—was making her ill.

Granted, there wasn't any definitive evidence linking Microbe X to Syndrome Q, but how could they not be connected?

An unidentified spore-encased microbe swept through the population, and then, all known human diseases vanished.

Then Syndrome Q emerged.

Correlation didn't prove causation, but—it was kind of a smoking gun.

She leaned in to inspect her handiwork. The worst of the dark circles were concealed, but now she just looked pale. She added some blush to add a touch of life to her face.

Hat. She needed a hat.

Returning to the other room, she hoisted her suitcase onto the bed. There, she noticed her T-shirt from last night peeking out from under the covers, mocking her. She snagged it and stuffed it into the case.

She hoped she wasn't sleepwalking naked. Not that it would explain why her pajamas were always neatly tucked under the covers. It was so bizarre ...

Kat refused to deal with that on top of everything else.

She just needed to find her hat.

After a few seconds of trying to find it in the mass of clothes, she gave up and dumped everything out.

Finally, she spotted her baseball cap and pulled it on, allowing her ponytail to hang through the back.

Then she crammed everything back inside the suitcase, using more force than necessary, but there were worse outlets for her frustration than dirty laundry.

Sometimes, life wasn't fair, and she needed to deal with it. It hadn't been fair that her twin had spent most of her life suffering from migraines, fatigue, and pain, either.

At least Beth Ann was feeling better.

And Kat was really, *really* thrilled for her. Really, she was.

And if she repeated it enough, maybe she could finally feel joy for her sister without the perverse dose of resentment that always seemed to follow.

She needed to let go of this vicious bitterness.

Beth was getting a chance to live a normal life.

And her goofball of a brother was in love.

Good things were happening to people she loved, which was terrific.

She couldn't help but chuckle. Danny *would* end up dressing that kid in stupid matchy-matchy onesies. It was going to be friggin' adorable.

She took a breath, then let it out.

It was time to start living again. To move on already.

Kat was no victim, not of circumstance or fate. Never had been and never would.

Step 1: Coffee with Claire. She steeled herself for the dose of tough love she was about to get from her no-nonsense best friend.

But she could take it. She was stronger than she'd been acting.

After a deep inhale, she plastered a smile onto her face.

I am not my sickness. I am not my failed career. I am not my stupid bitterness. I am Katharine fucking Miller, and I am a force to be reckoned with.

Snagging her purse, she braced herself and went out the side door to head for Zen.

THE
VALMORAN
CHRONICLES

7

INTO THE BELLY OF THE BEAST

EARTH, OMAHA, NEBRASKA

AUBREY HOPE, HEIRESS AND DIRECTOR OF PR STRATEGY FOR HOPE PHARMACEUTICALS

~

AUBREY HOPE's stilettos beat a satisfying click-clack as she crossed the marble lobby floor of Hope Pharmaceuticals.

Despite the warm sunlight streaming through the windows, a lingering chill from the brisk Nebraska spring morning clung to her bones.

The brief trip had drained her already dangerously low energy reserves. It also sparked the beginnings of another migraine, but her carefully applied makeup should conceal the dark shadows beneath her eyes.

The chatter of early-arriving employees, the modern chandelier hanging from the three-story ceiling, and even the slightly outdated sofas in the waiting area made this place feel like home.

She'd skipped across these marble floors wearing French braids and a tutu, walked through in a schoolgirl uniform ... and stormed in wearing a cap and gown the day her father missed her college graduation.

Today, she strode through in full war gear—tailored pencil skirt, silk blouse with several strategic buttons undone, fitted blazer.

Because today, her father would hear her out.

As she approached the security turnstile, she glanced down in dismay at the coffee cups in each hand and then at her Balenciaga handbag, which was slung crossbody.

Her security badge was inside.

"Shit," she muttered, her frustration slipping out under her breath.

But before she had time to sigh, Tony, the security guard, appeared by her side. "Here, let me hold those for you, Miss Aubrey! You're looking sharp today!"

"You're a lifesaver, Tony," Aubrey said, flashing a grateful smile. Tony had been a part of the team for at least a decade now, and Hope Pharma was fortunate to have him. "I guess I didn't really think this through."

She pulled out her card, scanned it, and kept it handy for the elevator.

"Thirsty?" he teased, handing the cups back to her.

"Nah—this one's for Helen. Early meetings, you know how it is."

He shook his head. "You work too much, young lady—you should take some time off."

Aubrey's heart skipped a beat.

Could he tell something was off with her? That she was sick? She'd need to check her makeup before meeting with her father, just to be sure ...

"Oh, but I'm sure you'll take some time off for the wedding, right?" Tony continued, shattering her focus. "You must be excited."

Relief hit her—he was just being friendly, chastising her for working too hard. Making small talk.

"Oh, absolutely!" she exclaimed, flashing him an extra-winning smile as she backed towards the elevator bay. "Dad hired a brilliant planner, and everything is coming together perfectly."

"Well, I'm truly happy for you, Miss Aubrey. You have a good day, now."

"You, too, Tony!"

With that, she strode towards the elevator bay, steeling her nerves for the confrontation ahead.

If her plan worked, she would meet with the CEO at 7:45 sharp.

But it had to work. Aubrey would meet with her father.

She envisioned success: handing the coffee to Helen, striding into her father's office with unwavering confidence, compelling him to hear her out.

It would work.

It had to work.

A couple of employees were waiting in front of the elevators, so she held back a few steps to wait.

Ever since Microbe X had turned the world on its head, employees had been showing up earlier and earlier, pretending to be busy even though there was less and less work to be done.

Hope Pharma hadn't laid off anyone because of this unprecedented upheaval and hadn't given anyone reason to worry. But Aubrey was among the few executives who knew things were about to change.

It was inevitable.

Microbe X had fucked over the healthcare industry, and then taken the global economy with it, just for good measure.

Companies in the healthcare industry had been going under, left and right.

Hope Pharma was screwed more than most pharmaceutical companies, since they developed—or rather, they used to develop—treatments for incurable diseases. She was determined to keep their doors open.

"Look, I'm just saying—it doesn't seem fair. He's already had his time," said the young man.

Aubrey didn't know him, but something about him screamed IT. Or accounting.

"But it's Tom Brady!" protested the older guy. Aubrey knew of him. He was from IT, and according to Javier, their CTO, he was a total pain in the ass. If the guy wasn't the only one who understood some obscure piece of software, he would have been fired long ago.

"I get it, I do—but if they keep letting old dudes come out of retirement, it's gonna mess up the whole system."

"It's a brave new world, kid. Don't look a gift horse in the mouth."

"I know," the young man answered, seemingly chastised. "My mom's cancer is gone. That's all that matters."

The older man scoffed. "Well, it's not the only thing that matters—I've worked in pharmaceuticals for thirty years, and now the whole industry has gone to shit. So much for that fancy pension, know what I mean?"

"Hey, Hope Pharma's still here," he replied. "We're not like all the others—"

"—kid, look around you—mark my words, the writing's on the wall." The way the jerk talked to the young man, they had to be from the same department, probably the same team.

The elevator door dinged, and Aubrey strode forward, shouldering her way between the two men. "Gentlemen," she said, nodding curtly as she approached the open elevator.

Behind her, she heard the older man stammer, "Oh, hey—morning, Miss Hope. Didn't see you there."

"You go ahead—we'll grab the next one," the younger man added.

Aubrey pinned one of the coffees against her body so she could scan her badge for the executive floor, then held the button to hold the door.

Meeting the younger man's gaze, she adopted her best sports banter voice. "Come on, if Tom is still the best, he deserves to play, right?"

Her gaze then shifted to the older man. "And Hope Pharma isn't going anywhere." She released the button and allowed the elevator door to close.

Away from observant eyes, Aubrey slouched against the back wall of the elevator.

The artificial lights pierced her eyes, and although the motion of the elevator was smooth as butter, her stomach lurched, and her head throbbed in protest.

Her morning cocktail of off-label drugs hadn't kicked in yet. Standing still, with a coffee in each hand, the trembling in her limbs became obvious. She braced her elbows against her ribs, checking her reflection in the mirrored wall to ensure she appeared nonchalant.

Following the technique she had perfected for concealing her tremors, Aubrey supported her limbs and avoided holding objects away from her body.

The elevator slowed, too soon, and Aubrey scrambled to assume a position of authority and poise before the door slid open.

Floor 14, Sales.

Two employees entered the elevator, wearing off-the-rack suits that could use tailoring. Aubrey thought she recognized the woman, perhaps from a previous project they had worked on. The other individual, who resembled a knock-off Ryan Gosling, exuded an inflated ego that barely fit inside the elevator.

The woman addressed Knock-off RG. "Your team has that big presentation today, right?"

"Yep," he replied, projecting his voice so Aubrey could over-hear. "Stayed up all night finishing it since Jared was out sick. Again."

Never mind that Hope Pharma had been clear in its support of those with Syndrome Q ever since the start of this whole fiasco.

Maybe he meant Jared in Sales ... if so, he was barking up the wrong tree. Aubrey had known Jared since she was a kid—he was one of their most experienced account managers.

She made a mental note to check in on Jared later, to see if he was ok and let him know his idiot subordinate was out for blood.

Trudy rounded the corner, slightly out of breath. "Hold the door," she said, then smiled at Aubrey. "You're going up?"

"Yep."

Trudy gave her a knowing look before scanning her badge. As the doors closed, Aubrey said, "Everything good to go on your end?"

"Yep," Trudy replied, lowering her voice even though they were alone in the elevator. "The government contract is in its final stages of negotiation, and almost everyone is on board with the acquisition."

"Almost everyone?" Aubrey's stomach dropped. Her father preferred executive consensus.

"It'll be fine. You just work your magic on those interviews and sell Richard on the PR plan, k?" Trudy assured her. "You still flying down to Texas for that meeting tomorrow?"

"Yep—her manager confirmed this morning."

Trudy shook her head, chuckling. "I still can't believe you had the guts to ask Hayley Jo to be our spokesperson."

"It just made sense."

"It's a good plan, Aubrey." Trudy reached out and squeezed Aubrey's shoulder. "Your mom would have been so proud of you."

Aubrey blinked rapidly and took a sip of her coffee. "Thanks."

Aubrey's mother had convinced Richard Hope to shift the company's focus towards finding treatments for chronic illness. When her father married a Lebanese supermodel, he couldn't have seen that one coming.

Some cynics viewed it as a smart business move, dealing with treatments rather than cures.

But that hadn't been how Aubrey's mother had seen it. Aubrey's grandmother had lived with multiple chronic conditions, and when her mom saw an opportunity to alleviate similar suffering in others, she made it happen.

She refused to let her mother's dream die.

The elevator opened, and Trudy prepared to exit, but apparently noticed that Aubrey wasn't following. "He finally let you on the calendar?"

"No." Aubrey sighed. "But he's meeting with me—he just doesn't know it yet."

Trudy let out a low whistle. "Gutsy."

"What's he gonna do?" Aubrey asked, projecting a confidence she didn't fully possess.

"Well, he always had a soft spot for you. Hopefully, he's in a good mood today." Trudy frowned, then continued, "Aubrey, I still think we should tell him—"

"—no," Aubrey interrupted, shaking her head. "People will take the idea more seriously coming from you and Jack. A lot of them still think of me as a kid."

"I'm not sure why he's been sidelining you, Aubrey, but it's not for lack of talent. I'm sure he has his reasons." After a brief pause, Trudy continued, "Well, if we pull this off, I'm telling him it was you."

"Oh, come on, it wasn't all my idea. It was a group effort."

"If you say so," she said, jerking her head towards the top floor."Good luck up there."

"I'll get it done—you guys just take care of your part."

"You got it."

The elevator doors closed, and Aubrey prepared herself for the last leg of her ride.

Unease swirled in Aubrey's gut at the thought of dissenters to the acquisition. The Wellify deal, the Microbe X contracts—it was an all-or-nothing package. Any opposition threatened to topple her carefully constructed house of cards.

If there were doubts, it was even more crucial that she secure Hayley Jo's celebrity sponsorship. Hopefully, that would be enough to tip the scales.

As the elevator doors opened to the small executive lobby, Aubrey was greeted by her father's long-time secretary at the mahogany reception desk.

"Morning, Helen." Aubrey handed her one of the coffee cups, and Helen returned the gesture with a warm grin.

Helen was the epitome of a morning person, almost sickeningly so. But though the woman didn't need coffee to wake up, Aubrey knew that coconut mocha from Zen was her weakness.

Helen greeted Aubrey with a bright smile. "Good morning, Aubrey. You're here early!"

Having been her father's gatekeeper since Aubrey was seven, Helen was practically family. It came with the territory when your only parent was the CEO of a major pharmaceutical company.

Helen's primary responsibility was to keep unauthorized individuals from bothering the CEO. So, at the moment, the kind-hearted woman was an obstacle—but Aubrey was determined to meet her father. Hopefully, she wouldn't need to raise hell to make it happen.

Psyching herself up, Aubrey gave Helen a warm smile and proceeded with her plan.

"Yes, I need to have a quick word with Dad before he starts his day."

Helen frowned. "Oh, Aubrey, he has a full schedule today."

Aubrey focused her mind, envisioning success. She had to make this work.

See it. Believe it. Create it.

She locked eyes with Helen and visualized success. She imagined Helen allowing her to pass without resistance. "He's expecting me."

Helen's entire demeanor shifted instantly, her expression morphing to ease and openness. "Oh, in that case, go on in. He'll be here any minute."

"Thanks, Helen. Enjoy the coffee—let's catch up soon," Aubrey said, already moving past the reception desk. As she walked past, a twinge of unease flickered through her. That had been too easy.

She hadn't actually expected to get in without a fight. A bitter confrontation with her father when he came in ... something.

But it was the outcome she'd hoped for, so she tried to put it out of her mind.

The opulent corner office, with its imported leather furniture and meticulously handcrafted mahogany desk, mirrored her father's persona to a tee. The antique clock on the desk was obscenely loud in the otherwise quiet room.

Aubrey despised that clock; every tick seemed to mock her for the countless hours she had spent waiting in this room, longing for a father who never seemed to have enough time for her.

Sunlight streamed through the windows, illuminating the ornate bookshelves that adorned two walls. Among the priceless rare books and cigar boxes, Richard Hope had carefully placed his most treasured possessions—pieces from his late wife's modern art collection, which he personally cleaned and maintained.

The scent of her father's sandalwood cologne filled the air, evoking a mix of comfort and anxiety for Aubrey.

She set down her coffee, removed her purse, and sank into one of the plush leather chairs. Her feet were already throbbing, but she resisted the urge to slouch in her seat.

No time to for weariness. Taking a gulp of coffee, Aubrey grabbed her phone to check her messages.

Derrick: Morning, beautiful! Good luck ambushing the old

man—you're gonna crush it. Maybe you can finally let me in on your clever plans once you win him over!

A flicker of irritation passed through Aubrey. It was so annoying when he acted like this. She couldn't help feeling like he was using their relationship to manipulate her.

Aubrey's fiancé, Derrick, was handsome, charming, and incredibly ambitious. However, he always got nosy whenever he found out she was working on something big without informing him.

But just because they lived together didn't entitle him to company secrets. Despite being one of their top project managers, he'd hear about it when everyone else did.

Glancing at the time, Aubrey tucked her cell phone back into her purse. Her father would arrive any minute now. She straightened her suit, putting on a façade of composure.

Ambushing her own father hadn't been part of plan A.

Or B, C, or D. But he'd been dodging her for weeks, and enough was enough.

For months, Aubrey had suspected that her father was sidelining her, but now she was sure.

Yesterday, she saw the retired VP of Marketing emerge from an executive planning meeting, one that she—the current Director of PR Strategy—had not been invited to.

Aubrey had no issue with Michael—he was practically an uncle to her after all these years. But how could she do her job if she was shut out of the decision-making process? It was an impossible situation.

Anger flared hot in Aubrey's veins. She'd had enough of this bullshit.

She was more than Richard Hope's daughter, more than a mere PR strategist.

Aubrey was the heiress to Hope Pharmaceuticals—its future CEO—and they were not going down without a fight.

THE
VALMORAN
CHRONICLES

8

SO NOT A CORPORATE TOOL

EARTH, OMAHA, NEBRASKA

VIOLET DAVIS-KOBAYASHI, DATA SCIENTIST AND CTO OF WELLIFY

≈

VIOLET ARRIVED at Wellify's office a few minutes before lunch. Today, she took the front door, hugging the wall like a spy so no one would spot her through the window.

Their small headquarters had that open-office-y startup vibe. The CEO refused to change it, even after Violet presented him with scientific proof that open offices hinder collaboration and destroy developer focus.

Not that he didn't believe her—Tom took all of her advice seriously these days—but he would sacrifice productivity if it meant visitors swooned over his trendy office space.

Which almost made it worse.

Violet's arsenal was in her messenger bag, along with her laptop. She pulled out two Nerf guns and checked that she'd loaded them. Her team always thought they would pull one over on her, but Vi was the queen of the Nerf-snipe.

The receptionist was not at her desk when she slipped through the door, so Vi ducked to take cover in front of it. She was positive she snuck in undetected.

She peeked out to see where her coworkers were. Time almost stood still for a moment, and all she saw were systems, patterns, trajectories.

Alice hadn't slept well last night, Jason was in a terrible mood, and Tabby was in a new relationship. Erika was having one of her superstar days. Awesome.

Something was off about their demeanor, and several must have been out for an early lunch. Or maybe a late coffee.

Violet didn't question this ability anymore. This hyper-perception thing—that's what she'd been calling it in her head—had been happening for months.

She'd take in information and then just know things. Her Syndrome Q seemed to have done more than make her hypersensitive and exhausted, but this near-precognitive intuition was bizarre.

Vi certainly hadn't told anyone.

About the hyper-perception or the Q. Not really a sharer.

Stashing her laptop bag under the desk, she flipped up the hood of her favorite Cowboy Bebop hoodie. Let's jam! Four years of Aikido in Japan and a decade of Jiu-Jitsu in the US enabled her to do showy stunts like the one she was about to do.

A side roll brought her to her feet to the left of the desk, and then she sprinted for the whiteboard across the room, firing on her team as she moved.

Tabby. Aiden. Celeste. Jason.

Hit. Hit. Hit. Hit.

She ducked behind the whiteboard and heard the room scrambling while she ran along the other side. She had to stay light on her feet.

Jason's shout rang out, "Crap—she's early, guys!"

Nerf bullets pinged off the other side of the board, and one whizzed past her legs, but she had already darted for her desk.

"Take cover, people!" someone called out—Celeste, maybe? No time to check.

Violet strafed sideways, taking advantage of years of footwork drills, and spotted Gigi heading out of the breakroom with her unicorn mug. Violet pegged her with a dart and heard her yelp, "Dangit, Vi—that one went in my coffee. Gross."

Once tucked away behind her desk, she reached under it to pull out her battery-operated mega Nerf cannon, nicknamed 'Vera'—because Firefly, duh—and plopped it on the desktop.

She pulled the trigger, preparing to rain fire down upon her team, and heard 'click-click-click-click-click.'

What the …?

"Looking for these?" The new guy, Bastion, called out from the dark conference room behind her … right before he and three others ran out, peppering her with projectiles.

Vi yanked her hood further down to shield her face, then held her hands up in surrender. "Yield! I yield—you guys got me. I submit to your superior battle strategy."

She stooped to gather ammo with the rest of the team.

"I hope you guys didn't waste all morning sitting in the dark," she joked.

"Oh, no worries. We set up our laptops in the conference room, and Erika said she'd text us when you got here. Besides, I like working in the dark," Bastion said.

"Yeah, I get that," Vi said, nodding. "It's a coder thing."

Jason piped up, "When Bas told us the plan, we told him he was crazy for touching your stuff, Vi."

Violet shrugged. "Eh, it was clever. I'll allow it."

She looked over at Bastion, the new guy. He wore an old-school Zelda shirt, bringing him up a notch in her book. Catching his gaze, she sent him an awkward smile.

Social interaction was a bitch, and eye contact was her nemesis.

Being the center of attention made her uncomfortable, but as the CTO, she had to suck it up.

This daily shootout ritual of theirs counted as team-building, and she'd much rather do this than sit around and endure some corporate bonding crap.

Trust falls? *Hellz, no.*

Violet went to the reception desk to retrieve her laptop bag and checked the time.

Ten minutes before her one-on-one with the CEO.

She pulled out her laptop and headed to the break room for a much-needed coffee.

Soft footsteps sounded as she rummaged through the fridge for her cream. Her martial arts training put her on high alert, though she knew it was just one of the team. She didn't turn around to check, and a moment later, Jason sidled up next to her.

He leaned in, not invading her personal space, but close enough to whisper, "Hey, Vi?"

"Uh-huh?" She checked behind half a dozen cans of Red Bull and finally located her cream.

"So what's up with all these investor types who keep coming around? We looking for VC funding or something? Financial troubles?"

"Couldn't tell you. Boss hasn't mentioned anything to me. Partners? Investors? Who knows ... but not financial troubles. That much I know."

She snagged a spoon from the drawer, and it clattered into her mug. Clink, clink, clink, as she stirred. Bright lights. The whirring of the fridge. Voices in the adjacent room. So many stimuli.

Jason hadn't responded, so she forced her attention back to the conversation. "If it makes you feel better, a round of funding would mean stock options for everyone."

"Yeah ...?"

"Hey, try not to worry about it. Just write some kickass code. Ignore the suit parade. They don't matter—it's all about the code."

Jason grinned. "Yeah, if you're sure. Thanks, Vi."

"No prob. Nice chat, but I gotta run. Time to meet with the boss man."

He chuckled. "Gotcha. Hey, can I swing by your desk later? I'm working on a comp of these API libraries and wanted your input."

"Sure thing!" she said, backing out of the breakroom. "I'll be back in like 10, maybe 15? Bring Erika and Gigi along. We can brainstorm."

She swung by her desk to grab her laptop before heading to the CEO's office—the only one with a door that shut, unlike the rest of them stuck in the bullpen—and rapped on the door frame.

Because even though he had a door, Tom liked to leave it open. *Eye roll.*

"Hey, Vi—come on in. Hey, close the door behind you, will you?"

Well, well, well. Look who decided to use his fancy-schmancy door.

Tom Alderson, the CEO of Wellify, dressed like a recovering corporate tool who was now trying to pull off 'Silicon Valley chic.' Khaki shorts, a fitted polo shirt, and Birkenstocks brought him oh-so-close, but it was all very 'uncanny valley'—like he was cosplaying as a tech geek.

The whole thing came off ... creepy.

But he was an okay guy. At least he gave a damn about the app—back when his wife had MS, anyway.

Now that Microbe X had cured her, the jerk was considering an acquisition by Hope Pharmaceuticals.

Part of her felt guilty for keeping Jason in the dark, but it wasn't like she was lying—Tom hadn't breathed a word to her about the sale. Thanks to Syndrome Q, she just knew.

Maybe it was the travel magazine she spotted on his desk the other day. Or the way he'd been slowly clearing out his office. Something in the body language during his meeting with those corporate goons from Hope Pharma last week ...

Violet couldn't pinpoint how she knew he was thinking about selling out. She just knew.

The entire situation was shouting the truth at her, even though no one had said a word.

It reminded her of the early days of the Microbe X debacle, when those first 'tainted blood samples' surfaced. A couple of weeks later, reports started popping up about people miraculously recovering from terminal illnesses.

There hadn't been much to go on, but the clues spoke to Vi and—though she didn't know it at the time—to her hyperperception.

Amid the chaos, she shorted the hell out of the medical industry—placing huge bets that Big Pharma and private hospitals would go belly up. Though, she could've made bank by shorting an index fund, because worldwide stock markets plummeted during the chaos.

But she'd known the medical industry was about to implode. Targeting 'Big Medicine' made her an absolute killing, and she was more than happy to take their investors' filthy money.

Vi had amassed a tidy little crypto fortune, all under the radar, thanks to her ... other skills. Skills she rarely used anymore, but getting wealthy at the expense of big pharma had seemed like an appropriate situation to make an exception and dust off her grey hat.

Then, while everyone else reeled from the financial collapse, Vi sensed the next big shift.

A month later, she waltzed into Tom's office, suggesting they add functionality for that bizarre new illness the media dubbed 'Syndrome Q.'

Because she knew, somehow, that Microbe X—though the press still called it the 'cryospore' back then—was gonna wipe out every disease ... except Syndrome Q.

He'd been a tough sell, so Violet told him she ran a statistical blah-blah model that predicted blah-blah growth in those with Syndrome Q over blah-blah timeframe.

'I have a hunch,' would not exactly have flown.

Fast-forward a few months, and the medical industry was in shambles. Wellify rolled out its Syndrome Q update and was suddenly the sole player in the game.

That's when Tom dubbed her 'the data whisperer,' because Vi's foresight had single-handedly saved the company. Now, he had investors and partners crawling all over the office, practically breaking down the doors.

Which made it all the more infuriating that Tom hadn't consulted her on this whole Hope Pharma thing. Deep down, he probably suspected she would flat-out tell him it was a terrible idea.

Which, to be fair, was 100% accurate.

She rolled the yoga ball out from the corner of the room and plopped down on it, then set her laptop on the edge of Tom's desk. "Whatcha got for me today, boss?"

"Hey, Vi! I was wondering if you could put together an estimate on how long it would take to prep our data for—"

Tom glanced down at his notes. "Third-party real-time integration. And another for a—"

He checked his notes. Again.

"—historical data export. How long, how much, how many people?"

Vi jotted down notes as he spoke. "Yeah, sure, Tom. Mind if I ask why?"

But she knew why—he was selling them to Hope Pharma, and the vultures wanted to know how quickly they could get their grubby little hands on Wellify's user data. Maybe he'd take this opportunity to fess up already.

"Is that important?" Tom sounded legitimately clueless, so Violet swallowed her exasperation and answered.

"Oh, for sure—the estimate can vary a ton depending on who the data is for. We need to know what data they need, the data models or format they prefer, if they expect us to push the data, or if we should build an API. That sort of thing."

He exhaled, looking relieved. "Gotcha. You've probably noticed we've had some visitors around the office. We've had inquiries from universities and research institutions about accessing our data for their Syndrome Q studies. That help?"

Right. 'Research institutions.' Like Hope Pharma.

Part of her couldn't shake the feeling that Tom was straight-up lying to her face, even though, rationally, she knew he was only being evasive. Falling back on old corporate toolishness.

"That's ... a start. I'll write it up assuming we're providing a basic REST API, and they'll pull the data on their end. When do you need the estimate?"

"Three days work? Heather will wrap it up in a neat little presentation for you. I don't want you wasting your time on that. Just get me the numbers."

Yeah. So maybe Tom wasn't all bad. When she was doing time at the tech giants, she always wasted so much time on grunt work.

It had been an *egregious* waste of resources.

Violet had to hand it to him—there was a reason she'd stuck around this long. But she was still peeved he was planning to sell the company without so much as asking for her opinion.

She'd been the first to join Wellify. The one who had discovered, interviewed, and cultivated the rest of the team. Vi believed in him and his idea back when no one else would give him the time of day.

The one with the skills to bring his dream to life. It felt like that should count for something, but apparently not.

This sale would mess everything up. Wellify was making a real difference. They had an epic culture and a fantastic team. Vi despised the idea of all this going away, thanks to something as basic as greed.

"Sure thing," she said, typing up the request. "Plenty of time. Anything else?"

"That's it—any updates for me?" He slapped his hands on his thighs, a Midwestern signal that the meeting was over.

"Nope, that's it for now," Violet said, standing up and rolling the yoga ball back to its corner. She snagged her laptop and coffee. "Actually, one more thing—I'm gonna round up the dev team in the bullpen tomorrow for some training. Wanted to make sure we won't have any suits dropping by."

"Nope, tomorrow's all clear. Keep up the great work, Vi."

"Yep, yep."

"Leave the door open on your way out."

Stupid sellout boss with his stupid door that he barely used.

As she stalked back to her desk, fury simmered in her veins. She was gonna loathe Tom if he sold out.

Vi's gut twisted with dread. Something about this whole situation felt off ... *really* off.

But her spidey senses were glitching out for once, sending her hyper-perception into a dizzying tailspin. Maybe she was still missing a critical piece of the puzzle.

Sure, she had a deep-seated hatred for corporate overlords and a secret anarchist streak a mile wide—not that she'd ever let that slip around the office.

But Violet was sure her political views and bruised ego had nothing to do with the sick feeling in the pit of her stomach.

Funneling all that Syndrome Q user data straight into the greedy clutches of some soulless pharma company was sketchy as hell.

That much, she just *knew*.

THE VALMORAN CHRONICLES

9

YOU WIN SOME, YOU LOSE SOME

EARTH, OMAHA, NEBRASKA

AUBREY HOPE, HEIRESS AND DIRECTOR OF PR
STRATEGY FOR HOPE PHARMACEUTICALS

~

THE OMAHA SUNRISE bled across the sky, casting long
shadows that danced over the lush furnishings in Richard
Hope's high-rise office.

Aubrey Hope braced herself against the chilly air and the
inevitable clash of wills. This confrontation with her father
would be a turning point, and failure wasn't an option.

The rich timbre of her father's voice hit her ears, followed by
crisp footfalls and a gust of air as he strode past her to his
desk.

Her father never simply entered a room. He occupied it.
Dominated it. Brought it to heel.

The blinding sunrise obscured the Omaha skyline in the floor-to-ceiling windows. Aubrey struggled not to squint as her father took his place behind the massive desk, steeling herself to stand her ground.

For a moment, she was tempted to make her excuses and flee. But she willed herself to stay seated and waited for her father to speak first.

If it surprised him to see her, he didn't let it show. Richard Hope took his sweet time settling in as if Aubrey wasn't there. He turned on his computer and didn't look up as he said, "Well, daughter—this is certainly a surprise. To what do I owe the honor?"

With a deep breath, Aubrey tried to sound confident in her reply.

"We need to discuss our PR strategy."

"Oh?" He raised his eyebrows, but didn't look away from his screen. "I don't recall requesting a revised PR strategy."

He was using his fake bored voice, the one she hated.

Aubrey clenched her fists under the desk, summoning patience.

She wanted to pound her fists on the desk and demand that he let her do her job, but she knew it wouldn't help her case. "We need to discuss the details of the PR strategy for the company's pivot."

"Pivot?" He raised his eyebrows in 'confusion'.

He had the nerve to pretend he didn't know what she was talking about. Aubrey's patience snapped. "Dad," Aubrey said, voice intense. "I'm your daughter. I love this company more than anyone but you. Just give me five minutes. Tell me what we're up against, and I'll tell you how we need to spin it."

She crossed her fingers under the desk.

Her father huffed, seemed to think for a minute, and then turned to face her.

"You want to know what we're up against? Fine." He crossed his arms and sat back, and for just a moment, his CEO mask slipped. Aubrey could see her father, weary, sitting across from her.

Then he started talking, ticking off the points as he went.

"First, we need to lay off 85% of our workforce—they don't fit the new direction."

"Second, we're taking on a government contract to field calls on Microbe X—the vacated space from all the people we're about to fire is becoming a damn call center."

"Finally, we're focusing everything we have on developing treatments for Syndrome Q, since it's the only chronic illness left. We're just days away from acquiring a small company with an app to help people manage their health, but we're actually after the user base and their data."

He sat back in his seat.

"Smart," she said. "Acquiring Wellify is the best play we have."

Ugh. Aubrey cringed every time anyone said that name—whoever named that app should be dragged out back and shot.

"It's the only play left. It's this, or close up shop. Honestly, some days, I'd rather just retire. But this plan buys us two years." Again, the mask slipped, and he just looked tired.

For a moment, Aubrey's heart ached for him. But she couldn't let emotion cloud her judgment. Not now. The company's future hung in the balance, and she had to stay focused.

He recovered his composure just as quickly, his tone taking on a biting edge.

"So, tell me, daughter—how do we spin this without looking like bloodthirsty bastards who abandon our employees, get fat off government contracts, and prey on the last remaining population of sick people in this godforsaken world?"

Aubrey leaned back in her seat and made a show of mulling it over.

She didn't need the time. Nothing her father had told her was news to her, but she took a few dramatic seconds before divulging her grand plan.

"Something like this: 'The medical industry has undergone a shakeup since the discovery of Microbe X. As longtime champions of the sufferers of chronic illness, we at Hope Pharmaceuticals would love to pack up our bags, declare victory over disease, and enjoy a well-deserved retirement.'"

Aubrey leaned in.

"But the battle isn't over yet. While most of the world basks in unprecedented health, we at Hope Pharm have not forgotten those who find themselves afflicted with Syndrome Q."

"Hmm ..." he said. "A decent opening, setting us up as the champions of the helpless." He nodded, expression unreadable as always. "Continue."

"Then we juxtapose ourselves with other companies. For example: 'While the rest of the industry closes its doors or turns its focus to more profitable life enhancement drugs, we choose to continue to fight the good fight. Today, we announce the acquisition of Wellify and the redirection of our firm. As of today, we are focusing 100% of our research efforts on finding a cure for Syndrome Q.'"

"Okay. What about the bad news?"

Aubrey gave a slight shrug. "The layoffs? We explain that hard choices were necessary to make the dream of a cure for Syndrome Q a reality. The government contract is easy enough to spin—it allows us to keep a close eye on any developments with Microbe X while buying us time and a source of funding while we search for a cure for Syndrome Q."

Time for the mitigation strategy.

"Then, we announce a comprehensive plan to retrain our workforce for the Microbe X Information team and the

Syndrome Q R&D team. We will continue to support our valued employees as we pivot company operations to stay true to our company's core mission—creating 'Hope' for the sick."

Her father nodded, then shook his head. "It's not bad, but there will still be backlash when the layoffs come. I can't see many research scientists and middle managers taking us up on our 'generous offer' to repurpose them as glorified customer service reps."

"Well, no—but the optics are much better if we at least give them an option to stay employed. Honestly, Dad, you have to stop beating yourself up—you did everything you could. Every other company laid people off months ago."

Her father grunted his assent, but Aubrey could see that she was losing him. He glanced at his computer. Probably scanning his email.

She needed to seal the deal, and fast. Thankfully, she still had an ace up her sleeve.

"So that's when we announce our partnership with Hayley Jo, and our joint campaign to raise visibility for the sufferers of syndrome Q."

"The pop star?" He lifted an eyebrow.

"Sure, Hayley Jo has a hit single, but she also has a huge following. She's also one of the most vocal sufferers of Syndrome Q."

Aubrey was hitting her stride. "Hayley's the ideal face for our new initiative—and our future customer base adores her.

This move also allows us to transition to ad campaigns once we develop treatments."

"Sounds like a long shot. What makes you think we can get her?" He looked intrigued, but more than a little skeptical.

Aubrey sat back in her seat and let a slow smile sneak into her expression. "Hayley Jo is already on board."

It wasn't precisely the truth, but Hayley's manager had agreed to set up a meeting. Close enough.

Her father gave her an appraising look, and she could practically see the wheels turning. He was just realizing that none of his 'top secret revelations' had been news to her.

Maybe that would get his attention. It was time for him to see her as the badass business strategist she was rather than the pigtailed little girl he remembered.

But she could tell he still had his doubts. Time to sell the vision.

Aubrey leaned closer, all avid excitement and sweeping gestures.

"Picture it: Hope Pharmaceuticals, continuing to fight the good fight. We will dominate the market for Syndrome Q treatments while garnering the support of its most beloved celebrity sufferer.

"It'll be like Michael J. Fox and Parkinson's—or Sarah McLachlan and puppies."

She paused and stared him straight in the eyes. And willed him to see what she saw, to feel it, to fall in love with the idea.

To buy what she was selling.

See it, Dad, see it.

He leaned forward and looked her dead in the eyes. And smiled.

"I'm impressed, Aubrey. This is excellent work. Be ready to present this to the board on Friday, and plan to go public next week."

A thrill of victory shot through her, but she kept her expression neutral.

It almost felt too easy.

No, it did feel too easy. Richard Hope usually put up a fight even when he loved an idea, playing devil's advocate and trying to poke holes in the plan. It was unusual for him to make such crucial decisions on the spot without even discussing them with the C-suite and board.

A nagging sense of unease crept into Aubrey's mind. Something wasn't right, but she couldn't quite put her finger on it.

Aubrey managed to keep the surprise off her face and responded, oozing competence and professionalism. "I have a five-step plan to ensure everything goes off without a hitch."

"Excellent. We need to stay in front of this, Aubrey." He wagged a finger at her and put on his CEO voice. "Employees hear it first, then we go public. We control the message."

He huffed and gave a partial eye-roll. "I'm already fielding rumors about us sniffing around the Wellify app, and I don't want news of the sale to leak."

She matched his no-nonsense tone, hoping to wrap this up before he changed his mind. "I'm right there with you. If we control the narrative, then we don't get stuck playing defense."

"Damn straight. Send Travis in on your way out." He turned his attention to his computer and started typing away.

Aubrey booked a hasty retreat to her office, careful not to broadcast her excitement as she went.

When she returned to her office, she pulled out her phone and saw two more texts from Derrick. Which was fucking weird. They'd never been connected at the hip.

> Derrick: Did you see my post on Insta? Can't wait for the wedding, babe. ;)

> Derrick: How'd it go? I'm excited to hear all about what you've cooked up in that brilliant head of yours.

Okay, what the fuck? Why the hell was Derrick acting so needy?

Then it hit her. Derrick was freaking out about his job like everyone else at Hope Pharm. Aubrey was preoccupied with working on her PR plan—meanwhile, all of Derrick's projects were drying up.

His people were likely updating their resumes and grilling him for info about the future of the company.

She was going to need to fix this. Derrick was ambitious and demanding, which was part of what attracted her to him. But she was finding out that when he had nothing to do and no one to command, he was all up in her business.

And that just wasn't gonna work.

Their relationship worked because they let each other have space to breathe. Derrick didn't get after her for working too much, didn't try to force her to be 'nicer' or expect her to put on a fucking apron and make him dinner.

As much as she hated to admit it, Aubrey would need to throw him a bone, give him something to sink his teeth into.

Then it occurred to her—even if Derrick weren't her fiancé, he'd have been one of her top picks to manage the Wellify Integration Project. It wasn't an obvious choice—he didn't come from a tech background—but he could manage anything.

His attractiveness and oozing charm made up for the fact that he was a brutal taskmaster. He somehow struck the perfect balance of being loved and feared in equal measure.

And his track record for bringing projects in on time and under budget was notorious.

It'd be easy to pull some strings and make sure he was the top candidate for the job ... and she realized she may have just found the solution to her little Derrick problem.

Aubrey: Nailed it! I know the suspense is killing you, but you'll have to sit tight for a few more days ...

Aubrey: But never fear—something big is coming down the pipeline, and we'll need your mad business skills to pull it off. Gotta run, see you tonight!

That ought to handle it.

After all, Derrick's ambition had been at least part of why they'd gotten together. And it wasn't like he wasn't qualified.

Maybe there was a little nepotism going on, but it was her dad's company. Her father wouldn't want her fiancé out of a job. Aubrey needed Derrick to be obsessed with work again, so he'd get off her back. Derrick would make sure the project was done right and on time.

Win. Win. Win.

Right?

But as Aubrey settled back into her chair, unease lingered. Her father's quick agreement, Derrick's sudden clinginess—something was off, but she couldn't tell what it was.

She wished she felt more confident in her decision. But she couldn't shake the nagging feeling she'd just been played.

Aubrey spent the rest of the morning delegating components of the PR plan to her most trusted employees before hopping online for a little quick retail therapy.

A new pair of strappy sandals could fix anything.

THE
VALMORAN
CHRONICLES

10

WELL-MEANING FRIENDS

EARTH, OMAHA, NEBRASKA

KATHARINE MILLER, MEDICAL MICROBIOLOGIST

~

As KAT EXITED her brother's walkout basement through the side door, the assault on her senses was immediate and intense.

The sunlight stabbed at her head, and her eyes filled with tears. Her nose itched from the blooming flowers, and the scent of exhaust was sickening.

Had birds and insects and lawnmowers and children always been this noisy?

These days, the world always seemed to claw at Kat's brain, and she wondered if it was a symptom of Syndrome Q or if she was just more irritable than she used to be.

She pulled out a pair of giant Audrey Hepburn-esque sunglasses and her Bose noise-canceling headphones. It wasn't exactly safe for her to block out the world while walking, but it couldn't be helped.

She turned on the last track she had been listening to, the new one by Hayley Jo, and even though it was an upbeat EDM piece, something that she would expect to grate on her senses, the heavy beat and repetitive sampling were shockingly soothing.

Kat usually hated angsty love songs, but this one was catchy, and ... well, she just liked it, so she mouthed the words as she made her way to the coffee shop to meet with Claire.

> The hunger ~
> Gnawing, clawing, gaping, aching,
> Searching, hoping, needing, breaking
> Oh, the hunger ~
> Do you feel it?
> Oh, the hunger ~
> Do you feel the hunger?
> Find me, save me, love me, take me.

She set the song on repeat, allowing herself to sink down into its hypnotic beat. Her sore body loosened up as she strolled through the suburban streets, heading toward her favorite coffee shop.

She almost felt normal in the relative comfort of her sunglasses and headphones. The spring air still held a refreshing crispness at this time of day, but it wasn't cold, just invigorating.

This had always been her favorite time of year, when the world was suffused with hope, life, and new beginnings.

The ping of a text message interrupted her reverie. Kat pulled out her phone and saw a text from Beth Ann.

Beth: Can you just confirm that you're still alive? I wish you would tell me what's going on with you. Besides, Daniel told me you've been sleeping at his place.

Beth: You know his basement is full of old baseball cards and vintage Hustlers. Vintage. Hustlers. Think it through and tell me it isn't gross. Anyway, love you, sis. Call me.

Kat smiled despite herself. She knew she needed to talk to her sister, but didn't know what to say.

She couldn't understand her own feelings right now, let alone explain them to her twin.

Her sister only wanted to help, but that was the crux of the problem. It didn't feel like talking about it would make any difference. But if she kept ignoring Beth, she'd think Kat was mad at her, which wasn't true.

If anything, she was pissed at herself.

*Kat: Ew, I had no idea our brother collected old porn.
Could have happily gone the rest of my life without
that little nugget, jerkface.*

When she hit send, she saw the three little dots showing her sister was replying, so she waited.

Beth: Who, me? I'm just looking out for your health. ;)

*Kat: Har har har. Hope your classes are going well.
Love ya, sis.*

There. Kat had let her sister know she was still alive, and that she even still had a sense of humor. Hopefully, that would buy her some time to figure things out.

Beth: You, too ... I wish you would come home.

Kat frowned and put the phone away. Beth wasn't trying to guilt trip her—that wasn't her style—but Kat felt guilty all the same. There wasn't a good solution here.

If she had stayed in that apartment one more day, she would have snapped at her chipper and sweet sister for no good reason. But staying away was obviously making Beth worry.

The guilt gnawed at her stomach. Why couldn't she just be happy for her sister?

Everything was so messed up. Beth had done nothing wrong. She was only ... being happy.

But every grin, every little dance, every time she had acted overjoyed about some mundane thing, had been yet another among a thousand tiny paper-cuts. After years of being sick, Beth deserved to be in love with life.

The problem was Kat.

If she couldn't be happy for Beth, she needed to stay away.

～

KAT WAS STILL STUCK on those melancholy thoughts when she plopped herself down across from Claire in their favorite booth at Zen.

Claire was rocking scrubs and tennis shoes, but the look was offset by a diamond tennis bracelet and what was undoubtedly the latest designer bag. Her makeup was pristine, and her brown hair shined with fresh honey highlights.

With a perfect French manicure, she looked more like a supermodel doing a photoshoot as an OB/GYN rather than the real deal.

Kat glanced down at her own outfit—ratty band tee, yoga pants, hoodie, baseball cap—and cringed. Next to Claire's polished perfection, she felt like a hobo.

The two friends couldn't have been more different. If Kat and Claire hadn't bonded during med school, they would never have spoken to one another, let alone become besties. But Kat was glad that they had.

Claire slid a steaming paper cup across the table at Kat as she stuffed her sunglasses and headphones into her bag.

"Jesus, Kat, what's with the getup? You look like you're on the lam." Claire gestured at Kat's disheveled appearance. "And you look like shit."

"Gee, thanks. Love you, too."

Claire leaned forward, slamming a hand down on the table. "Omigod—everything makes sense now. You're on drugs."

"Keep your voice down." Kat hissed. "This is my favorite coffee shop, and I'd like to show my face here in the future."

Claire leaned in, reaching a hand across the table, "It's okay, Kat—lots of people—"

What the hell? Was this an intervention?

"—Geez! I'm not on drugs, Claire, I just haven't been sleeping well. You know, on account of my life imploding and everything."

"Ugh," Claire rolled her eyes. "Don't be dramatic. It's just, you know—" She made a dismissive gesture. "—a bump in the road. It'll all work out."

Then she leaned closer, studying Kat like a bug under a microscope.

Kat resisted the temptation to squirm in her seat.

"You're sure you're not on drugs? Because I know this great program—"

"Oh. My. God. I'm not on drugs, I've never done drugs, I barely even drink. I'm a boring person who spends all of her time reading technical papers and working in the lab—"

She cut off and looked down at her coffee.

"—well, I used to, anyway."

Awkward.

Kat pasted on a smile and tried to change the subject. "So, how's your practice faring after—well, you know."

"The cryospore?"

It was Kat's turn to roll her eyes. "I wish that stupid name would die already. I swear, one guy comes out with a theory that it came from polar melt, and now we're stuck with ... I mean, how hard is it to call it by its proper name? 'Microbe X'. Until we manage lysis and can do a proper DNA analysis, the responsible—"

She noticed Claire shaking her head and chuckling.

"—What?"

"It's just nice to see that my best friend is still in there somewhere. I barely recognize the morose sack of self-pity you've turned into." Claire smiled, and there was no malice in her words. "Go on—educate me. What's new in the exciting world of Microbe X?"

Aaaand ... now she felt silly for nerding out.

Claire made a rolling gesture for Kat to continue. "No, seriously. I've been so distracted by the changes in my practice that I'm barely keeping up with the research end of things."

Kat shook her head and chuckled. "I can't. You made it weird. So, what's going on with your practice?"

Her friend leaned back and took a gulp from her latte.

Kat noticed that beneath her shiny facade, Claire looked tired. No, more like exhausted.

"Well, of course, there's everything that changed since now there's no cancer or STDs, but we sorted out most of that."

Kat laughed. "There's more? I do not envy you, trying to keep a medical practice up and running right now ..."

The words died in her throat when she noticed the serious look on Claire's face. "What is it?"

Claire lowered her voice and leaned in to ensure they weren't overheard. "Okay, so this is all just speculation right now, but ..."

"But what?"

"Okay, so a couple of months ago, my periods started getting irregular. But they've always been like clockwork."

"Yeah, mine have been messed up, too. I thought it was just stress," Kat said.

Claire shook her head. "Yeah, I thought so, too. And I figured the same thing when I noticed a small uptick in patients seeing me for amenorrhea a couple months back. But more and more patients are coming in now—you know how we tell them not to worry unless it's painful or they miss three periods in a row, right? Well, that means there's already a lag effect here."

Kat felt a chill run down her spine and leaned in to whisper back. "Are you saying what I think you're saying?"

Claire ran a hand through her hair. "Right now, all I have is data from my practice, and similar anecdotes from my OB/GYN friends. At first, it didn't seem so bad—patients with lifetime dysmenorrhea, or PCOS, even hormonal acne kept coming to my office to get taken off medication. We thought it was just the cryo—sorry, Microbe X—healing them. But now lighter periods are turning into no periods in a lot of young, healthy patients."

Maybe there was a positive explanation. There had to be. The alternative was ... too alarming to think about.

"Maybe it's changing our biology, removing our need to shed the uterine lining every month? Aren't humans one of the only species that doesn't just reabsorb it?" Kat offered, her mind whirling with the implications.

"That occurred to me, too, but then I looked at my monthly stats for new OB patients."

Kat's stomach tightened. "And?"

"It was gradual, and there was so much chaos with everything else, so I didn't notice at first."

"Mhm ..."

"But my number of new OB patients has been declining over the past three months. It's now under 70% of last year's average."

"But that's just your practice—it could be a coincidence, or maybe people just don't want to have kids because the economy is such a mess ...?"

"Except when some of my friends looked over their records, they saw the same thing."

"How is no one talking about this?"

"They are—well, some are—some random social media groups, a couple of those big data period and fertility tracker apps have blogged about it—but you know how it is. No one wants to talk about 'female stuff.' People only stop cringing again when we're talking about babies. And that data won't be collated by the CDC until ... well, it'll be over a year before the drop in live births starts to show in the vital stats."

Kat sat back, stunned. This was going to cause a shitstorm. The world had barely got its bearings, and this—she didn't want to think about it.

She realized Claire was still talking. "... I'm not sure what it will mean for my practice. I'm thinking of taking a research job."

"You should—we need people like you working on this to figure out a solution."

"Well, yeah, that—but also, I had Jillian remove my IUD last week. Erik and I have been fucking like bunnies. A research job would have much more stable hours."

Kat wanted to be annoyed with her friend. She was a bit annoyed with her for focusing only on how this situation affected her personally rather than the bigger picture—human fertility might be dropping precipitously.

But that was just Claire. She cared deeply for the people close to her, but 'didn't overburden herself with the weight of the world,' as she put it.

"I thought you wanted to wait a few years before having kids."

"I did. But if this is my last chance to be a mother, I don't want to miss out. So we reassessed our priorities."

"Um ... congratulations? Good luck? I'm not sure what to say in this situation."

Claire smiled. "Thanks. We'll see how it goes, I guess. I stopped taking new OB patients, so I could phase out of practice, so now it's just fingers crossed that I can get knocked up. Everything's been so weird since all this happened. Anyway, I'm bored of worrying about all this. Tell me what's up with you."

Kat shrugged. "Not much to tell. Just taking some time to regroup."

Claire narrowed her eyes at Kat. "Regroup, hmm?"

"Yep." Kat popped the 'p' as she said it and looked around the coffee shop. It was only about half full at this time of day. There was a guy on a laptop in the corner armchair, bobbing his head to music only he could hear. A woman sitting at a window table, jotting something down in a Moleskine—

"Oh, no, you don't—you don't get to check out on me. Fine, if you're not going to tell me what's going on, then I'll tell you. You are a fixer, Kat, and I mean that in the nicest of ways. But sometimes you focus on other people's problems, so you don't need to figure out what you want. Your whole life revolved around fixing Beth Ann, fixing her illness. And now you don't know what to do with yourself, so you're moping—"

"—but—"

"—Not finished yet." Claire used her 'doctor voice' and held up a hand. "The way I see it, there are two ways to fix this. One, you find some new lost cause to devote your life to, or you finally focus on figuring out what you want in life." She gave a curt nod and smiled. "Okay, now I'm finished."

Claire had a point. Without her work and without needing to dote on Beth Ann, Kat felt like a boat without an anchor, tossed about. But lame as it sounded, all she wanted was to get back into the lab. Her voice was quiet when she responded.

"What I want is to work on Syndrome Q."

"Then do it! You're the perfect woman for the job. You love studying weird diseases and germs and shit." Claire shuddered.

Kat had always found it amusing that her friend could deal with abdominal surgery, all the fluids in the delivery room, baby barf—but mention the flu, and she was dousing herself in hand sanitizer and backing out the door. She wondered if Claire still used hand sanitizer now that no one got sick anymore.

Kat huffed and continued, "Claire, I want to work on Syndrome Q, but there's no way anyone would hire me. Have you looked around lately? The job market is flooded. It's just," she shook her head, "it's never going to happen. I need to be realistic and figure out a Plan B."

Claire wrinkled her nose. "So it turns out I'm not quite finished yet—that bullshit about the job market is a cop-out, and you know it. How many jobs have you even applied for?"

Kat stared down at her coffee cup. "I haven't gotten around to it yet."

"That's what I thought. So I got you an interview."

Kat leveled a stare at her. "You what?"

Claire got a sheepish look and picked at the sleeve of her coffee cup. "So ... one of my old sorority sisters is the daughter of the CEO of Hope Pharmaceuticals—"

Well, shit.

"I dunno, Claire ..." Kat set down her cup, trying to choose her words at least a little diplomatically.

"I have complicated feelings about big pharma. And it's not even a good fit. They manufacture and sell drugs, right? I was studying etiology, diagnostic tests ... things that would help people prove they were sick, actual cures ..." She let out a frustrated sigh. "You know how I feel about bandaid medicine."

But Claire would not be deterred. "Hope does in-house R&D, too."

Then her perky friend took a deep breath and said the following sentence so fast Kat could barely make it out. "And so I reached out to Aubrey and told her your background and how you're great at programming, and she'll be here in ten minutes to interview you."

"Claire! What the hell? I look like a bum today!" Kat gestured at her disheveled appearance.

Claire scrunched her face. "Maybe a little. But it won't matter. Aubrey won't give two shits what you look like—she's all about hiring people who get the job done. Just be you. Let that geek flag of yours fly, and you'll be perfect."

Kat tried to summon a glare to throw at Claire, but her lips ruined the effect by cracking a smile.

"I can't tell if I hate you or love you more right now," she mumbled into her latte.

"You'll be singing my praises when you get the job, because you need this, Kat. You're a champion without a cause, and I can't stand to see you like this. The world needs you to be solving its problems again, and you need problems to solve. So, like, go kick ass and stuff."

Kat's mind raced. An interview? Now? She wasn't prepared, looked like hell, and wasn't even sure she wanted to work for a pharmaceutical company. But Claire was right … what other options did she have?

She took a deep breath, squared her shoulders, and nodded. "Okay. I'll do it. But if this goes sideways, I'm blaming you."

Claire just grinned and sipped her latte, looking far too pleased with herself. "That's my girl. Go get 'em, tiger."

As Kat mentally prepared herself for the unexpected interview, her thoughts drifted back to the troubling revelations Claire had shared about a potential fertility crisis. First, Microbe X showed up like a miracle, then Syndrome Q, and now this?

Kat couldn't shake the feeling that something sinister was lurking beneath the surface, waiting to be uncovered. The world had been turned upside down, and every day seemed to bring new challenges and uncertainties.

She had to find a way to get back into the game, to be part of the solution. While waiting for Aubrey to arrive, she silently vowed that no matter what happened with this interview, she would stop at nothing to unravel the mysteries that plagued their world.

The fate of humanity might just depend on it.

[PART 3]
POMP AND PAINFUL CIRCUMSTANCE

THE
VALMORAN
CHRONICLES

11

THESE SUFFOCATING ROBES

Valmoran Republic, Planet Kronai, Temple of the Seven

Matthai Valtrellin, Future High Priest

~

When Matthai returned to his quarters after meeting with Callum, he felt lighter. Perhaps everything would work out.

If anyone could help him figure out how to navigate the maze of politics and public opinion, Callum could. They would find a solution.

He was sure of it.

But as the attendants braided his hair into a complex knot, then placed the silver zanchion onto his head, doubts crept back in.

The gleaming circle of bejeweled Obelisks—worn only by the High Priesthood of the First Temple—looked out of place on his head.

He was just Matthai, not a leader—the zanchion didn't seem to fit.

As they draped and shrouded his body in the layers of silver and blue cloth that made up the ceremonial robes, then wrapped his waist in an elaborate belt, it became harder to breathe.

The thick robes were too warm. The weight of them tugged Matthai into the ground.

With each layer, the burden of his responsibilities seemed to settle more heavily on his shoulders.

By the time his guards came for the procession, it was an effort to push his nerves to the back of his mind.

But Scion Valtrellin did, because his parents, the priests, and the rest of the galaxy were waiting, and he would not let them down.

～

As Matthai exited his chambers, the normally gleaming halls of the dormitory appeared almost mystical in the dim ceremonial candlelight.

Lines of kneeling priests framed both sides of the curved hall-way. The space thrummed with their chanting tones, candles flickering as the song permeated the air.

Matthai's personal guardians trailed behind him, affording him an unobstructed view of the devotional scene.

There was a stillness within these walls, where none but the priests could enter. A sense of refuge from what awaited him in the courtyard.

As he walked along the corridor, each person acknowledged him before lowering to the floor as he passed. All wore the blue and silver of the Valtrellins in honor of the First Temple, with sashes in the colors of their originating temples setting them apart.

He ambled forward, wanting to acknowledge each of them, knowing that most had crossed the galaxy to be here for the occasion. But he soon realized the futility of the task.

There were simply too many, not enough time to pay them the respect they deserved.

As their faces blended together, he noticed Priest Jarron, the man who had trained him in defense since childhood. Matthai smiled at him, relieved to see a familiar face.

While his former trainer did smile back, his expression had a disconcerting reverence that had never been there before.

There had always been a distance between Matthai and the other adepts. Yet somehow, he pretended he was one of them ... most of the time.

As Jarron bowed before him, the ground shifted beneath Matthai's feet, setting him above and apart from everyone and everything he had ever known.

With only the barest falter in his steps, the Scion continued forward, leaving the man behind.

A dull ache bloomed in Matthai's chest, and the thick robes and the stuffy hallway made it difficult to fill his lungs.

He felt like an imposter, playing a role he wasn't meant for.

How had his mother borne this, the day she donned these robes, the day she walked these halls?

As he walked past the priests who knelt in genuflection, Matthai longed to tell them they didn't need to bow, that he was just another adept. Just another priest, the same as them.

But the Scion held his composure and did his best to project the dignity these priests deserved from their future High Priest.

~

THEIR FOOTSTEPS ECHOED on the ornate lobby floor as Matthai and his personal guardians emerged from the dormitory hallways.

The courtyard door was propped open, granting a terrifying glimpse of the massive crowds that awaited outside.

A shaft of light cut through the dim room onto the shining crest of the House of Valtrellin, emblazoned on the stone floor.

As Matthai stepped forward, his personal guardians encircled him. A group of priests from the Order of Protection joined them, forming a second circle.

Another barrier to separate him from his people.

His heart rate quickened.

Perhaps it was from being confined on all sides by watchful guards. Or that once he greeted the pilgrims outside, there would be no turning back.

As he walked through the doorway, the guards adjusted to his momentary hesitation at the threshold, as if it had never occurred.

For Matthai, the ultimate step that took him from the sanctuary of the priests' private home into the future that awaited him required a burst of sheer will.

Matthai's eyes struggled to adjust to the brightness of the late afternoon sun.

The spacious courtyard spanning the inner and outer walls of the citadel had been transformed for his procession.

The first thing that caught his eye were the drones meandering through the skies. Capturing the footage that would be broadcast throughout the galaxy.

Memorializing the day from every angle.

As he dragged his feet forward, he checked his posture, striving to project the peaceful dignity expected of him.

Matthai had accompanied his parents to the Temple, had sat behind them as they shared the wisdom of the Gods with the people, so he knew precisely how the future High Priest should carry himself.

But it was difficult to remain impassive, standing on display for this sea of people.

He had never seen such a large assembly. In vids, maybe, but that hadn't prepared him for the sudden awe he felt in their presence.

People gathered along both walls, brightly dressed Valmorans from all over the galaxy. Priests lined the footpath, separating him from the masses.

The crowds, the priests, and the path they created curved gently out of view, revealing the way to the cathedral.

Teeming crowds made the inner and outer walls feel like they were closing in, as if the throngs might burst free and consume him.

Roaring cheers and waving arms greeted him as he passed. As his march wore on, the initially pleasant sunlight became harsh, and Matthai sweltered under his heavy robes.

One foot in front of the other—graceful, dignified, and—

A commotion on his right had his guardians closing ranks. He heard the shouts before he peered through a small gap in their formation.

"Take Back The Obelisks!"

Matthai spotted a man, arms spread to display a large cloth sign emblazoned with the same perplexing words.

"Take Back the Obelisks!" the man shouted, face red and brows knit with rage.

Matthai's guardians ushered him along.

In his peripheral vision, dozens of priests converged on the man's position. They surrounded him, then moved to exit the temple grounds.

Matthai made out a few last words before the man's voice faded.

"The Obelisks belong to the people!"

As Matthai resumed his procession, he puzzled at the man's fury, though he didn't allow his bewilderment to show on his face.

The Obelisks did belong to the people—of course, they did. The Temples were wide open to pilgrims who wished to commune with the Gods.

Why would anyone need to take them back?

A seed of doubt took root in his mind. Was there something he was missing, some discontent brewing that no one had informed him of?

The journey became a blur of faces, shouts, and steps as he and his guards parted the sea of people on the road to the cathedral.

The robes and zanchion were a heavy burden, each step more arduous than the last.

Matthai wished he could talk to the pilgrims, maybe even cross the fence, to join them. At the very least, he longed to smile and wave as he passed.

But the Scion dutifully propelled himself forward, the brief raise of a hand or a mild nod his only outward reactions as he resumed his march toward fate.

~

As Matthai approached the cathedral, it loomed over him.

The gaping mouth of the ancient Temple waited at the top of the staircase.

It was peculiar for such a thought to enter his mind. He had always imagined this building held a sort of magic—that walking through that door was like traveling to the distant past.

Today, it might swallow him whole.

His guard fell in behind him as he ascended the stairs.

The ceremonial chamber accommodated only a few hundred dignitaries. They stood when he entered, respectfully quiet.

As the heavy doors shut behind him, the distant roar of the crowds broke off.

The cathedral was eerily silent and bathed only in the light of ceremonial braziers.

Matthai spotted his destination—the stairwell beneath the altar. The High Priest and Priestess stood solemnly behind it, the Council of High Priests lined up at their back.

Everyone was still, the silence in the room oozing into every dark recess.

Matthai forced his feet towards the staircase.

Dignitaries covered their faces with respect as he passed.

He spotted Callum out of the corner of his eye. The man smiled at him before bringing both hands to shield his face like the others.

Matthai wanted to smile back, but the Scion stared straight ahead as he traversed the aisle.

When he reached the front of the room, he paused momentarily, taking comfort in the sight of his mother and father.

And then he descended into the Chamber of the Obelisk.

THE
VALMORAN
CHRONICLES

12

WORDS, ONCE SPOKEN

Valmoran Republic, Planet Kronai, Temple of the Seven

Matthai Valtrellin, Future High Priest

~

THE CHAMBER of the Obelisk held a slight chill, providing relief from the sun's heat, still trapped in the layers of his robes. The domed ceiling loomed overhead, and stone walls curving up to accommodate the towering Obelisk in the center of the room.

Seven braziers encircled the room, casting flickering light over the inky surface of the relic.

As Matthai knelt before it, glowing blue patterns over deep black morphed and mutated, random and endless.

The sheer size and wonder of the Obelisk made Matthai feel insignificant by comparison. The reverence, the sheer sense of the history of this object which had spoken to his ancestor in epochs past, humbled him. Today, his awe was only magnified. He knelt before it and reached out a hand to caress its glossy surface.

The patterns on the Obelisk flared as their glow intensified. Matthai bowed his head and waited.

A voice rang out, as if from everywhere at once ... and simultaneously, as if the origin was within his mind.

"Words, once spoken, cannot be unspoken."

His hand fell from the stone, heart racing, chest too tight. With a sudden wave of lightheadedness, he leaned forward to rest his forehead on the cool stone.

Were the Gods trying to tell him he should not take his vows today? Or maybe they were warning him he should not have trusted Callum?

Millions of people waited—just up the stairs, lining the courtyards, swarming the pavilions of the outer gardens.

Billions throughout the galaxy were watching in real-time—throughout the Republic, the Federation, Ioria Prime, Anaris Station ...

Everywhere.

He felt sick. His skin felt clammy, the robes too warm.

Unmoving save for the too-quick rise and fall of his chest, he pressed his forehead and hands against the smooth stone floor.

The zanchion tugged at his hair, but he ignored the pain, willing the room to stop spinning.

Matthai's mind whirled. This felt wrong.

He couldn't do this. It should have been Liyara.

A tingle rose to the back of his skull, quickly becoming an itch.

He couldn't do this.

Then the quaking began, the first warning tremors as his body prepared to jump away from a perceived threat.

If he didn't calm himself, he would jump to the gardens. He would jump back to this room, naked, in a few minutes. But the robes and zanchion were too complex to put on alone.

Panic clawed at his throat. He couldn't let that happen. Couldn't let everyone see his failure, his weakness. Couldn't disappoint his parents.

He forced his mind to stillness, his quaking body to calm. In through the nose—one, two, three, four. Out through the mouth—one, two, three, four, five, six, seven.

The chill, damp air filled his nose, and the earthy odor grounded him as he clung to the here and the now.

"I am here. I am now. I will not jump away," Matthai repeated the mantra, praying for strength. For calm.

Eventually, he swallowed, then took a normal breath. Then another.

Slowly, he raised himself to kneeling, staring up at the Obelisk.

He didn't allow himself to think, didn't give himself a chance to doubt. If he gave himself that opportunity, he wasn't sure he would do what must be done.

The Scion spoke his solemn vow to the Gods, stood, brushed off his robes, and smoothed everything back into place.

Matthai thought of Kat-a-reen's smile, and his lungs seemed to relax. He didn't allow himself to worry about the future. Instead, he imagined her face and allowed thoughts of his mate to shift his expression to contentment.

Then he ascended the stairs to confront his fate.

∼

AFTER EMERGING from the Chamber of the Obelisk, Matthai knelt in front of the altar, head bowed as he waited for the ceremony to commence.

The High Priestess's voice reverberated through the cathedral, authoritative and resonant.

"Matthai Valtrellin, blood of my blood, Scion of the House of Valtrellin, descendent of the First High Priestess of the First Temple, Future High Priest of the First Temple of the Temple of the Seven.

"217 generations ago, our ancestor discovered the Sacred Obelisk of Kronai. She saw that it was beautiful, and set hands upon its gleaming surface."

Matthai's voice joined the call and response.

May they shine forever in the darkness.

There was peace in these sacred words.

"The First Priestess trembled at the voice which rang into her mind, saying 'The Second Epoch has begun,' and she knew it was the Gods who had spoken."

May the Gods speak to us always.

"She fell upon the ground, and the Gods spoke to her for seven days and seven nights. And the knowledge from the Gods was so great she could not move."

May we gain wisdom in stillness.

"In the darkness of the seventh night, the Gods spoke again: You must not separate those bonded by matehood. You must protect the young and birth new life. You must never harm those gifted with great powers of mind and body. Heed these three commandments and earn the knowledge of the stars."

For the stars would lead us to our brothers and sisters.

"And so she returned to the village where she was struck with a great hunger, and she followed its pull. And the hunger was not for sustenance but for a man. And when she touched his skin, they grew warm, and they were marked. For they were the first of the mates, bonded by the Gods."

And together, they led the others to obey the words of the Gods.

"And they were blessed with three children, and those children held the secrets of time and space. And they knew these children had been touched by the Gods."

May we honor and protect those whom the Gods have chosen.

"And the Valtrellins led the people to obey the words of the Gods, to take comfort and guidance from the words of the Obelisks. And in this way, they multiplied, flourished, and became wise for 160 generations."

May we multiply, flourish, and be wise.

"And the Obelisk knew they had obeyed its commands well, so it spoke again to the High Priest of the age, saying, 'Arise, Herald! The Third Epoch has begun.' And he knew it was the Gods who had spoken."

May the Gods speak to us always.

"And the Obelisk rewarded their obedience with the knowledge of the stars, mathematics, and everything great and small, seen and unseen."

May our obedience be rewarded.

"And so it was that seven worlds met one another in the stars. And they traveled far on the paths of the Gods to seek the Obelisks. And they shared the knowledge of the stars with their brothers and sisters there."

May we honor our brothers and sisters from the stars.

"And they knew their Gods were the same Gods and that they were good. And they built rich temples to honor the Obelisks and vowed to keep them sacred."

May we honor the Gods and guard the Obelisks.

"Matthai Valtrellin, blood of my blood, God-touched Scion of the House of Valtrellin, descendent of the First High Priestess of the First Temple, Future High Priest of the First Temple of the Temple of the Seven. Speak your solemn vows."

Matthai raised his head, facing the High Priestess.

"I, Matthai Valtrellin, Scion of the House of Valtrellin, of the 217th generation in an unbroken line of the faithful, do vow to guide and protect the Valmoran people, to respect and obey the will of the Gods, to uphold the sacred texts and guard the Obelisks to keep them sacred."

Matthai hesitated, feeling as if he were about to speak an untruth.

But Scion Valtrellin took a breath and recited the words he knew by heart, projecting them with the confidence and gravity of the future High Priest.

"I vow to keep sacred the mate bonds, to carry on the Valtrellin line, and to cherish my God-touched sons and daughters. And when it is time, I vow to ascend to the role of the High Priest of the First Temple of the Temple of the Seven."

The words tasted like poison in his mouth, but he forced them out anyway.

"This is my sacred vow."

"Arise, Ordained Scion Valtrellin, future High Priest of the Temple of the Seven. May you learn well so you may guide the Valmoran people to peace and prosperity."

~

As HE JOINED his parents in the recession from the Temple, Matthai felt himself recede, shrinking to make room for the Scion.

Down the stone stairs of the Temple.

He observed himself walking, as if in a trance.

Through the crowds gathered in the courtyards, through a door in the outer wall.

Up the elevator. Onto the gleaming metal ramparts. A roiling sea of Valmorans, as far as the eye could see.

Forward, to the first oratory platform overlooking the outer grounds of the First Temple. The crowds surged towards the outer walls of the Temple like crashing waves.

Something deep inside him—something that he had buried deep but could no longer ignore—shattered.

Matthai screamed inside his skin, inside these suffocating robes—

I am just a man! I am no one!

Under the weight of the gleaming silver zanchion and the screaming of the crowd,

The crushing weight of duty and the secret he bore on his chest,

The vision of Kat-a-reen, bloodied and broken ...

... of Liyara, bloodied and broken and dead.

Under the weight of all these things, Matthai despaired.

I will let you down. I have failed you all.

But Ordained Scion Valtrellin took measured breaths, set his expression in a serene half-smile, and raised his arms to acknowledge the cameras and the adoring masses gathered below.

Matthai hadn't felt so lonely—so utterly helpless and hopeless and wrong—since the day Liyara's blood stained the tiles of the Temple courtyard.

THE VALMORAN CHRONICLES

13

POISE, POWER, AND PLEASANTRIES

Valmoran Republic, Planet Kronai, Temple of the Seven

Callum Torion, Representative Arbiter for the Valmoran Republic

~

It had been an interminable day, and it was far from over. Callum couldn't remember the last time he spent this many hours around so many people, and the emotional burden had long since robbed him of the effortless poise he so prided himself on.

He would have preferred to go home for the evening, but that would have been unspeakably rude. Also, tonight afforded him an unprecedented opportunity to rub shoulders with the most influential people in the galaxy—and one he might never get again.

After attempting to muddle through and recognize the various diplomats and dignitaries for several hours, Callum caved and enabled one of those CelebSpy overlays on his Hix. After all, everyone else was using them—he couldn't very well be the only person out of the loop.

But Callum could not wait to get home and turn the blasted thing off again.

The group the Temple had assembled for the investiture was alarmingly powerful—a who's who of not just planet Kronai or the Republic, but the entire galaxy. Dignitaries from the Federation, Ioria Prime, Anaris Station, and the Republic were there.

Captains of industry, musicians, actors. Representatives from the Peacekeepers. There was even a Threllian Ambassador in attendance.

Callum almost felt humbled to be included.

"Representative Torion, we thank you for your support of the temple and invite you to dine with us this evening," a smiling priest greeted him as he reached the grand entrance to the banquet hall. "Please allow me to show you to your seat."

The room was a grand stone hall, one of the more ancient places in the Temple, impeccably maintained despite its age. The Temple's Hix overlay—which all visitors enabled on entry to the grounds—generated a pop-up on the side of his mindscreen, inquiring if he wished to learn about the chamber's history.

Not right now. Perhaps if Callum's dining companions turned out to be dull.

An attendant led him to one of dozens of small round tables, already set with complex dinnerware. He groaned as he enabled yet another irritating Hix overlay, this one to guide him through the etiquette of a formal Valmoran feast.

Guests were seated in four of the six seats at the table when he arrived. He quickly pulled up his dinner companions' details on his Hix while making himself comfortable at the table.

Arilla Rennor, from the Anaris Station Spacefolding Syndicate, sat to his left. He turned to introduce himself, but she started speaking before he got the chance.

"Representative Torion, I absolutely adore your vid series!" the woman gushed. Her awkward manner and inability to sustain eye contact seemed out of place among such company.

A quick peek into her emotions showed she was shockingly attracted to him—maybe even had a bit of a crush. That explained it—nothing to worry about, just not something he cared for.

"Nice to meet you—"

"Arilla. I'm the administrator of the space folding syndicate on Anaris Station. I love your vids. Oh, I already said that." She flushed and tugged a stray bit of hair behind her ear. Her embarrassment surged through Callum, and he needed to put her at ease, if only so he wouldn't have to experience her discomfort.

"I'm glad you enjoy them. I sometimes forget that people actually watch those things," he replied.

He was rescued from the rapidly devolving conversation when the man seated on her other side cleared his throat, loudly.

"Vargus Trix, at your service." The man bowed mockingly, ignoring Arilla as he introduced himself to Callum. This motion pointed his horns directly at Callum, and the subtle threat disguised as pleasantry did not go unnoticed.

This was a man who needed no introduction. The unofficial leader of Ioria Prime, Vargus, was often in the news, and not a man to be trifled with. His ruddy skin and pointed horns marked him as a Vultrai, and rumor had it he was God-touched.

His kind had the horrifying ability to influence the levels of pain and pleasure experienced by those in their vicinity.

Callum couldn't imagine what the Gods had been thinking, granting such a terrible power to a man destined to rule a mob planet. The man's leathery wings curled behind him as he leaned back in his seat with a smirk. A tentative peek into Vargus's emotions exposed simple amusement.

Great, that's just what the universe needs—another powerful man who views the world as a game.

Callum returned the bow, suppressing the chill that threatened to run down his spine. "Callum Torion."

"To be sure," Vargus said, sounding uninterested. "I suppose you'll want to be meeting the rest of the crew." He threw a half-hearted gesture to the man sitting to his left, straight across from Callum. "This one's just a missionary from the Federation. And that lovely creature is—"

"—I can introduce myself, if you please," the woman interjected. She wore sharp, formal business attire and had a no-nonsense air. "Regla Dresh, I run—"

Callum nodded emphatically. "—Valmar Defensive Tech. Yes, I know. It's an honor to meet you."

"Regla is fine. We're all friends here. Well, except him," she said dryly, jerking her head in Vargus's direction. "That one's already proving insufferable."

"Me? I'm a delight," Vargus replied, and the barest eye roll was Regla's only response.

It made sense that a woman like Regla would be in charge of the most advanced defensive tech firm in the Valmoran Republic. She had a commanding presence, and was obviously fearless, taking jabs at Vargus Trix with such nerve.

Regla's firm had a reputation for skirting the definition of legal "defense tech" and flirting with more offensive weaponry. Callum had been called in on several votes involving her company during his tenure as a Representative Arbiter.

As a student of military history and theory, Callum would have loved to pick her brain for hours and get her thoughts on the Peacekeepers, de-weaponization, and the role of defense in maintaining peace.

Instead, he remembered his manners and returned to the quiet missionary Vargus had dismissed as unimportant. "And you are?"

"No one of consequence, although you may call me Priest Ollem." The man bowed his head and smiled. When Callum reached out to the man's emotions, he found a placid sea of calm tinged with a hint of sadness. Why he was here in such illuminated company was an intriguing question.

But it was soon forgotten, because their last companion was joining the table.

None other than the Threllian Ambassador. As far as Callum knew, no Threllian Ambassador had visited Valmoran Space in over twenty generations, not since the Valmorans caused their near-extinction—horrifically and decisively ending the Threllian Wars.

Callum burned with curiosity—how was it that the Temple managed to re-open communication with them when all Republic attempts at diplomacy had failed?

Yes, this was going to be a fascinating dinner, indeed. Callum wouldn't need to entertain himself with the hall's history, after all.

The Ambassador rolled up to the table in his adaptive apparatus, a robotic contraption that adjusted as he approached so his seat was at table height. Threllians were nothing like Valmorans, but Callum had never seen one up close. Before today, he'd never seen one outside of ancient recordings.

Threllians were small creatures with a large head and a mass of tentacles at their base. They were rumored to speak to one another through their color-changing skin.

Right now, the Ambassador's skin was a muted brown, morphing and changing with the minor undulations of his body.

Threllians were supposed to be hardy little creatures, proving nearly indestructible during the wars. Well, until the Valmorans unleashed a virus on their population and killed almost their entire race. The Republic and Federation were still paying reparations for the accidental near-genocide.

"If I may please have your attention," High Priestess Valtrellin's voice rang out as she addressed the gathered dignitaries, and Callum turned to the table at the front. She was next to the High Priest and Matthai, and the Council of High Priests sat along either end of the table with them.

"Our deepest gratitude to you for making the journey to honor the investiture of Matthai Valtrellin, now Ordained Scion of the Temple of the Seven. We appreciate your support and patronage and are delighted to host you for this momentous occasion. Please know that you are among the most indispensable allies of the Temple."

Callum noted the genuine pride radiating off the High Priestess as she gazed at her son, applauding his new role in the Temple. But there was something strange, something wrong with Matthai. On the surface, his face was a mask of serenity as he nodded his head in acknowledgment of the High Priestess's words. Inside, he was ... disturbingly blank.

When Callum left their meeting that afternoon, Matthai radiated a tentative sense of hope. He had exuded chaotic turmoil beforehand, but his emotions had always been visceral and real.

Now, Matthai's emotions, previously so vibrant as to be overwhelming, were muted, as if someone reached inside him and diminished the very essence of who he was. The stark contrast between Matthai's earlier emotional state and his current emptiness set off alarm bells in Callum's mind.

What could have changed in just a few hours?

It grated on Callum in a way he couldn't fully grasp. Something had corrupted the deep ocean of feeling that was Matthai Valtrellin.

Callum wished he could find out what was wrong and correct it, but this was neither the time nor the place.

Matthai accepted his mother's invitation to address the room, his appearance the perfect simulacrum of a gentle, humble, and gracious Ordained Scion.

"Thank you for being here with us today. As Ordained Scion, I assure you I will approach this role with the humility and sincerity it deserves. Those in this room are cherished allies of the Temple, and I look forward to meeting each of you over the next phase. Please, eat, drink, and celebrate."

Even as Matthai smiled and greeted everyone, to Callum, it was as if Matthai locked his own emotions away so thoroughly that he could not even experience them.

Callum's suspicion grew as he watched Matthai, searching for any hint of the vibrant emotions he sensed earlier, but finding only a disconcerting emptiness.

He watched the boy out of the corner of his eye, still trying to get some hint of the issue, but there was not much to go on. Matthai was barely there, emotionally.

Callum absentmindedly took the tiniest sip of his wine with the other guests. It was excellent, and doubtless cost a fortune, but there was no way he would deliberately dull his senses at an event like this. Not that he was much for intoxicants.

"Well, this is all very posh, now, ain't it? They even have Iorian fare on the menu," Vargus said.

Priests carrying trays began circulating through the room, bearing delicacies from across the galaxy. This was not your typical temple food, simple and healthy. No, this meal was the most ostentatious display of wealth that Callum had ever seen.

He had always known that the Temple was prominent, wealthy, and connected. Heck, his sister Zalila had been telling him forever that the Temple was more powerful than they let on, that they had secrets. He should have believed her.

As one of the galaxy's foremost researchers of the Obelisks, she would know. But Callum had not accepted the full extent of that truth until now, sitting here among these people, dining on the most exquisite cuisine the galaxy had to offer.

The influence of the Temple of the Seven transcended the lines of government, subspecies, and philosophy.

Their direct control was only over their own land and priests, but Callum was beginning to suspect that the true extent of their power may as well be absolute.

THE
VALMORAN
CHRONICLES

[14]

DIGNITARIES AND DELICACIES

VALMORAN REPUBLIC, PLANET KRONAI, TEMPLE OF THE SEVEN

CALLUM TORION, REPRESENTATIVE ARBITER FOR THE VALMORAN REPUBLIC

～

THE POMPOUS ASS had been bad enough sober, and now the fool was starting in on his third glass of Iorian wine. As if this hadn't already been the longest, most wearying day in memory, Callum had to contend with Vargus Trix on top of it.

The scent of fermented fruit wafted across the table, mingling unpleasantly with the delicate aroma of the Temple's incense.

Unfortunately for everyone at the table, the wine further loosened the crime lord's vile tongue. While Callum typically prized his empathic senses, he was currently cursing the fact that he had the added displeasure of experiencing the man's megalomania and sadistic tendencies grow with his inebriation.

He could not, for the life of him, understand why the Temple would choose to associate with such a monster.

Thankfully, Vargus didn't appear to be using his powers to inflict pain or pleasure on anyone yet—Callum had been monitoring his dinner companions' emotions for signs of the man's signature antics—but the nonsense falling from his lips was bad enough all on its own.

"But slavery just makes fiscal sense!" He punctuated the assertion by slamming his fist on the table, rattling the wine glasses. The man's emotions revealed that his indignation was an act. On the inside, Vargus brimmed with gleeful anticipation.

Callum gritted his teeth, his jaw clenching so hard he could almost hear his molars crack. The bastard was baiting them, trying to provoke a reaction.

Callum resisted the urge to roll his eyes, then took a calming breath and focused on the soup course. He wasn't hungry—at this point, he only wanted to find a transport, head home, and sleep for three days straight.

It's not that there was anything wrong with the banquet. Priests played uplifting instrumental music, the room was a kaleidoscope of joy, excitement, and reverence, and the pleasant chatter of polite conversation filled the hall.

Callum's gaze drifted to the head table, where Matthai sat among the High Priests. If only Matthai didn't seem so off this evening. The contrast between Matthai's vibrant emotions earlier that day and his current emotional void was jarring. Where there had been a tempest of feeling—fear, hope, determination—there was now ... nothing.

Outwardly, Matthai was eating, drinking, smiling. Inwardly, he was ... gone. Callum was aware of Matthai's empty presence at the head table behind him like a hovering ghost, and couldn't seem to stop monitoring the Scion's emotional state. It was as if someone had erased Matthai's spirit, leaving behind a shell performing the motions.

It was unnerving, and Callum was further annoyed by how much it bothered him. After all, he had only met the man this afternoon—why should he care if something was wrong with Matthai? Yet the wrongness of it all gnawed at him, a persistent itch he couldn't scratch.

He turned around, hoping to catch sight of the Scion, but before he spotted him, Vargus made a loud announcement.

"Fine. I'll say it."

Callum turned back to the table and wished he hadn't when he caught the glint in the crime lord's eye.

"It's about time we address the obvious problem with this picture." Vargus glared at the Threllian Ambassador, his leathery wings rustling with barely contained aggression.

The Threllian Ambassador had spent most of the meal sitting quietly, observing. Its skin rippled with subtle patterns of blue and green, the meaning of which Callum could only guess at.

Callum assumed he had been content to do so, but couldn't be sure—Valmoran powers didn't work on Threllians, and he didn't know how to read the alien's body language. It was a strange sort of emotional blindness, being unable to know or even guess at the Ambassador's emotional state.

He hadn't spoken much to the Ambassador this evening, regrettably. The opportunity to broker communication between the Republic and the Empire was tempting, but how could he have guessed there would be a Threllian at Matthai Valtrellin's ordination? Without ambassadorial authorization, his hands were tied.

Callum had worked hard to distinguish himself as an expert war historian and strategist—often considered a useless specialty after generations of Peacekeeper oversight—so he would have been the perfect candidate for the role of Ambassador.

It was a shame, but he could get himself in a galaxy of trouble if he acted without voters' approval.

"What are you going on about now, Vargus?" Regla spoke as if to an unruly child, her fingers drumming an impatient rhythm on the table.

"I'm just saying, now that we've got past the pleasantries, it's about time we all admit that there's a parasite sitting at the dinner table, right?"

Callum's shock was mirrored by Arilla, Regla, and Priest Ollem. Arilla's face paled, Regla's jaw clenched, and Ollem's eyes widened in horror. Many Valmorans still mistrusted the Threllians, even twenty generations after the ceasefire. And while some still used derogatory terms such as "parasite" or "space bug" to describe them, it was not done in polite company.

And this moron had the gall to say it to the first Threllian Ambassador to grace Valmoran space since the war. Centuries of careful diplomacy, teetering on the edge of ruin because of one drunken, bigoted idiot.

The Republic had been trying to reopen communications with the Empire for several generations, and was almost desperate to gain access to their superior medical technology. Vargus was likely the last Valmoran Callum would want to represent their species.

Ambassadorial approval or not, he couldn't allow Vargus's comments to stand.

Callum turned to address the Ambassador—X'ilxis was his name, according to his Hix overlay. He had no clue how to pronounce it, and his Hix wasn't helpful—information on the Threllian Empire was still sparse.

"Ambassador ...?" Callum began.

As the Ambassador spoke, the effect was unlike anything Callum had ever seen. Every inch of the Threllian's skin morphed in bright colors as his robotic chair projected a male voice, speaking eerily perfect Valmoran Standard.

"Zil is fine, Representative Torion. I understand that our language is quite challenging for Valmorans."

The Threllian Ambassador was genial, almost scarily diplomatic, in the face of Vargus's brazen rudeness. It was remarkable how his synthetic voice mimicked good-natured amusement.

Callum still found it unsettling to feel nothing coming through his empathic senses. Yet somehow, even without, he got the impression that the Ambassador was ... pleasant.

"Ambassador Zil, I apologize for my dinner companion's unforgivable rudeness. I assure you, he does not speak for all Valmorans, and most certainly does not speak for the Valmoran Republic. We deeply regret our ancestors' actions during the Threllian Wars, and hope to one day call ourselves friends of the Empire."

The Threllian's skin morphed through a soothing pattern of green and blue tones. "Thank you, Representative Torion. We are very pleased to make your acquaintance, and see that your reputation precedes you. As for you, Vargus Trix, we are content to address your concerns."

The silence hung in the air, but it didn't take long for Vargus to shatter it. When he did, he didn't even deign to address the Ambassador. Instead, he turned to each of the Valmorans in quick succession, his wings flaring with each accusation.

"Are we just going to sit here and act like it's not a big deal that there is a Threllian in our space? In our holy Temple? These ... things ... used Valmoran females as hosts to their filthy offspring."

For the first time tonight, Callum felt something other than pride and amusement from Vargus. This was no simple shit-stirring—he was well and truly disgusted.

"They enslaved Valmorans, on our own homeworlds—"

"—undiscovered homeworlds—" Callum interjected.

"—and stuck their spawn inside our women! Why the hell didn't they just use their own females? Just the thought makes my skin crawl."

This was getting out of control.

"Vargus," Callum raised his voice, leveling his gaze at the crime lord. "Perhaps we should move back into the realm of facts, lest we cause a scene for the Valtrellins. In their holy Temple."

Vargus snarled and shot Callum a look so deadly that he braced for pain reflexively. The crime lord had a reputation for correcting those who displeased him.

Instead, Vargus lurched to his feet, nearly toppling his chair in the process. "You bug-lovers can do as you like. I'm getting another drink."

Then he stormed off.

Callum let out a breath, relaxing now that the threat of pain had literally gone away. Then he turned back to Ambassador Zil. "I sincerely apologize—"

"—No need, Representative Torion. Master Trix's reputation is well known to us. As is yours. Our Emperor finds great inspiration in your political philosophies."

Callum wasn't sure how to respond to that. How did the Threllians have so much intel on Valmorans, when none had visited Valmoran space in over twenty generations?

Also, the thought of the Threllian Emperor following his political platform was so strange, so completely outside the realm of anything he had considered possible, that he didn't know what to think.

The Threllian Empire remained an enigma, shrouded in centuries of isolation. In texts from the time of the Threllian Wars, their Empire had been brutally hierarchical—a far cry from the progressive ideals Callum championed.

Things must have changed a great deal if their current Emperor appreciated his progressive philosophies.

"That is … unexpected. Granted, my understanding of Threllian culture is quite outdated. May I ask—"

"—you are wondering how we know so much, fearing what it could mean."

Callum couldn't deny it. Any military strategist would be wary to hear the Threllians had been secretly gathering intel.

"I assure you, our interest is nothing nefarious. Our Emperor is an avid student of philosophy, and his curiosity soon surpassed our own cultural and sociological technology. Valmorans have had many governments, many philosophies to study and compare."

Callum relaxed slightly, but he would need to report this information to the Republic. That would mean explaining why he had broken protocol and spoken in an ambassadorial capacity. Navigating bureaucracy would be a headache, but he couldn't think about that right now.

"Fascinating. May I ask—"

"—you may ask the Emperor when he visits the Temple. We have been invited, and Our Great Emperor would like to accept. He will want to meet with you during his visit. For now, I must go. We have seen all that we need today."

With that, the Threllian Ambassador made his farewells and left the hall, his electronic chair gliding across the polished floor.

That had been ... unsettling.

Then again, the Ambassador hadn't seemed threatening. He had been perfectly reasonable. More than reasonable, with the way he handled Vargus.

Of course, a cunning enemy would present themselves in the best possible light. It didn't matter—it wasn't Callum's responsibility or right to decide how to handle foreign affairs.

However, he should handle this delicately. Others might blow this incident out of proportion if he gave the wrong impression. Callum wasn't sure why, but he didn't think the Threllians were a credible threat.

Urgency level 2, then, and security level 1. That would show that Callum was taking the matter seriously but wouldn't raise any alarm bells. He asked his AI to request a meeting with the Department of Foreign Affairs.

Such an unexpected turn of events. Now that Callum had time to reflect, it was odd that the Ambassador could speak perfect Standard, since Threllians used a combination of visual and electromagnetic communication.

The initial conflict with the Threllians had unfolded from a series of misunderstandings—two species, with a nearly insurmountable language barrier, and stark cultural and theological differences.

Violence had been the unavoidable and catastrophic result, and it seemed many Valmorans still hadn't learned their lesson.

"Do you travel often?"

He started at the sudden question Arilla directed at him and turned to look at her. "What was that?"

Arilla cleared her throat and blushed, a rosy tint creeping up her neck. The wine seemed to be getting to her, though Callum was sure she hadn't imbibed as much as Vargus. He may be the only sober person left in the room, which meant he would have the pleasure of watching the evening devolve around him.

She gave a self-deprecating smile. "Oh, I was just wondering ... you must travel a lot as a politician, right?"

Callum suppressed a sigh. Small talk was mind-numbingly inane, but snubbing the woman beside him would be rude.

"Some, though not as much as you might think," he answered, in a flat tone he hoped would discourage further inquiry.

"Oh? I figured someone like you would be in our VIP network."

Tamping down his irritation, Callum applied his best "politician smile." Public image was important, after all. "That's right—you said you work for Anaris Station, didn't you?"

"Mhm—for the Anaris Station Spacefolding Syndicate. I was in charge of coordinating all the travel routes for the ceremony today." She grinned, and there was a glint in her eyes. "It was quite the logistic puzzle, actually."

Interesting. Callum spared her a closer look. Arilla was an unassuming sort of woman—quiet, unremarkable, and slightly underdressed for the occasion, as if she hadn't known quite what to wear to this event.

Her fingers fidgeted with the stem of her wine glass, betraying her nerves.

Hearing her talk about her role in the travel arrangements, he would bet that they had invited her as a thank-you for a job well done, not as a dignitary. That she was here on merit made her infinitely more fascinating.

A second look into her emotions painted an intriguing picture —this woman may be awkward, but she was excited about her work, almost to the point of obsession.

He had never given a second thought to how difficult it would be to coordinate the sudden influx of billions of extra Valmorans to planet Kronai. Still, now that he was thinking about it, his interest was piqued.

"That sounds like quite a puzzle—did you complete the project alone?"

"I led a small team. Have actually been working on this project my entire career." She gave a shy smile, and Callum could feel the mix of excitement, pride, and embarrassment radiating off her. "Got promoted because of it."

"Congratulations! I'm guessing the project was a success, then?"

She nodded emphatically, her earlier nervousness giving way to animated enthusiasm. "Oh, yes—there were a couple of hiccups with some of the rental orbitals, but we had backups lined up, so no one noticed."

Arilla was so earnest, so obviously invested in her work, that Callum almost wanted to pat her on the head. Almost. "So, what's the new job?"

She grinned. "You're looking at the new Junior Director of Forecasting and Scheduling. It's not easy, you know—since folders are immobile and take so much energy. We have to plan the trips to be as close to capacity as possible. And it's a huge investment if we recommend a new set of endpoints to the Syndicate."

"I think I read something a while back about issues with people sneaking into the fold zone?" Callum asked.

"Oh, slinkers? Yeah, they're kind of inevitable." She leaned in, her voice dropping to a conspiratorial whisper. "Don't tell anyone, but we actually plan for it."

"Oh?" Callum raised an eyebrow, his interest genuinely piqued.

"Yeah, there's always a few small ships that slink into the zone right before the fold. We ignore it as long as the trip isn't too full, and they're not too obvious about it."

Then she made a face. "Well, mostly. It's too expensive to monitor every fold for freeloaders, so we have random inspections."

She assumed a mock authoritarian voice and gestured like a teacher. Her hand chopped the air for emphasis, nearly knocking over her wine glass.

"If you get caught slinking during one of those, that's it—blacklisted. That's enough to keep slinking to a manageable level. It's a bunch of math to minimize costs. Anyway, I'm rambling." She looked at him sheepishly. "Sorry."

"That's fi—"

"—oh, hey—let me give you my contact info, and if you ever need help with travel, I can hook you up."

Her notice came across his Hix, and he hesitated. He rarely added strangers to his contacts. Off-planet travel was rare for him, since he conducted all his voting duties from his home Ansible chamber. It was one of his favorite perks of being a Representative.

Space travel was a nuisance—hours or days cut off from communication networks, followed by the tedious catch-up with delayed messages. Only Ansible allowed for instantaneous interplanetary communication, and its exorbitant cost made it impractical for routine use.

Then again, he didn't have any contacts at the Spacefolding Syndicate, so he decided it couldn't hurt.

As soon as he accepted, he wondered if he had made a mistake.

Arilla leaned in closer, her body language suddenly much too familiar. The scent of wine on her breath was cloying as she invaded his personal space. "You know ... if you ever want help with travel, or anything else ..."

Callum coughed and resisted the urge to jerk away from her. His skin crawled at the unwanted proximity, his empathic senses irritated by her sudden burst of attraction.

He never knew how to act when people insisted on flirting with him. Being considered classically attractive had its benefits, he knew that, but after a childhood where everyone treated him like a pariah, he was still very unused to—and uncomfortable with—people coming on to him.

He glanced away, searching for an excuse to end the conversation.

And immediately wished he hadn't.

Vargus was back, drink in hand, staring right at Callum. A cruel smile crept across the crime lord's face.

"Looks like I made it back just in time for dessert."

THE
VALMORAN
CHRONICLES

15

THREATS, TORTURE, AND TARTS

VALMORAN REPUBLIC, PLANET KRONAI, TEMPLE OF THE SEVEN

CALLUM TORION, REPRESENTATIVE ARBITER FOR THE VALMORAN REPUBLIC

~

CALLUM STRUGGLED to keep an impolite grimace off his face as Regla Desh picked up her berry lancer, then used it to pierce the skin of the crimson fruit. The thick red syrup cascaded down the sides of her tart like a revolting waterfall.

"I do love julee berries!"

He had always found the delicacy somewhat nauseating, especially knowing how absurdly expensive they were. The air was thick with the intoxicating scent of the exotic fruits, their sweet-tart aroma mingling with the odors that lingered from dinner and the stale perfume of the wealthy.

Glancing around, Callum realized he might be the only person not relishing the hedonistic dessert. The banquet hall hummed with gossip and laughter, a symphony of decadence that echoed off the stone walls.

As if they needed additional mind-altering substances at this party. Though he was perversely curious how a mild empathogen would affect a sociopath like Vargus Trix.

Callum gently removed the swollen red berry from his dessert and pushed it to the side of his plate, careful not to puncture the skin. He had no interest in partaking.

Apparently, Vargus was watching.

"What? You're not going to eat that? Give it here, then." Before Callum could protest, the mob boss loomed over the table, plate in hand, impatient.

How unspeakably rude. Though it was probably easier to just give him the damn thing than argue about it.

Callum stood, somewhat awkwardly, and carefully transferred the fruit to Vargus's plate, his mind conjuring bizarre images of the thick juice spilling out over the table like blood. A moment later, he was comfortably seated again.

Vargus sat down, like a king claiming his throne, looking—and feeling—smug.

As if the entire episode had nothing to do with the berry.

It was a struggle for Callum to stifle his groan. He had long since run out of patience for Vargus's childish dominance games.

By not making a fuss, Callum had just lost this one, and he was surprised by the flash of irritation he felt at the realization.

Just a few more minutes.

Once they started collecting the dessert plates, he could make his polite excuses and finally head home. He was thoroughly exhausted and couldn't remember the last time his nerves had felt so fried.

Vargus caught his gaze, stuck an oozing bite of julee berry tart into his mouth, then spoke around it. "So you're one of them out-cyclers, I hear." His voice held a hint of challenge, emotions laced with malice.

Callum's blood boiled.

He never hid his out-cycler status, though these days he could have. He had been just entering puberty when the last generation entered the mating season, but now, especially since he took good care of himself, he didn't look particularly old compared to the current generation.

He could blend in if he wanted to.

But he didn't do that, because he refused to be ashamed of it. He owned it, was an outspoken advocate. A proud figurehead.

It had been a long time since someone tried to publicly humiliate him over his birth status, and he was horrified at his own reaction.

He could actually hear the blood rushing in his ears. For a moment, he froze, no longer the well-respected Arbiter Callum Torion. Instead, he was an orphan, unwanted and—in the eyes of others—unclean. He wanted to disappear.

No!

This was nothing new. A childhood fraught with bullies had taught Callum that the best response was nonchalance. He mastered his expression and outwardly recovered his composure.

"Most certainly, I am."

He forced himself to take a small bite of his own dessert.

Vargus used his spoon to point at the missionary from the Federation. "If you'd been born in his territory, they'd have sold you off to get rid of you. Me? I like out-cyclers. They're cheap." His face broke into a wide, nasty grin. Then he shoved another bite of tart into his filthy mouth.

Before Callum could react, the Federation missionary lurched forward in his seat.

Outwardly, the man was composed, but inside, he was furious. "You go too far, Master Trix. The Federation no longer tolerates the sale of Valmoran children, not from the brute species, nor out-cyclers. I have devoted my life to running orphanages to raise unwanted children, and I won't sit here and listen to you—"

"—ah, calm yourself. It was a joke. No need to get all tetchy."

That sneaky bastard. One insult, two targets.

Regla's biting tone rang out. "Vargus, I've had about enough of your games for the evening. Can we please enjoy our dessert in peace?"

"Games? I'm just making conversation." He flashed his eyebrows. "You'd know it if I were playing games."

Regla's stare turned severe. "Oh, yes—my people have told me all about the games you like to play when you're drunk, Vargus Trix."

Ignoring her ire, Vargus leaned closer to Regla. When he spoke, his voice had a seductive edge, "What can I say? I do so love to play."

Callum watched in horrified fascination as the two squared off.

Regla leaned in, mirroring Vargus's body language, voice slow and breathy. "Imagine a scenario where Valmar Defensive Tech fulfills 63% of Ioria Prime's yearly contracts, yet those same purchase orders account for a mere 2% of our sales."

All hints of warmth dropped from Regla's face as she fixed Vargus with a look that could freeze blood. "Try your little pain games on me, and we'll play a game I like to call 'Ioria Prime can't maintain its planetary defense grid.'"

Vargus lifted a hand to his heart, apparently affronted, though Callum read only amusement from him. Not one shred of intimidation. "I would never inflict pain on women—"

"—I know exactly what you like to do to women, Vargus. Pain or pleasure, it's a violation." She leaned back, picked up her wineglass, and made a show of looking bored. "Try it. I dare you."

Regla held no fear of Vargus, only unmitigated contempt. Callum couldn't help feeling impressed at her ability to go head to head with Vargus. He couldn't say he exactly liked the woman—her emotions felt cold and uninviting, like metal left out in the rain—but her negotiation skills were formidable.

Vargus stared at Regla for a moment longer, though she no longer paid him any attention. With a slight jerk of his head, he moved his focus back to his meal.

Huh. Apparently, Vargus did have the ability to control his impulses.

Unfortunately, Vargus Trix was no longer calm. The man clearly did not appreciate being ignored.

Callum felt Vargus's icy rage slithering through him. He suppressed a shiver as a smile crept across the crime lord's face.

Vargus's eyes snapped to Callum.

Zap.

A shock of pain lanced down Callum's left side, shoulder to wrist. Before he could contain it, he twitched in reflex.

If not for the satisfaction emanating from Vargus, he might have written it off as a random twinge. A flurry of emotions sped through Callum at the unprovoked attack, but he pushed them all aside.

This wasn't the first time he'd been attacked for no reason. If Vargus planned to force Callum to react, he would be sorely disappointed. Physical pain was nothing compared to the emotional load an empath shouldered. Callum had a lifetime of practice concealing his empathic pain from others.

Zap.

This time, Callum didn't react. Instead, he took a bite of his tart and hummed to himself as in delight, though the food tasted like ash in his mouth.

If he was smart, he'd mind his business, get through dessert, and head home straight after. Vargus would tire of this soon.

To his horror, words tumbled from Callum's lips before he could bite them back. "I'm surprised a man such as you is a friend of the Temple, Vargus."

"A man such as me?"

Zap.

Callum ignored the pain and nodded.

He cursed himself for losing control of his tongue. It was the exhaustion. It had been beyond stupid to provoke this asshole.

"I'm not sure what you're implying, Callum—that because we don't believe in the draconian rule of governments, we're somehow less pious than you Republic-types? I'm offended.

Why, I believe in the Gods. How could I not, when they have seen fit to bless me with such power?"

Zap.

"Oh, the Gods blessed you with a power, then? I wasn't aware you were God-touched." Callum said, voice flippant. Now that he had started, he couldn't seem to get his sharp tongue in check.

Zap. Zap. Zap.

Callum could feel Vargus's irritation and confusion. It was driving him crazy that Callum wasn't reacting to his torture. Who's winning now, asshole?

Zap. Zap.

His tormentor let out a huff of breath. "We have a great many temples on Ioria Prime and provide generous financial support to the Temple. It's only fitting that they would honor me with an invitation."

"How are things on Ioria Prime lately? If you listen to the news reports, the whole slave trade isn't working out so well for you these days. Perhaps it's time to adapt to the times." Callum's words came out before he could stop them. It was reckless, a product of an interminable day and too long in this asshole's company.

He was playing with fire, but part of him reveled in it.

Zap.

Vargus set down his spoon and wiped his face deliberately with his napkin before folding it and setting it on the table.

"Is that so? Enlighten me, Representative Callum—what exactly are they saying about my planet?"

Zap.

Callum knew he should stop, but the pain only fueled him. "Oh, you never know how much you can believe from the news vids." Callum gave a dismissive wave. "They're making it sound like you've got a full-on uprising on your hands."

Vargus's nostrils flared. "No uprising. We had some trouble a while back, but I'm taking care of it."

"Oh?" Callum feigned innocence, even as he recognized the dangerous game he was playing.

"Yeah. One of my lords just doesn't know how to control his property."

Arilla piped up, apparently oblivious to the tension at the table. "Oh—you're talking about Braxtor the Liberator, aren't you? I saw that story on the—"

"—Braxtor the Terrible has been a pain in my ass for far too long."

Callum's gut twisted at the name, a cold sweat breaking out along his spine. He forced his breathing to remain steady, his face impassive, even as his mind flashed to the Blood Pits of Ioria Prime.

Arilla shrunk back in her chair at his chilling tone. There was something about the dead calm of it that set off alarm bells.

The table had gone silent, and Vargus continued, "That brute should never have been allowed to escape. His fool of a master just never learned how to properly leash his dog. Back when his mother was in the next cell over, things were copacetic."

He looked at Regla and spoke to her as if sharing insider business secrets. "A woman like you understands leverage, I know you do. You wouldn't be stupid enough to let that woman off herself."

Arilla gasped, and Callum felt Priest Ollem's horror at the declaration. Callum forced himself to relax his jaw.

Vargus shrugged and picked up his spoon again. "For a while, we had to make due with hostages—that simpering fool wasn't about to disobey if we threatened poor, innocent children." He rolled his eyes.

Callum's hands clenched involuntarily under the table, his knuckles turning white. Fourteen Children to be exact. The casual way Vargus spoke of threatening innocents made his blood boil, but he forced his face to remain neutral.

"But here's the thing—that sort of leverage isn't sustainable. I mean, who goes to the trouble of kidnapping and training a god-touched Vraxai, making him into the most efficient killing machine the galaxy has ever seen, and doesn't make sure he controls whatever that monster loves best?"

He turned back to Arilla and smiled. "I'm telling you—get your hands on what a person loves most, and they'll do whatever you want."

Callum's gut clenched as Zalila's face flashed across his mind. He kept his ward-sister's relationship to him a secret for this exact reason. That someone would use her to get to him was unconscionable.

Vargus shrugged, acting unaffected by everyone else's discomfort, though Callum could feel him reveling in it.

"Problem is, that wily bastard refused all our gifts. We just had to stick it out until mating season, see? Because a man like Braxtor, powerful as he is—is definitely mateable."

"But you can't force a bond!" Arilla said.

"Can't I? Way I see it, we've got a lot of whores on Ioria Prime. I was all set to run the whole lot of them through his cell come mating season. See, once we held his mate, there would be no more of this 'Braxtor the Liberator' bullshit."

Callum could hardly believe what he was hearing. And Vargus had the nerve to call Braxtor a monster.

He had witnessed Braxtor's sorrow once, had seen him stealthily mercy-kill a man he was supposed to execute, before tearing the corpse apart in a bloody show for the spectators ... and the masters.

But Callum hadn't known the full extent of Braxtor's suffering.

Slavery was horrific—but what Vargus described was something out of a nightmare.

"But there's a problem, see? That worm didn't liberate himself—he had help. We rounded up a whole gaggle of the slaves that got out that day, along with whatever they love

259

best. But the guy they pointed to is just a merc—I want the bastard who caused this mess. The mastermind."

Callum's heart raced, but he kept his face a mask of mild interest. His paranoia flared, even as he reminded himself that Vargus had no way of knowing he was involved. He silently cursed Captain Zephyr and his inability to stick to a damned plan.

If the man had just followed instructions instead of inciting a full-blown rebellion ...

"If your true target is the one who planned it, why put the bounty on Braxtor?" He knew he was treading dangerous ground, but he couldn't stop himself.

"Yeah, well—we need him back to quell the damn uprisings. Can't let him go free, can't kill him—need to shackle him up proper and let the others see no one escapes."

His voice turned steely. "The mastermind—I don't want him to see me coming. But when I hunt down the prick with the nerve to steal my prize fighter?"

Callum's heart felt like it was beating loud enough for the entire table to hear, but he forced himself to sit impassively for Vargus's final verdict.

A fleeting recollection of fourteen out-cycler children, now safely tucked away in a Republic ward, flitted across his mind. Vargus's earlier taunt about out-cyclers being "cheap" resurfaced, and Callum felt a surge of righteous anger.

Those children deserved better than to be used as leverage in Vargus's sick games.

"When I find that man, I'm going celebrate by making Braxtor tear him to pieces in the Blood Pits. Because nobody fucks with my planet."

[PART 4]
ANARIS STATION, LOGISTIC CENTER OF THE GALAXY

THE VALMORAN CHRONICLES

16

VRAXAI MAKE THE BEST BODYGUARDS

VALMORAN SPACE, ANARIS STATION, THE BLACK SWIRL BORDELLO

TOR, AN EX-SLAVE IN HIDING

~

TOR STOOD guard inside the suite door, ensuring Delilah's safety as she entertained her newest client. Her entertaining room's elegant colors, lavish bedding, and soft lighting provided a stark contrast to the subtle violence unfolding before him.

Watching, but trying not to see. Listening, but trying not to hear.

The musky odor of sweat and cologne mingled with her delicate scent of flowers and sweetness, a jarring contrast that set Tor's nerves on edge.

This was different from the rampant prostitution on Ioria Prime. The Black Swirl was a niche bordello on Anaris Station, the most prominent tourist hub in the galaxy. No one here was a slave, but it was still jarring, transitioning from pleasant conversation to watching Delilah like this.

With some of her regulars, once Tor watched her interact with them, it was enough to stand near the door and listen instead of watching. On those days, he might even use his Hix implant to practice reading while he kept an ear out.

The interface was still a struggle, and reading was challenging, but he was determined to learn.

But something about this new client unnerved him, so he was on edge, watching the creep's every move.

Tor had good reason to trust his instincts. As a Vraxai—a God-touched Vraxai—he was gifted with intuition. His mind picked up on little things as long as he paid attention.

Which he always did. Vigilance was his default state. A lifetime of brutal combat training and harsh punishments had honed his vigilance into an instinctual reflex.

Memories of his past life ignited a tremor of repressed anger in his hands, but he shoved it down, refocusing on his current task—protecting Delilah.

As he observed them, a knot tightened in his belly, a miserable reminder of his growing affection for her. Getting attached was a dangerous game, but maintaining emotional distance from Delilah was proving impossible.

There were moments when he almost thought they might be friends ... as much as two people could be, while keeping so many secrets.

She was remarkably coy about her subspecies whenever anyone brought it up, which was often.

With her striking red hair and skin so pale it was almost translucent—not to mention her strange name—she was mysterious and exotic. Delilah held a particular allure that she shamelessly exploited when wooing patrons into her bed.

He didn't dare ask what he most wanted answered—did she remember him from before?

Long ago, Tor's former master offered her as a "gift," which Tor refused, as he had all others. Was it possible he was so unrecognizable in his new life?

Part of him liked to dream that she secretly knew who he was, and it didn't matter to her. But it was a fantasy. He struggled to live with the things he had done—how could anyone else see him as anything but a monster?

Especially someone as gentle as Delilah.

Tor tensed as the new client snaked his hand up from her hip and grabbed her hair, wrenching her head back and arching her spine at a painful-looking angle. It wasn't an overt threat, and it wasn't uncommon for the clients to play a little rough, but that didn't mean he liked it.

Violence always put him on edge, but it was becoming unbearable when inflicted on his petite client.

Tor's heart nearly leaped out of his chest, his feet involuntarily propelling him forward as the client wrapped his other hand around Delilah's throat. He gritted his teeth and forced himself to retreat when she carelessly gave the hand signal that she was ok.

He wished she would take this more seriously, but she seemed almost flippant about her own safety. Maybe because she assumed he would keep her safe, but it couldn't all be on him—she needed to do her part.

Tor's eyes bored into the back of the man's head, his gaze shifting to scrutinize every twitch of his shoulders and back. He was a coiled spring, ready to unleash his fury at the first sign of real danger. Didn't she realize how easily that man could end her life with his hands on her throat?

He repeatedly clenched and unclenched all four fists, reminding himself that Delilah didn't want his help. She had not been pleased the last time he interrupted after she'd already given the 'all clear' signal.

This part of the job was sheer agony. Somehow, standing back and watching the clients manhandle her was infinitely worse than any torment in the Blood Pits.

Memories of Ioria Prime flooded him with a furious rush of shame. For the things he had done, for the people he left behind.

He still didn't know why he'd been chosen to be liberated, or who orchestrated it. But someone risked sending a smuggler down to that hellhole to free him, then set him up with a cover story here on Anaris Station.

His new life wasn't glamorous, but it meant he got paid to use his former skills without having to kill people. For the first time since he was a child, Tor was free—or as free as he could be.

Freedom was an illusion when he was still hiding, waiting for his mysterious benefactor to call in that life debt.

And when his past weighed so heavily on his soul.

The next several minutes felt endless until, finally, Delilah reclined nude on the bed while the client dressed. Tor itched to drape her robe over her exposed skin, but it would be overstepping.

Delilah, perfectly comfortable in her own skin, crawled forward and kneeled at the foot of the bed, showering the client with affection and sweet nothings. She had a way of making each patron feel like the most important person in existence, as if they meant more to her than anyone else in the galaxy.

She was a master at her job.

After what felt like an interminable wait, the man left. Tor fought the urge to slam his fists into the door, instead drawing a deep breath before turning to face Delilah as she lounged on the luxurious bed. The way her eyes moved showed she was engrossed in something on her Hix.

Gods, he envied her ease with the Hix implant. His former master had never allowed him to have one. Access to the galactic web would have armed the slaves with forbidden knowledge, and the masters couldn't risk that.

But he and the others found alternative ways to share information—whispers in the heat of battle, pillow talk with pampered tourists. It had allowed them to piece together a plan. But those plans hadn't been finished when Zephyr broke him out, and leaving was a choice he still agonized over.

He'd set their plan in motion too early. Some of the others escaped at the same time he did. At least he and Zephyr had managed to save the children.

But it hadn't been enough. Tor slammed those thoughts away. It was done, and now he had to live with it.

He pressed his eyes shut tight, unsure if he was more irritated with himself or with the woman sprawled naked on the bed. When he spoke, his voice had a grumpier tone than he intended. "No more choking, Delilah."

She tore her gaze away from whatever she was doing on her Hix and looked at him, wide-eyed and innocent. "Hmm?"

He tried to make his voice gentler as he repeated, "No more choking," although it still came out rougher than he meant.

She smiled at him and shrugged. "Oh, that? He wasn't actually choking me, Tor. He was just holding my neck."

Delilah swept her hair back and tilted her head from side to side to demonstrate. "See? No marks or anything."

Tor shook his head vehemently. "No more neck-holding, then. He could have killed you."

And she would have been dead before he could cross the room. He had escaped his old life and was determined never to kill again. Aside from one glaring exception—that monster deserved every bit of retribution Tor planned to unleash. But Delilah needed to understand that some things were too dangerous to allow.

She pouted and made a dismissive gesture. "Psh ... it's harmless. Besides, it takes a while to suffocate someone, doesn't it? I'm sure you would rescue me before it got serious," she said as she slid off the bed and walked over to retrieve her delicate robe. She turned her back to him while she dressed.

Tor wasn't sure how to respond. He didn't want to tell her he knew over a dozen techniques the client could have used to kill her in an instant—Tor didn't want her to fear him. But he also didn't want to budge on this.

She turned around, carelessly giving him her back. Her unwavering trust in him was mystifying.

"Delilah ..."

"Tor, do you know what it is that I sell here?" she asked, voice contemplative, as she fastened her belt.

Sex was the obvious answer, but he knew it wasn't what she meant. "You give people what they want."

She turned her head and beamed at him over her shoulder. "You're so clever, Tor."

A warm flush crept into his cheeks at the compliment. No one called him smart, not ever. He wasn't dumb, just uneducated, and not by choice.

Delilah continued, "You're right—I give them what they want, and then ..."

She turned around, raised her eyebrows, and spoke as if imparting the divine secret of the universe. "... then, I give them what they need, the one thing they need so desperately they won't even allow themselves to want it."

Delilah looked him dead in the eyes and winked. "And then they need me."

"But if choking you is what they need, you don't need them," Tor protested.

She waved him off. "Oh, that?—the rough sex is never the part that they need. That's just what they think they want."

"Delilah, please." He huffed a breath, trying to think of words that might change her mind. "It's ... dangerous."

She tilted her head and gave him an indulgent smile. "Oh, fine—you win. Sometimes I forget you're a gentle giant."

His heart clenched, more troublesome affection bubbling up.

No one had ever called him a 'gentle giant' before. He longed to embrace the title, but his past made it seem like an impossible dream.

"I'll update my profile to exclude choking—will that satisfy you, Tor?"

Tor cleared the lump in his throat, then grumbled his approval. "Thanks."

Delilah sat down at her vanity, brushing out her long red hair before securing it with some sort of metal comb. All Tor saw was how well it would function as a weapon.

Gods, he wished he could view the world without his mind always preparing for battle. Why couldn't he just see a beautiful woman twisting her hair up, exposing her nape ... without seeing every vulnerability on her body, every makeshift weapon in the room?

"Tor, if you keep making me add to my limits, I won't need a bodyguard anymore." With a quick glance over her shoulder, she grinned. "And then, who would keep me safe?"

She had a point. Tor wasn't sure why she agreed to fulfill such dark requests from her clients. Sure, some clients were almost doting, but the ones who wanted to tie her up or hit her enraged him.

He wanted to hit back.

But the idea of her working without a bodyguard was even more disturbing than the thought of her with sleazy clients. The Black Swirl had a certain ambiance of manufactured danger that must appeal to its clientele.

People who had never known actual danger.

Delilah sauntered over to the door, slipped her dainty feet into tiny slippers, and reached up to pat him on the cheek. Almost as if Tor was a pet, even as he towered over her.

He struggled not to lean into her touch, which was soothing and familiar. It was miraculous to have another person approach him without fear. He couldn't remember anyone touching him so casually since his mother.

"You take good care of me, Tor," she said, her warm smile lighting up her eyes.

He would have stood taller, but didn't dare move. In that moment, he was the most important person in the universe.

It was no wonder Delilah's clients always returned. She was using her charm on him, giving him what he needed, just as she did with the patrons. He knew it. And yet, her easy affection felt so euphoric he didn't care whether it was genuine.

Tor remained motionless, savoring every second, wishing the moment would stretch forever. But all too soon, it ended.

"I don't have any other appointments today—let's go downstairs to see who's hanging out," she suggested, taking hold of his wrist and tugging him towards the door. He liked it when she treated him like a friend. It was an unfamiliar and not unpleasant feeling.

But he knew better than to grow too attached. From a tender young age, Tor had learned that everything and everyone he cared about would be used against him as leverage.

Possessions didn't matter to him—they'd always been the first things taken when he refused to comply with the masters. So he learned to need little. But people ...

... people had always been his weakness.

Tor refused to put anyone at risk again. Especially not Delilah.

THE VALMORAN CHRONICLES

17

CHANCE AND HAPPENSTANCE

VALMORAN SPACE, ANARIS STATION, RING 88B
PROMENADE

ZEPHYR, CAPTAIN OF THE SHINING FATE

~

ZEPHYR WHISTLED HAPPILY as he made his way down the promenade level of Ring 88B. His shine was turned up, and he wore his skin in his favorite shade, a deep brown, which offset the white shock of his hair in the most pleasing way.

Far overhead, the vid screens on the ceiling projected a blue sky so convincing that he'd have almost sworn he was planetside. Colorful birds swooped through the air, and a chitterling darted out of a tree to snag some food someone had left on a bench.

He grinned at the adorable little bio-engineered janitor.

They should get a chitterling for the Shining Fate ...

Hah, Fera would hate that. She never let him have pets on the ship.

As he continued ambling spinward, the ground sloped gently up, and the centerline tram disappeared behind the ceiling. The sight was a dead giveaway that he was in a space station. Zeph tried not to examine it too closely.

He'd been on Anaris Station hundreds of times, but his skin crawled whenever he imagined himself as a tiny bug pressed against the inside of a giant spinning ring. It made him feel trapped and insignificant.

He turned up his shine a little more, smiling at the additional attention he drew from passersby. Not even the myriad VR overlays, flashy and ever-present on Anaris Station, could compete.

Of course, none of the people nearby would have a clue that he was using his power on them. They would simply be more likely to notice him in a crowd.

A woman walking in the opposite direction caught his attention as she moved in his direction. He switched off the advertisements on his Hix to get them out of his way so he could get a better look.

She was one of those cybermod kids, a mod kit over one eye and a full silver replacement arm proudly on display.

Cute, and a little rough around the edges in a way Zeph certainly approved of. The way her lithe body moved, with graceful intentionality, he imagined this one could hold her own in a fight.

Unlike other cybermod kids, who wore faux combat gear for fashion rather than function, this pretty little monster was decked out in the real deal.

The girl gave him a once over and flashed her eyebrows in approval. Too cool to smile, but definitely into him. This woman looked like 18 shades of trouble and—

A voice rang out in his head.

> *Fera: Just because we're on Anaris Station doesn't mean it's safe. Stop being an attention-whore and try to blend in. We're smugglers, for fuck's sake. We have enemies, remember?*

He stopped in his tracks and glared at the fake sky in exasperation.

Fera. The state-of-the-art AI he had liberated from an all-but-abandoned personal museum, even though she claimed it was her who did the rescuing. Though calling Fera an AI was like calling a supernova a 'pretty light.'

Usually, he enjoyed her snarky commentary, but sometimes, he wished he could be alone in his own head. Since she lived in an organic matrix in a secret hold of the Shining Fate, Zeph often served as her portal to the outside world. He didn't have the heart to ask her to leave, except on the rarest occasions.

Partly because she was his best friend. Also, when a sophont-level AI holds the keys to your accounts, manages your entire smuggling business, and knows your ship better than you, a smart man keeps her happy.

> *Zeph: Fera, stop worrying. The birds are chirping, the crowds are smiling, and we just made enough to remodel the galley AND buy that upgraded memory module you've been eyeing.*

Fera needed to chill. He wasn't even doing anything illegal right now.

Well, probably. Zephyr didn't actually know what was on the disc in his pocket. And there was the small matter of the highly illegal Threllian AI on his ship. Also, the contraband stashed on the Shining Fate in case they ever needed to barter …

Ok, so maybe he was doing some things of questionable legality, but he wasn't doing anything wrong.

> *Fera: An intelligent man would turn down his shine and make himself unnoticeable. Especially when he still has Nulma's data delivery sitting in his pocket.*

She had a point. Annoying little brilliant AI. She sucked all the fun out of things with her whole 'being right all the time' thing.

> *Zeph: Where's the fun in that? I like people. I enjoy looking at them. I like it when they look at me.*

Fera didn't answer.

Zeph turned down his shine—not all the way like she wanted, because then he may as well be invisible—but to more normal levels. He could turn heads without using his power.

That settled, he continued down the path towards the nearest tram station. Nulma's was about a quarter of the way spinward from here, and he didn't have hours to spare, so walking was not an option.

He glanced around, trying to spot the cybermod girl who had so intrigued him. They had a moment back there ... he was sure of it, but she must have already moved on.

Not that he had time to socialize. He huffed, annoyed that Fera was right again. Nulma had paid for an expedited personal courier for the encrypted data disc, and might even pay extra for early delivery. That thought brought a smile back to his face.

Come to think of it, wasn't Nulma the one who sometimes got worked up over little things like late deliveries? Zephyr picked up the pace, arriving at the riser just as the spinward tram pulled up. Lucky. Lady Fate was smiling down on him today.

He took the riser to the tram level and boarded the train. It was busy today, but not overly so, and he was able to grab a seat near the back rather than stand for the ride.

Artificial gravity did funny things on the trams—spinward made you feel heavier, antispinward lighter.

The effect wasn't too overt, but noticeable, like being pressed into your seat while feeling pulled backward as the train hit speed. Zephyr despised it, though he'd never admit it out loud. What sort of captain would he be if he had a meltdown over centrifugal gravity?

He looked out the back of the car, watching as the promenade became a blur out the window. The awful sensation faded once they got up to speed, and he relaxed back into his seat.

Fera: Better?

Zeph: All good. Need me to pick anything up while I'm down here?

They had a routine. Fera stocked the ship, negotiating with various merchants for the best deals. But there was always some price-gouging with shipside delivery, especially for luxury items.

Fera: We're all topped up on nutritional substrate, but the prices on flavor additives today are absurd, and we're running low.

Zeph: Got it—I'll order some and have it sent to the Fate.

His eyes wandered—and snagged on the cybermod girl from before! She was sitting on the other end of the tram. It was tempting to go sit across from her, but he would look ridiculous, lurching and swaying his way over there.

It had to be fate, seeing her again.

He'd been waiting, impatiently, for mating season to begin. The Shining Fate could crew seven, but it was only home to him and Fera. He wasn't interested in taking on crew—it was just a four-letter word for people who end up selling you out —but a mate would be different. He was sure of it.

Even with Fera's homey touches, it could get lonely on the Fate. The ship was gorgeous, but achingly empty sometimes. Not that he ever told her that—it would just hurt her feelings.

Fera: It's that weird girl from before. Stop staring at her. It's creepy.

Zeph: She might be the one.

Fera: Not this again—it's not even mating season.

The girl looked up and caught him staring at her. He flashed her his most winning smile. She smirked and nodded in his direction before looking away.

Zeph: Out-of-cycle matings are possible—

Fera: —and rare as fuck. And generally considered bad luck.

Zeph: Lady Fate wouldn't steer me wrong.

Fera: You're an idiot. That woman is tailing you.

Could she be following him? If she was, it was because she felt it, too. Whatever this thing was between them. Excitement prickled down his spine.

Wait. What if they got off at different stops, and Zephyr lost her?

He should make his way over there, the motion of the tram be damned—his future mate wouldn't care if he acted foolish on the day they met. It would just be a cute story they told the next generations. 'I remember the day I met your father—he fell flat on his face trying to get to me on a public transport. That was the day I fell in love—'

The transport slowed, and gravity weirdness ensued. Zephyr took a deep breath, shutting his eyes against the queasy feeling.

Shoot, this was his stop!

As he got up to leave the tram, he saw the girl was getting off there, too. But by the time he made it past the others on the platform, he had lost sight of her. Again. He whirled around, searching the bustling promenade.

Fera: Focus, Zeph. You only have a few minutes to get to Nulma's on time.

He wanted to growl in frustration. But Fera was right. Again.

Groaning, he turned toward Nulma's Emporium and made a beeline for the entrance.

A bell chimed as he entered the musty shop. Nulma's always reeked of grease, dust, and general dankness, and Zeph always wondered what in the galaxy he was keeping in the back room to cause such an odor. It didn't matter.

Crossing to the tiny counter, Zeph reached into his pocket for the data disc, then presented it to Nulma with a flourish and a bow.

"Well, well, well—we had a wager going, whether you would be late this time. Looks like I lost." The old Zeltai's scarred face pinched in what looked like a grimace, but was actually his version of a smile.

"Hey—I'm not late that often!"

Nulma scoffed and took the disc.

> Fera: *You sort of are. Three of the last five times, Zeph.*

> Zeph: *Only by a minute or two.*

> Fera: *That's why he picks you. You show up almost on time, and he can dock our pay, anyway.*

Nulma fished a handful of credit chips out of his pocket and held them out over the counter.

When Zeph reached for them, he jerked his hand back, a sly glint in his violet eyes.

"I may just have that information you asked for—about Vargus Trix."

Zeph's ears perked up at that. He'd been trying for years to get an in with Vargus. They'd be set if he and Fera could find work smuggling hrelex next season.

Hrelex were illegal and delicate and needed to be delivered discreetly. Each had to bond with its new owner within a tight window, or the entire growing cycle would have to be restarted.

It was one of the most coveted smuggling jobs around. A lucrative job like this would bring in life-changing credits. More importantly, running the little murder-pets would finally cement him as a real smuggler in the eyes of his peers.

"How much?"

Nulma held up the chips and divided them in half.

> Fera: No, Zeph. That's for the galley remodel. Besides, I'm not sold on working with Vargus.

> Zeph: This is our big break, Fera. We'll make it up ten times over when running hrelex next season.

> Fera: We don't have time for this. We have 14 crates of julee berries due on Ioria Prime—the client paid triple for rush delivery!

"Deal." Ignoring Fera, Zeph held his hand out to Nulma to retrieve the now smaller payment. "How do we get a meeting with Vargus?"

Nulma pocketed the other chips, then leaned over the counter. "He's opening a new club tomorrow—fights, gambling, sex, drugs—just like his places on Ioria Prime, but more classy-like for the tourists. The grand opening is tomorrow night, right over in Sector 73."

Zeph scowled. "What am I supposed to do? Just walk up to him and say hello?" As if he hadn't tried to track Vargus down in one of his clubs a dozen times already. No one got close to Vargus Trix without Vargus's say-so.

Nulma waved off the comment. "No, no, no—you have to know his weakness. He has a penchant for beautiful women —the more exotic and seductive, the better. You show up with a rare beauty on your arm, and he'll take notice. Then you tell his people Nulma sends his regards."

An endorsement from Nulma? This might work.

"Just don't fuck it up. You're cashing in on my good name, don't make me regret it. And bring some muscle to look important-like."

Zeph was practically skipping when he left Nulma's. Lady Fate was smiling down on him today. He knew exactly who he needed in order to pull this off. The Black Swirl was just a few minutes' walk. He took off in that direction, heady with anticipation.

He could almost taste the money and fame this new job would bring him.

Fera: Absolutely not. It's dangerous for her to be seen with you, Zeph, and you know it. And if we jeopardize

Braxtor's cover, you-know-who will be pissed. It's bad enough that you set him up guarding a woman you stole from Ioria Prime.

Zeph didn't slow his steps. He hadn't been so sure of himself in ... well, a few days, at least. He had a really good feeling about this.

Zeph: I'm just gonna swing by—if they're not interested, I'll head back to the Fate, and we'll leave.

This was it. No more listening to other smugglers snicker about how he was just a rich boy playing at being a captain. Hrelex runs required finesse.

Fera: What about the julee berries? If we stay another night, we'll be late.

Zeph: If we take a space fold instead of the gates, we have plenty of time.

Fera: And no profits!

Zeph: We're just going to check in with them. If they aren't interested in the job, we'll leave. See? Now, it's up to Lady Fate.

He crossed under the sky tram, passing the stalls that blanketed the center of the promenade this time of day. He ignored the various vendors who called out, peddling food and baubles for the tourists.

Fera: I don't like it.

That was as close to a 'yes' as he was going to get. Triumph surged through him as his eyes locked on the sign outside The Black Swirl. He barreled forward with a single-minded focus and reached out for the door—

"Captain Zephyr, fancy meeting you here," a voice purred from his left.

Zeph nearly jumped out of his skin, turning to find the owner of the sultry voice lounging against the front wall of The Black Swirl Bordello. He blinked. It was the cybermod girl, his dream girl. In the flesh, talking to him.

Wait.

How did she know his name?

THE
VALMORAN
CHRONICLES

18

HEROES AND DEMONS

VALMORAN SPACE, ANARIS STATION, THE BLACK SWIRL BORDELLO

TOR, AN EX-SLAVE IN HIDING

~

TOR TRAILED after Delilah through the dim, burgundy interior of the hallway. The thrumming background music barely masked the inevitable sounds in a bordello. Tor would never get used to it. It was the soundtrack of slavery.

Sex, sobbing, and screams ...

The memories clawed at his mind, threatening to drag him back into the darkness.

He reminded himself that the workers here were not slaves—they chose this profession and could leave here if they wanted to.

Any discomfort he felt was his problem, not theirs. There was nothing wrong with sex work—those who enslaved and coerced others were the ones with something to be ashamed of.

And yet, it set him on edge. He couldn't help remembering the 'comfort slaves'—a cruel euphemism—on Ioria Prime. They never had a choice. Their hopeless eyes conveyed it more clearly than words ever could.

It ate at him, the people he hadn't been able to save.

Emotion boiled beneath his skin—guilt, fear, rage—so much helpless rage. But he didn't let it show, never let it show. Tor was a master at hiding his emotions, observing them, naming them, and concealing his thoughts and reactions.

A mantra drummed into him since childhood.

Reveal nothing to the masters.

His vision swam, pulse pounding in his ears. No one deserved to be enslaved. His nails cut into his palms as he balled his four hands into tight fists.

No one.

"Tor?" Delilah's musical voice brimmed with concern. Damn. She had picked up on his sour mood. His control must be slipping.

He relaxed his fists and cleared his throat. "Sorry. Lost in thought." He glanced back down the hallway to confirm it was empty, then stepped in front of Delilah and opened the door.

He scanned the room. One attendant, mixing drinks at the bar. Six off-duty employees lounging on couches by a vidscreen. Four women, two men, all known. This was the only entrance. Safe.

He stepped to the side so Delilah could enter.

Her expression said she thought he was being overprotective. He ignored it, as he did every time—it was his job to protect her.

Tor didn't mind the employee lounge. Once he checked in, he didn't need to worry about being recognized or being on high alert for potential threats. He only had to monitor the door.

"Lila! Get your tight little ass over here—we need you to settle something!" Delilah's friend, The Loud Woman, waved her over.

Delilah ran over to sit next to her friends on the couch. Loud Woman and Quiet Girl. Tor headed to the bar to grab her a drink, overseeing both her and the door out of the corner of his eye.

"Heya, Tor—what can I get you?" Of the three people who worked the employee lounge at night, Tor liked this guy the least. The Pusher.

"The usual—Talorai Moonset." He settled himself next to the bar, forcing his posture into something approximating casual. Everyone around here liked to tease him for being 'too tense.' Especially The Pusher.

"And for you?" The Pusher raised an eyebrow in what felt like a challenge.

Tor ignored it. "Just water, thanks."

"Come on—you're off duty, man. Live a little, I've got this great new—"

"—Just water."

"Suit yourself." The Pusher pulled out a tumbler and set it under the dispenser before turning around to work on Delilah's drink. Thank the Gods. Water hissed out into the glass.

It was crazy to think that the water pouring into his glass came from the station's recycler system, which ran through all the walls. The logistics system shipped it around from ring to ring, section to section, using it to keep the station balanced.

It was nice, finally having a Hix and being able to learn new things whenever he wanted. Anaris Station was delighted to look things up for him, which was helpful since he still wasn't a fast reader. Also, Anaris loved to talk about herself.

A massive AI ran the station. Or maybe Anaris was the AI? Was she the station or the AI? Tor wasn't sure, but she ran the entire station, and anyone inside could ask her anything using their Hix. She said most people only ever asked for directions. Tor thought she might be lonely.

He looked her up on the galactic web the other day—it said she wasn't sentient, just very complex. But when he asked her if she was sentient, she'd responded, "Are you?"

Kinda hard to argue with that.

It was a relief to talk to Anaris. At night, when his mind flooded with horrific images, he'd started asking her to explain her systems. It seemed to make her happy, and her soothing voice in his head occupied his mind enough to allow him to fall asleep.

"Here you go." The Pusher slid a tumbler of water and a frosty glass of purply-blue liquid to Tor. "You know, you really should learn to have a little fun—"

"—Thank you." Tor gave the man a nod, picked up the drinks, and then headed over to give Delilah hers, keeping the door in his line of sight.

He hadn't been paying attention to the conversation in the room, but as he approached the couches, he couldn't help hearing one of the male voices cutting through everyone else's. The Handsome Man.

"—no way, not risking it. Not seeing any female clients until after mating season is O-VER."

"But it hasn't even started yet," Delilah said.

Tor handed over her drink, and she gave him a gracious smile.

Handsome Man kept talking, arms flailing about as he spoke. He had obviously had plenty to drink tonight.

"No kids for me—no, thank you—don't have any parents to pass 'em off to, and not everybody has those cushy Republic benefits to fall back on." The man cast an accusatory look at Delilah.

Tor wondered how Delilah would handle this situation. According to her story, she was a Republic citizen who moved to Anaris Station for the excitement of the tourist destination. But he was pretty sure she'd never been to the Republic. He never had, and he was also supposed to be from there.

"I haven't spoken to my parents in years." She replied flatly.

Bit of a conversation-killer, but effective.

Handsome Man shrugged it off. "I'm only keeping the clients I'm willing to get shackled to for life."

The Loud Woman scoffed. "As if you're even at risk."

Everyone gaped at her.

"What? We're all thinking it. How many of us have mated parents?" She raised her eyebrows, looking at each of them. "Any fancy God-touched types in your family tree?"

Tor watched as each person's body language broadcast their discomfort.

"You don't know anything about me," the Handsome Man said.

"Look, all I'm saying is we're worrying about nothing. Changing how we do business over something that just will not happen is stupid. It's not like we chose to live on Anaris Station because of our impeccable bloodlines."

The Loud Woman's statement hit Tor like a bucket of ice water.

The others may not be God-touched, but he most certainly was. Braxtor the Terrible had been famous for it, so Tor made sure everyone thought he was just a nobody. But the truth lurked there, never far from his thoughts.

He had a high risk of being mated.

He could not allow it to happen.

Tor remembered his master's plan after his mother had ...

He squeezed his eyes shut against the memories.

... how they planned to mate him, then hold his mate as hostage.

He would need to stop touching people now that mating season was about to start.

Delilah sat on the couch laughing with the Quiet Girl. Tor suppressed a shudder at the thought of putting her in danger.

Tor could not—would not—allow anyone to become tied to him. It would mean a fate worse than death. No more gentle touches from Delilah. He was putting a stop to it, no matter how much it might upset her.

No matter how much he would miss it.

The Handsome Man turned on the vidscreen and started flipping through his favorite creators.

"Oh—see if Fashion Diva has something on the newest mating season collections!" The Loud Woman called out.

Vidscreens held little interest for Tor. Most of what people watched was loud, flashy, and pointless, so he didn't bother to enhance the flat wall screen with his Hix.

Most people did—made the images 3D, but he never did—he didn't want his senses clogged up by things that weren't even there. Besides, he still wasn't used to it. Most people grew up with Hix implants and used them for everything.

The masters never gave them to slaves, didn't want them learning.

Tor forced his jaw to relax. That part of his life was over. He was free now.

"Wait—go back!" The Loud Woman said. "What was that Braxtor one?"

He tensed, heart racing.

Tor couldn't watch this, didn't want to see it—but he also couldn't draw attention to himself. No one here had recognized him yet, and they probably wouldn't. He didn't act like the psychotic murderer pictured in the vids.

Living those horrors had been bad enough ... why did everyone keep watching them? It felt like everywhere he turned, people gloried in the carnage of Braxtor the Terrible, the monster with the bounty on his head.

Bile rose, burning his esophagus.

"See if you can find the one where he rips that guy's guts out with his bare hands! I love the feral look he gets when he smears the blood on his face at the end."

His throat felt thick, like something was stuck in it. He tried to swallow, but his mouth was dry as dust. Where had he set his water?

Tor forced his vision to focus and noticed Delilah. She was watching him, a curiosity burning on her face. He wanted to leave.

He needed to calm down.

Suddenly, Delilah downed her entire drink all at once, then shook the empty glass in the air.

"Tor, darling—be a dear and fetch me a refill?" She smiled as he hurried over to take it. Was that pity in her eyes?

Right now, he didn't care—he was grateful for any excuse to put distance between himself and that accusatory vid screen.

Tor monitored Delilah from the bar while waiting for The Pusher to fix another round of drinks. And tried to block out the vidscreen. He wished he knew how to use his Hix better —there had to be a way to obscure it from view. But he didn't know how.

He focused on his breaths, on his heartbeat. Tensed and relaxed each muscle in his body. Reminded himself he was safe. But the past clung to him like a shadow, devastating and horrific.

The memories of everything they forced him to do flashed through his mind, refusing to be forgotten.

"—calling him The Liberator, yeah?"

Tor turned to face The Pusher and realized the man had been speaking to him. How had he missed that? He needed to pay better attention to his surroundings.

"Sorry, what was that?"

"I said it's crazy that everyone's started calling him The Liberator now."

"Who?"

The Pusher rolled his eyes. "Geez, man—do you live under a rock? Braxtor. Apparently, he's like this big hero and shit."

Tor stared at the man for too long, unable to make sense of what he was hearing. "I, uh ... no, I hadn't heard that." He did his best to sound disinterested. "Isn't he that murderer?"

The label tasted like ash in his mouth.

"You really are out of touch—it's all over the newsvids." He shook his head, as if it weren't worth the trouble to explain it to Tor. "Whatever, man—here's your drinks."

Just then, one of the male doormen, Fake Tough Guy—who obviously had no actual fighting experience but pretended he was a badass—stepped into the room.

"Hey, Delilah, you have a visitor in the main lounge."

She pouted at Fake Tough Guy, eyes wide, pink lips glistening in the vidscreen's light. "But it's my night off."

"I know, I know, but this one says he's a friend of yours. White hair, brown skin, a bit of a dandy, " His voice rose at the end, and he raised his eyebrows in question.

Tor would have frozen in place if he hadn't already been standing still.

The room tilted, and he forced his breathing to remain steady. Adrenaline flooded his system, and his mind mapped out the building. Only one exit. He would need to fight his way out.

No. They couldn't have found him. Not now.

Delilah ran over, and then he felt her tugging playfully on his lower arms. "It's Zeph—it has to be! Oh, I haven't seen him in ages!"

Tor blinked, trying to bring his attention back to Delilah's words, to the enormous grin on her face. Calm. Fear was a useless emotion here.

He took a deep breath, focusing on her smile, the press of his feet against the ground, and the scent of perfume in the air. It was a little too warm in the room. Glasses clinked as The Pusher gathered them up.

Tor's attention snapped into focus. Clarity.

He forced a casual smile for Delilah though his senses remained on high alert. "You think so? I wonder what he wants?"

"Let's go find out!" She wove her fingers between his, leading him towards the door. He looked down at their interlaced hands, remembering his vow to stop touching people.

Tomorrow. Tor would put an end to it tomorrow.

Maybe Zeph was here for a visit. That would actually be ... fun. He was probably over-reacting.

Zeph had been the one to unlock his cell door on Ioria Prime and had helped him lead the children back to the ship. Had ensured every child was relocated to an orphanage in the Republic. He was a decent man, from all Tor had seen. Good with the kids, too.

And not afraid to cause a little mayhem.

Tor felt a grin creep over his face. They had caused a hell of a lot of mayhem that night on Ioria Prime. It wasn't enough—not near enough—but it had been a start.

Trailing after Delilah, he used his free hands to pat himself down, confirming that all of his concealed blades were where they should be. Hopefully, this was just a social visit, but he would never wander into an unknown situation without being prepared for a fight.

When they reached the door to the main lounge, Tor maneuvered Delilah so she was tucked safely behind him.

He drew in a steadying breath.

Steeling himself, he opened the door.

[PART 5]
EARTH GOT … EVEN WEIRDER

THE VALMORAN CHRONICLES

19

HOUSE OF CARDS

EARTH, OMAHA, NEBRASKA

AUBREY HOPE, HEIRESS AND DIRECTOR OF PR STRATEGY FOR HOPE PHARMACEUTICALS

∼

AUBREY'S HEAD throbbed in protest when her phone started buzzing on the nightstand at 5 AM. She silenced it and sat up to make sure she didn't fall back asleep. Everything hurt.

Mind over matter.

She grabbed yesterday's purse and trudged into the en suite. The heated ceramic tiles soothed her aching feet.

She turned on the water in the shower, then pulled out her pill case and fished out several pills.

She downed them in one gulp before stashing the pill case back in her bag.

Most days, Aubrey showered at the gym after an early-bird spin class. But one day a week, she met her friend, Ace, at his favorite local breakfast spot before they headed to The Hole in the Wall for private shooting lessons. So, no workout this morning.

It was more of a relief than she cared to admit. A glance in the mirror showed dark circles under her eyes, and her skin held a sickly pallor. She looked exhausted. Thank fuck for makeup and coffee.

A weaker woman would have taken a week off, or at least a day or two, to rest and recover. But Aubrey was not—and would never be—weak.

Stepping into the steamy glass-walled room, Aubrey sighed as the multiple showerheads soothed her aching muscles. She needed to hold it together for another week, maybe two, and then she would take a break. A couple of days off.

She needed to slow down, eventually. Working herself ragged like she had been on this Wellify deal wasn't sustainable. After months of research, networking, and legwork, it was finally all coming together.

The Wellify merger would happen, they would pull off the world's fastest data integration, and they would find a way to diagnose and treat Syndrome Q. Hope Pharma would be saved. Aubrey would make sure of it.

It had to work. Failure wasn't an option, because if this deal fell through, Aubrey didn't have a Plan B. Her family's legacy would just ... end. She refused to entertain the possibility. Headquarters was like home.

She finished her shower, dried and straightened her hair into a svelte power bob, and made up her face.

Flawless. Classy. Powerful.

If only she didn't feel like she was unraveling on the inside.

Crossing to her walk-in dressing room, she selected one of many sleek skirt suits and a pair of designer pumps. She selected a bright red patent-leather Dolce and Gabbana bag and transferred everything from yesterday's bag to it.

Wallet, makeup, phone, keys, Hope ID badge. Emergency kit —tissues, hand sanitizer, mini sewing kit, bleach stick, tampons, fingernail clippers. Pill case.

And finally, she opened the hidden zippered pouch on the back and pulled out her Springfield XDS.

Out of habit, she checked the ammo, enjoying the heft of the sleek weapon in her hands.

She would never admit it out loud, but holding the pistol made her feel more in control of her life. It was almost meditative, feeling the cold metal against her palms.

She could handle this.

She could handle anything.

Sliding the gun into the zippered holster in today's purse, Aubrey double-checked that yesterday's bag was empty before returning it to the shelves.

Since today was range day, she also grabbed her protective ear muffs and slung the purse strap over her head, cross-body.

Ace insisted if she carried off-body in a purse, she wear it cross-body and never let it out of her sight. He was sort of anal about it. Had drilled it into her head so hard she had been tempted to call him 'Sir.'

Aubrey smiled at the memory. Ace always had her back.

She grabbed the carry-on bag she'd packed last night for her overnight trip to Dallas, since her flight would leave this afternoon. All set. Everything under control.

Derrick was still sleeping when she passed through the bedroom on her way out to meet up with Ace at Barb's Diner. Her fiance could roll out of bed at 7:15 and show up at the office before eight, looking like he stepped straight out of GQ. She should text him later today to remind him about her trip.

～

She parked her Mercedes in the lot at Barb's Diner, then set the car alarm before heading in to meet Ace.

Aubrey knew she looked out of place in the diner—which was a bit of a greasy spoon—but she and Ace had been coming here since high school. The decor hadn't changed at all, and coming here each week was like walking into their past.

If her dad had paid enough attention to notice, Ace was the friend he wouldn't have wanted her to have. He wasn't rich and had never been a model student. He also rode a motorcycle, had tattoos, and joined the Marines straight out of high school.

They had kept in touch and reconnected when he left the Marines to start a PI firm and personal defense training business. Aubrey was a loyal customer of both. Once a week, they met up for breakfast and target practice.

And reminiscing.

"Aubs!" Ace stood when she entered, and he threw her a million-dollar smile.

He wrapped her in a warm and friendly hug, something most people would never dare to try. Aubrey basked in the simple comfort of the embrace, a fleeting moment of safety in the war zone called life.

"I already put in your order."

The place served giant stacks of pancakes and future heart attacks Barb called omelettes. However, she allowed Aubrey to order off-menu—avocado toast, scrambled egg whites, and sauteed spinach and mushrooms.

Barb served it alongside strong opinions about Aubrey's boring taste in food.

She and Ace slid into their old-school diner booth, and Aubrey poured herself a coffee.

"How's life?" Aubrey asked, adding two French Vanilla creamers to her mug. She thought about adding another, but decided she shouldn't.

Drinking shitty diner coffee, sitting here with Ace, it was almost like they were back in high school.

Any minute, they'd hop on the back of his bike and go looking for trouble, or fun. Or both.

"Same old. The world may be fucked, but people still pay me to spy on their spouses. Some things never change," Ace replied, lifting his mug.

"To cheating spouses." She threw Ace a smirk, and they clinked mugs.

"Oh, hey—we should review that intel you asked for before she brings our food," Ace said as he reached into his messenger bag and pulled out a manilla envelope. He un-looped the string and pulled out several paper-clipped dossiers.

Each one had a photo and name at the top and a summary of online activity below. He allowed her to look them over while she drank her first cup of coffee.

Violet Davis-Kobayashi, Hayley Jo, Katherine Miller—all three were lynchpins in her Wellify plan.

Violet was the CTO and architect of the Wellify app. Hayley Jo, America's newest pop starlet, was essential to their PR and marketing efforts. And Katherine Miller—well, she was a beautiful bit of serendipity.

Last week, Aubrey met with Javier, the man in charge of hiring for the Wellify Integration team, to find out if he needed her to start a discreet search for specific skill sets.

His answer: as long as the deal brought Violet with her entire team, their only gap was someone with experience modeling medical data for analysis.

His ideal hire: someone loyal, with years of experience using patient-reported and lab-confirmed data to run bioinformatics experiments. An expert with Python, a pro at HIPAA guidelines, and familiar with the data structures they would need to build.

Some higher power must have had Aubrey's back, because an hour later, her friend Claire had pinged her with Katherine Miller's resume. Apparently, the woman had been studying fibromyalgia, chronic fatigue syndrome, and migraine disorder to see if they were related.

And then—poof! Microbe X hit—no more patients, no more research, no more postdoc.

The woman must be desperate, because Claire had offered box seats to Hamilton if Aubrey agreed to meet.

It hadn't been necessary—Katherine Miller's resume was a gift, wrapped and delivered by the universe herself. Miss Miller had dedicated her life to studying unexplainable chronic illnesses—illnesses just like Syndrome Q.

Katherine had the right experience and was local. Hope would get her for a steal rather than paying a fortune to a headhunter for a similar skill set if she was as desperate as Aubrey suspected.

According to Ace's background check, Katherine Miller was a Girl Scout. Played the clarinet in high school, mathlete, Salutatorian, graduated from Creighton University Magna Cum Laude, then Creighton Medical School with honors before completing a PhD in medical microbiology with a focus on Bioinformatics and in silico experimentation methodology.

The only dirt Ace had dug up on Kat was an old teenage LiveJournal.

"What was in the LiveJournal?"

"Eh, a bunch of emo crap about how hard it was to have a sick sister. She probably forgot the thing existed."

So, not only was Katherine Miller a Girl Scout, but healing people was personal for her. They had a preliminary interview later this morning, and Katherine Miller was essentially a sure thing.

"What's your general impression of Katherine?"

Ace shrugged and slipped into that semi-militaristic voice he used sometimes. Like he was delivering a briefing, and she was his superior. "Model employee. Idealistic, hard-working, will probably work herself half to death for a good cause. Just don't ask her to do anything illegal or immoral, and you're good."

Aubrey nodded. Yep, Kat Miller was perfect.

Next was Hayley Jo's file. It contained little that Aubrey hadn't already found online.

Hayley had been a small-time EDM artist with a small but loyal following before blowing up earlier this year with her hit single 'The Hunger.' Hayley Jo was queer, and loud and proud about it. These days, she was also the most high-profile sufferer of Syndrome Q.

She held up the file. "Kinda thin ...?"

Ace nodded. "Yeah, she's got her own PR team, and they're obviously managing her online image. Also, she's on tour, so I couldn't observe her in person.

"But she still writes her own tweets, because the writing style is the same as it's always been. She loves music, loves her fans, and uses her platform to try and change the world. Her tweets are open and authentic—always have been. Best guess? Don't act corporate with her, and don't try to bullshit her. And make sure to listen to her album, if you haven't yet."

Aubrey nodded. "Good to know. That's helpful." She'd take that into account for tonight's meeting with Hayley Jo. The album wasn't a problem—she knew it by heart.

Next, she pulled out the file for Violet Davis-Kobayashi, Wellify's technical genius. Without Violet, the Wellify Integration project risked going over budget and taking years to complete.

They didn't have years. More like months.

Middle school in Japan, high school in the US. Made good grades, studied Computer Science at MIT, and got a Master's degree from MIT specializing in Data Management. Worked for one of the 'big five' tech companies for a few years post-graduation, then took a few years off before signing on with Wellify seven years ago.

Ace had no info on her three-year employment gap—barely anything was listed under online activity.

"This is all you have on Violet?"

Ace grimaced and shook his head. "Yeah. Something's off with her if you ask me."

"How so?"

"She's practically a ghost. Her only, and I mean only, online presence is LinkedIn. No Facebook, no Instagram, no Tweets, no defunct LiveJournal or MySpace page from her stupid teenage years. Nothing. It's strange, especially for someone in her line of work."

Aubrey chuckled. "What, is she a spy or something?"

"Nah, nothing like that. Spies curate their online image. Violet just doesn't have one. She's either paranoid, or she's hiding something."

Just then, Barb marched over to their table with a tray of steaming food, so Ace tucked the files back into the envelope and handed it to Aubrey. She tucked it into her purse while Barb greeted Ace with a motherly smile, setting his insane meat lover's griddle in front of him.

"Eat up, put some meat on those bones." She instructed him, just as she did every week.

Then she set Aubrey's plate in front of her with the same concerned scowl as always. "You need to eat more, missy, put some meat on those bones. Live a little, eat something that tastes good."

Aubrey didn't argue, just thanked Barb for letting her order off-menu and told her it looked delicious. Sure, pancakes would be divine, but Aubrey didn't let herself eat crap like that.

Aubrey knew better than to argue with Barb about food, which was basically the woman's religion.

They put aside business while they ate, and Ace regaled her with stories of his latest shenanigans as a PI, his most ridiculous self-defense students. Aubrey drank another coffee, ate half of her food, and relaxed into the simple companionship.

After they finished and she had paid the bill, she and Ace crossed the street to The Hole in the Wall, where Ace used his keycard to let them in. He had a deal with the owner to use the range during off-hours so he could train Aubrey.

Ace insisted Aubrey practice each shot with the draw from her purse.

So they did as they always did. Ace drilled her on gun maintenance, and then they started in on a box of hollow points, Ace adjusting her form on every draw.

Grip. Rip. Slap. Press. Aim. Fire.

Aubrey loved spending time at the range each week. It was her meditation. For a few blessed minutes, everything was pure. The thrill of firing a weapon, pulling her finger here and hitting the target way over there, was like magic.

Ace had her put down the gun and take off her muffs. "Geez, Aubrey, your hands are shaking like crazy. You ok?"

Her hands *were* shaking like crazy today. Was it sleep deprivation? A side effect of the meds? Too much coffee?

"I'm fine. Probably just too much coffee," Aubrey answered, not meeting his eyes.

Ace wasn't buying what she was selling. He grabbed her shoulders to face him.

"Aubs, I'm serious. You can talk to me—you know that, right? You don't have to be strong all the time." He moved his head to catch her gaze. "You don't have to be perfect."

And there it was. She could spill her guts right now, tell him she was exhausted. That she felt like the future of her family's company was all on her shoulders, that she couldn't lose Hope Pharma because it had been her mother's dream before she died.

Aubrey could confess that Syndrome Q was awful, and that she felt like she was coming apart at the seams.

Instead, she forced her most winning smile. "Didn't sleep well last night, and shouldn't have had that third cup of coffee."

Ace gave her a look that made it clear he knew she was lying. But he didn't press the issue.

He jerked his head at the gun she had placed on the counter. "You'll be shaking if you ever have to use that thing, too. Let's finish our drills."

Once they finished, Aubrey pulled off her protective ear muffs, and they cleaned up, locked up, and made their way back to their vehicles.

Her Merc next to his cruiser.

She had an impulse to hop on the back, reach into the saddlebag, and pull out the helmet, which he almost certainly still kept there. But pencil skirts and motorcycles don't mix, and her bad girl days were long over.

They stood by his bike, hesitating, before Ace broke the silence. "You need anything else from me?"

Take me away from here, she thought, before saying aloud, "Would you be able to follow Violet, see what she's up to? If she's going to be a problem, I need to know."

He threw a leg over his bike. "Sure, but I won't find anything before the deal goes through."

"That's fine—her staying on as the technical lead is part of the deal. So we're stuck with her. But ..."

"So you want dirt on her?" His voice wasn't judgy, just matter of fact. He was looking for clarity.

"I want information. If there are skeletons in Violet's closet, I need to know they won't bite us in the ass. And if those skeletons happen to provide me with leverage ..."

He gave her another 10,000-megawatt smile and winked. "Consider it done. I've got you, Aubs."

THE VALMORAN CHRONICLES

20

SOME CORPORATE BULLSHIT

EARTH, OMAHA, NEBRASKA

VIOLET DAVIS-KOBAYASHI, DATA SCIENTIST AND CTO OF WELLIFY

∽

VIOLET's black combat boots clomped along the sidewalk as she made her way to the office. Her trusty trench coat, a la Trinity in The Matrix, staved off the morning chill.

The mental image of herself as a badass cyberpunk heroine brought a smirk to her lips.

Her phone buzzed in her pocket. Probably the team checking in.

> Jason: Team's all here, pizza's on the way, boss-lady. Time to get up. =P

Vi: Sweet. Be there in 5. Hey, let's save the Nerf war for after the meeting today—spread the word.

Jason: Roger that.

It was working out to be an epic day.

Now, if Tom would only fess up about the impending sale to Hope Pharma ...

She should bring it up in their next one-on-one.

Yeah. If he didn't confide in her by next Tuesday, she was going to corner him, find out what was going on, offer to look things over, and make sure the team was taken care of.

Mind made up, Vi popped in her earbuds and queued up her favorite podcast.

'Hey, all my fellow nerds and nerdettes, you're listening to Big Effing Questions with JJ Zimmer.'

'Today we've got data guru Nate Gold and futurist Emily Tanzer on the show to talk about how fucked up and weird the world is lately, haha. Hey guys, great to have you on the show.'

As Violet finished the short trek to the Wellify offices, the host and guests made obligatory small talk, and JJ poked fun at them as he always did. Both guests were good sports about it, and the dude Vi had just walked past probably thought she was a weirdo for laughing out loud.

Meh.

The podcast had barely gotten to the good stuff when Vi rounded the corner to Wellify.

Dang.

> 'So, level with me, guys—should I be worried about the shit I'm hearing in the news? Like, which one is it—are we gonna be overpopulated since people are living longer, or are we going extinct because people aren't having babies?'

People weren't having babies?

Something niggled at the back of her mind, her hyper-perception kicking in. But nothing clicked. She'd need to do some research.

> '—so, like, just how screwed are we? Will the economy ever recover? And what is this I hear about people getting superpowers—I mean, that's total bullshit, right?'

> 'Whoa, slow down there, JJ—how about we start with the long-term effects of Microbe X on lifespan and go from there?'

With a sigh, Violet paused the podcast and put away her headphones. She wanted to keep listening, but the team was waiting for her.

When she strode into Wellify, her team was already gathered in a semicircle in front of a whiteboard in the bullpen, laptops ready.

Gigi had the Chaos Horn—a bullhorn she'd decorated with rainbow ribbons and puffy paint—ready to go in case the debate got out of hand.

"Morning, guys!" Vi called out as she booked it over to her desk to drop off her things.

"Lol, it's almost lunchtime, Vi." Gigi hollered back.

"It's eight o'clock somewhere," Vi replied with a smirk. They didn't have set hours at Wellify, and everyone knew Vi did her best coding in the middle of the night. Morning people were a strange breed.

She went over to the whiteboard, grabbed a marker, and turned to the team.

"Okay, so you know why we're here today. For those of you who weren't on the team last year, some of us—you know who you are—couldn't agree on the app's coding standards, so we had to refactor basically every file to make it compatible with Jason's code generator."

There were grumbles and groans around the room. That refactor had been a major pain.

"Yeah—never again, amiright? I get that we each have our preferences, tabs and spaces and all that jazz. I don't actually care what you all agree on, but we're not leaving this room until you hash out the standards we're going to use for the

API." She turned to write 'REST API' on the top of the whiteboard and underlined it.

"This is some corporate bullshit," someone muttered. It had to be the new guy, Bastion.

Violet hated this part, but couldn't let that comment slide, or it would poison the team culture. She froze with her back to them, then lowered the marker and placed it on the tray.

"Uh-oh," Jason said, voice dripping with mock severity.

"Someone's about to get schooled." Gigi added in a sing-song voice.

Violet turned around and then spoke in a calm, quiet voice. "I don't know who said that, and I don't actually care. But you're wrong.

"Corporate bullshit would be if someone you had never met who worked in another building sent you new company coding standards after your team had already finished an entire project and said you had a week to implement them."

"This?" She gestured to the team, to the whiteboard, and back to the team. "—this is the opposite of that. Every person who had to dig through the refactoring backlog last year is sitting in this room, plus the new hires—everyone gets a voice. I don't even care what you settle on, because I trust you will agree on something brilliant.

"This—" she again gestured to the team, "—is not corporate bullshit. This is having high standards, because we're goddamn awesome. If you can't tell the difference, you know where the door is." Violet raised her hand lazily to the side, pointing at said door.

"Damn right, we are!" Erika hollered.

Jason raised his fingers to his mouth and gave a whistle. Others laughed, whooped, and otherwise affirmed their quirky brand of solidarity. Vi had endeavored to foster a culture of working hard, playing hard, and having open communication. But sometimes, they got a little carried away.

Gigi blew the Chaos Horn, and Vi gave a dismissive wave to get them to quiet down.

"Seriously, though, it's an honest mistake, right, guys? We're not kicking anybody off the island today. Bastion, how about you take the marker and write down ideas as the team shouts them out?"

Bastion, still a bit red in the cheeks, shuffled up to the front of the room to take the marker.

Violet leaned in so only Bastion could hear. "Shake it off. You're not the first I've called out like that, and you won't be the last. Welcome to the team."

Bastion took the marker, and the team started calling out ideas and arguing back and forth.

Violet sat in the back and pulled out her laptop, hands shaking imperceptibly. It was way more comfortable back here than up there. Public speaking would never be comfortable for her, but she had learned to fake it for her role as CTO.

Violet watched as Bastion recovered from his embarrassment, hamming it up with the team as he scribbled their rapid-fire ideas on the board. The minor hazing he had just endured would either cement him as part of the team or encourage him to find another job.

Watching Bastion smile and joke with the team, she suspected it would be the first.

She kept an ear out to make sure the team was fighting fair while they debated the finer elements of API design and naming conventions, but their team dynamic was so solid that Vi probably didn't need to be in the room at this point.

Violet pulled up the spreadsheet she was using to assemble the API and historical data export request for Tom and continued filling in her estimate—lovingly referred to by software geeks as a SWAG—Software Wild-Ass Guess. She was just plugging in the final numbers—

And then it all went sideways.

"Oh, great—you're all here!" Tom, the CEO, walked up to the front of the room, all big-dick energy, and stood next to Bastion.

He turned to study the whiteboard and raised his hand to rub his chin thoughtfully—as if he understood a damn word of it —then turned back to the team with an indulgent grin. "Doing great work, as always, I see."

What the fuck was this noise? Why was he bogarting her meeting?

"Hey, son—why don't you hand me that marker and take a seat?" He gestured to Bastion, who shot a nervous look in Violet's direction, so she nodded, and he hurried back to his seat.

That was when Violet noticed the receptionist standing behind Tom, an enormous stack of thick envelopes in her arms.

Oh, hell, no.

He was announcing this in front of the entire team without even giving her the courtesy of a heads-up? She leaned back in her seat, glad she was sitting in the back, because she was having tremendous difficulty keeping a furious scowl off her face.

"I'm sure you all have noticed that we've had a lot of visitors in the office, and I'm sure you're all curious why that is. Well, you'll find out today, but first, we have a quick little NDA for you all to sign."

He turned to the receptionist. "Jeannie, why don't you just set those down on that desk over there so you can hand out the forms?"

Jeannie scurried around the room, beaming as she handed each employee a form and a pen.

"Okay, all this form says is that what I'm about to tell you cannot leave this room." He gave everyone a stern look. "You'll be able to tell anyone you want in a couple of weeks, okay?"

The team members nodded, and a few threw 'wtf?' looks in Violet's direction. She merely shrugged in response, but the struggle to keep her demeanor professional was an exercise in sheer will.

It was a good thing Vi got super-perception and not laser eyes, or the ability to explode heads, or Tom would be the one having a bad day.

She read over the paper, saw it was indeed a short-term NDA, and savagely signed the stupid thing. Jeannie collected the forms and checked that every person had signed.

"We all good?" Tom asked Jeannie.

"Yes, sir—everyone signed," she said, swinging her legs cheerfully in front of the desk where she was perched.

"Fantastic. I have great news to share with you. I've been itching to tell you this, but I couldn't say anything until we hashed out the details. It's the day all startups dream of, folks. Wellify is being acquired by Hope Pharmaceuticals.

"And before you start to worry—I've negotiated it so each and every one of you has been offered a full-time salaried position with a raise at Hope. In addition, you will each be getting a generous bonus as your share of the profits from the sale in recognition of your hard work.

"These packets have the details of your bonus and your compensation package at Hope. Come see me if you have questions. My door is always open."

∾

Violet followed Tom back to his office and slammed the door shut.

"What the hell was that, Tom?"

"What the hell was what? This is wonderful news, Vi—I don't see why you're upset."

"Maybe because I knew about the sale and was waiting for you to bring it up. If not as your CTO, then as the first employee willing to take a chance on this company."

She caught herself when she realized she was pacing, then stopped.

"I mean—fuck, Tom—I stood here in this office with you, and we talked about how Big Pharma was taking advantage of sick people, how we were going to change things. 'Democratizing medicine'—you remember that? You said that."

"I did say that."

"So what the fuck, Tom?" She shook her head, then exhaled, calming herself.

She sighed, then changed gears. This wasn't the end of the world. "Whatever. I have some money saved up—I guess I can just dust off my resume and find another—"

"—What are you talking about?" Tom's voice had an edge, a little panicked, the pitch a bit too high. "You wouldn't quit—you love this team."

"Tom, you know how I feel about corporate crap. I can't do it. I *won't* do it. I'll get you my letter of resignation tomorrow, and we can work out the transition plan—"

"You can't." There was a finality in his tone that didn't compute.

She cocked her head at him. "Um, yes—I can. Watch me." She turned, intent on stalking out of the room.

"No, I mean—the deal is contingent on you."

The ground dropped out from under her as her heart plummeted. Tom couldn't possibly mean ...?

Violet slowly raised her head as she turned back to face him. "I'm sorry—I must have misheard you. Perhaps you should elaborate." Blood thrummed in her ears, and her cheeks heated. This couldn't be happening.

"I, um, well—Hope—had a bad experience acquiring a software company without the architect a few years back, so they refused to move forward without you on board."

That was pretty smart on Hope's side. But she still fucking hated them. And right now, she hated the man standing in front of her.

"But I'm not on board, Tom. You would have had to ask me for that to be true." Violet's voice dripped with venom, and she didn't care.

Tom fidgeted, his eyes darting around the room. He was cornered, and he knew it.

His voice took on that wheedling quality of someone who is covering their ass. "Of course, I countered by saying they would need to hire your entire team. I said you would never take the offer if they didn't keep the team together. They wanted you so much that they agreed to take the entire team, and I even got them to bring the salary offers up by 5%."

He continued in a rush, apparently trying to get every last excuse out before she could cut him off. "And Hope didn't want to cut the team in on the profits, so I did it myself—I split 50% of my own earnings with the team, to make sure everyone got a piece of the pie.

"I even set up a meeting for you with one of their people, someone named Audrey or something, so you can talk team culture. She wants to work with you. You can keep the Nerf guns ..."

She tuned him out as he continued to ramble on. This was beyond the pale. Did he seriously want credit for keeping his word that he'd share profits with the team if they were acquired? What a douchebag. Vi glared daggers at him, calling on her martial arts training to slow down her heart and find her center. It wasn't working.

"... If you walk, Vi, this whole thing falls through."

Now, there was an idea.

She hated the idea of the Wellify data going to Hope, and here was her chance to nuke the entire thing. Tom had handed it to her on a silver fucking platter.

"Maybe I should do that, then."

His eyes went wide. "You wouldn't do that to your team ... they're all out there celebrating. I mean, Jason—his mom has all those bills from her cancer treatment. Annie's six months pregnant. You wouldn't do that to them."

Violet glared at him and took a step closer to the desk. "Maybe I'll just pay their bonuses myself, Tom."

He laughed. Laughed, as if she had just said something stupid.

"It's sort of a lot of money, Vi, there's—"

"—Remember what you call me? 'The data whisperer'? Did you honestly think Syndrome Q was the only market trend I've ever predicted? Of course, maybe you're right, and I don't have the money—"

She leaned in and put her hands on the edge of his desk, never breaking eye contact. "But maybe I do."

Tom's Adam's apple bobbed as he swallowed hard, his eyes widening in realization.

"I thought you would be happy about this. I'm keeping your team together, and—"

"—you want to stop talking, Tom." She took a beat to calm herself, looking down at her hands on the desk. "If you thought I would be happy about this, then you wouldn't have felt the need to manipulate me."

She lifted her head, and her response was deadly calm.

"Fuck this. I'm out."

Violet walked to the door, and as she opened it, she heard Tom call out in a cheery voice, "Okay, great talk, Vi—take the rest of the afternoon, and we'll chat tomorrow!"

She tried to look as normal as possible as she gathered her things. The team was in high spirits, everyone talking about what they were going to do with the windfall.

Annie, leaning against her desk, said to Jason, "I mean, Hope Pharma is one of the best employers in Omaha, especially for working parents. I think it will all work out. Vi won't let them mess with the team dynamic."

"This will cover my student loans and most of my mortgage." That was Gigi.

"I mean—fuck, guys—this is like a 40% raise or something ..."

Violet felt an ugly twist of guilt and rage and knew she had to get out of there before she lost it. She let the team know something had come up and asked them to continue the REST API meeting after lunch and show her what they came up with the next day.

She couldn't quite suppress her scowl as her eyes locked on the whiteboard.

No. What Tom had just done to her—

Now that was some corporate bullshit.

THE VALMORAN CHRONICLES

21

UNCONTROLLED VARIABLES

EARTH, OMAHA, NEBRASKA

KATHARINE MILLER, MEDICAL MICROBIOLOGIST

~

KAT HATED SITTING ALONE in public, and Claire had abandoned her at the coffee shop to wait for Aubrey. What if some rando came over to talk to her?

She fished out her phone and pulled up LinkedIn.

Aubrey Hope had an MBA from Creighton University, which explained how she knew Claire. She was the Director of PR Strategy. Was Aubrey any good, or did Daddy just give her a pretty title to go with that dazzling smile?

She shook her head, chastising herself. That was uncalled for —for all she knew, Aubrey Hope was brilliant. Plus, hadn't Claire said they were close friends?

The bell on the door of the coffee shop jingled as it swung open, bringing in a chill and a loud man.

"—can't do it, bro. Wish I could, but tonight's hosed." His white button-up was wrinkled, skinny red tie loosened around the collar. Salesman, most likely. Or some sort of middle manager.

He rushed over to the counter in the manner people do when they want to look important. "One sec, dude, gotta order." He jerked his head at the barista. "Triple espresso with cream, to go."

Kat hated guys like this. His voice carried through the entire shop, grating on her brain. Fucking douchebags and their Bluetooth headsets. She reached for her purse, ready to pull out her headphones—

"No, swear to god—half my fuckin' team called in sick today, lazy fuckers." He had backed away from the counter and was leaning against the wall, blabbing away.

Kat froze, her hand still in her purse. Had she heard that right?

Wait, sick? That's weird. She pulled out her phone again so it wouldn't be obvious she was eavesdropping. Not that it should be considered eavesdropping, with the way his voice carried.

"Damn right, they're lying. But I can't—" Dude-bro cut off and nodded to himself. "—no, that's what I'm saying, dude—it's an HR nightmare."

It hadn't occurred to Kat that people would fake Syndrome Q to get out of work, but it made sense. She clenched her jaw. Why did people pull crap like that? All those times when people ignored Beth or insinuated she was faking ...

"Nah, man—it's real. Suzie's sick, it's fuckin' obvious, man."

Well, that was something. Maybe this guy wasn't all bad. It sounded like he was standing up for—

"I know, right? She used to be so hot."

Or not.

The front door jingled again, prompting Kat to glance in that direction.

A woman in a sleek skirt and blazer strode inside, filling the room with an unmistakable aura of power. Even the woman's ridiculously high heels struck the ground with authority.

Aubrey Hope was possibly the most intimidating woman Kat had ever seen, and she hadn't even looked over yet. Kat suddenly wished she were anywhere but here. She didn't want to meet a woman like Aubrey while wearing a ball cap and an unwashed hoodie.

Maybe she could duck out and apologize later? She glanced towards the bathroom. Maybe there was a back exit? Then Aubrey's eyes locked on her, recognition clear.

Kat froze.

Aubrey smiled and started towards the booth. Crap, this was happening.

As Aubrey approached, Kat hurried to her feet and extended a hand in greeting.

"Katherine Miller?"

Aubrey raised her sharp eyebrows, then darted her eyes to Kat's outstretched hand. "Nothing personal, I don't shake."

Lowering her hand, Kat tried to put it in her pocket, then remembered she was wearing yoga pants. Real slick, Kat. "Of course." Her cheeks heated, but Aubrey didn't seem to notice. Or if she did, she didn't let on.

"I'm gonna get a coffee. What can I get you?"

Kat snagged her coffee from the table and held it out awkwardly. "All set, thanks."

Aubrey grinned. "Well, I need another coffee—be right back." Geez, even her smile exuded confidence.

Scrambling back into the booth to wait, Kat cradled her coffee between her hands. It wasn't hot anymore. She should have taken Aubrey up on her offer.

She could go meet her in line, say she changed her mind. Nah, this one would be fine. She wasn't thirsty, anyway.

As she waited, she watched Aubrey out of the corner of her eye. She was the living embodiment of that one Cake song. Or maybe 'Boys Wanna Be Her.' Kat had always been envious of women who could command a room. Even dude-bro was starting at Aubrey, slack-jawed.

There was no way this was going to end in a job offer. It's not like she wanted to work at a place like Hope Pharma. Besides, how could she take a full-time job when she was this sick? She could barely stand the noise in the coffee shop. And as poorly as she'd been sleeping, she could never manage an eight to five.

She looked over at Aubrey, commanding even as she stood there, waiting for her coffee. Someone like Aubrey probably worked twelve hours daily and expected the same from everyone around her.

Yeah, this wasn't going to work.

As she watched Aubrey pay and collect her coffee, Kat tried to devise a polite way to get out of this meeting. She had yet to come up with anything that didn't sound rude by the time Aubrey returned.

Aubrey slid gracefully into the booth and settled her purse next to her before taking a sip of coffee. "Ah—that's better. So, I checked out your LinkedIn—you've got quite the resume there. I especially enjoyed your latest paper on CFS, fibro, and migraines. Good stuff."

Huh. That was unexpected. "You read that?"

Aubrey quirked an eyebrow and shrugged. "I can muddle my way through an abstract. Besides, it was very well written. Not too jargon-y. What made you decide to use Python?"

They spent the next several minutes discussing her research. Aubrey's questions were surprisingly insightful. Although this wasn't her area of expertise, she was honest about what she didn't know.

Kat liked that. People who tried to fake their way through science drove her crazy. Aubrey was curious and unintimidated by Kat's knowledge. To her surprise, Kat found herself warming to the other woman.

Sure, Aubrey was curt and never apologized for herself in the ways women were socialized to do, but Kat kinda admired her for it. Why should Aubrey be meek just because she was a woman?

Aubrey jumped in as Kat finished a lengthy explanation of the data models she used in her experiment.

"—and that's why we need you at Hope Pharm, Kat. We need someone to serve as our data modeler and the liaison between the lab and data teams. I can't go into the details until you sign an NDA, but we're about to launch a project that needs your expertise."

Kat took a deep breath. "Aubrey ..."

"—before you talk yourself out of this, at least give me a chance to convince you." Aubrey's eye contact was piercing, and Kat struggled not to look away.

"Okay ..."

"We're going to find a cure for Syndrome Q."

Kat couldn't keep the incredulity off her face. "A cure? I don't mean to be rude, but I find that hard to believe."

"What? Since we're a pharmaceutical company, you assume we'd rather develop treatments than cures?"

"Well, wouldn't you? That's always been your company's business model. And it means you have a vested interest in keeping people sick."

To her surprise, Aubrey laughed. "I like that."

"What?" Kat furrowed her brows.

Aubrey's voice took on a mischievous tone. "You're all quiet and meek, but get you talking about medicine, and you turn into this total ball-buster."

She leaned forward, voice serious. "Look, I won't apologize for Hope's role in improving people's quality of life, but that's not important here. Think about it—human disease is all but eradicated. Whoever cures Syndrome Q will go down in history."

"We want that to be our legacy, Kat. Our last contribution to the world. One sec." She held up a finger for Kat to wait, then fished a pen out of her purse. Aubrey scribbled something on a napkin and slid it over face down. "Don't say this out loud."

Hayley Jo is on board.

Kat's eyes widened. If Hayley Jo had agreed to this, it had to be legit. After the controversy with her old manager, she couldn't imagine Hayley allowing anyone to exploit her beliefs again.

If Aubrey was telling the truth, this project might be ... perfect.

Kat looked Aubrey square in the eyes, searching for signs of deception. Aubrey held her gaze, waiting.

An unexpected image flashed into Kat's mind, vivid and enticing—Aubrey, Hayley Jo, and Kat stood with their team, popping champagne and cheering.

She blinked, then looked away. Her heart rate quickened, and she felt a rush of exhilaration she hadn't felt in months. The thrill of discovery, of contributing to something that mattered. She could almost taste it.

Meanwhile, Aubrey scribbled something on another napkin.

Aubrey slid it over. Kat's heart leaped into her throat when she saw the number Aubrey had written there. "Is this a joke?"

Aubrey shook her head. "Absolutely not. You have the skills we need, you're local, and I like you. The project is slated to start in less than two weeks, and we need a data modeler to ensure we get it right. Our tech manager already agreed—that's our offer, if you're willing to start on short notice."

The number written on that napkin was six times her postdoc salary.

Astronomical student debt balances popped into Kat's head. Medical school, the PhD program—none of it had been cheap.

She thought of Beth, worried about her own college tuition bills. If she took the job at Hope, Kat could afford to help Beth, too. Her sister had always dreamed of being a teacher. Beth had just started her first semester of college, now that she wasn't sick anymore.

Kat's daydreaming came to a screeching halt as she remembered her Syndrome Q. She couldn't take this job, no matter how much she wanted to. There was no way she could keep up with the workload or the hours.

Her heart sank, and she slouched back against the seat. "I … can't. I actually want to, but I can't."

Aubrey frowned and leaned back, fixing her gaze on Kat.

Silence hung between them, begging to be filled.

"It's just …" Kat sighed, leaned forward, and mouthed, "I'm sick."

Aubrey's eyes flashed, and her face held an odd expression for a microsecond before settling back into calm professionalism. What was that all about?

She grinned at Kat, shaking her head. "You can't even see it, can you?"

"See what?"

"How perfect you are for this job." She leaned in conspiratorially. "We need people who are invested in making this a reality, Kat. We can work with you on hours or remote work —whatever accommodations you need. I'm 100% confident you won't drop the ball on this."

Remote work might actually make this doable. Hope bloomed through her—was she actually going to do this?

Yes. "I'll do it."

Aubrey pumped her arm. "Damn straight! You won't regret it, Kat." She leaned forward again. "Don't worry—I won't tell anyone. But you know there are treatments, right?"

"I don't like taking medicine—"

"—fair, I'm not a drug pusher. But if you ever change your mind, I know a doctor treating people off-label. No reason to suffer through it if you don't have to, right?"

"Thanks, but no. I'll be fine."

∿

ON THE WALK HOME, Kat rocked out to the new Hayley Jo album with more hope than she had felt in months.

Imagining herself back at work, she couldn't keep the smile off her face. Her chest felt tight, but with excitement rather than the guilt and anxiety that had been plaguing her.

It was time to get her shit together. Once she returned to Danny's place, she needed to pack her stuff and head home. She'd talk to Beth, and—

Kat's eyes caught on the sight of naked flesh. She halted, trying to make sense of what she was seeing.

Wait. Beth?

Why was Beth standing naked in the middle of the sidewalk?

She pulled off her hoodie, then ran to Beth's side, yanking it down to cover her body. Good thing it was oversized, but it was still obscene. Glancing around, she spotted an alley and grabbed Beth's hand to drag her into it.

Once they were tucked away in the alley, she whirled on her.

"Beth! What in the world? I know you're the life of the party now, but this is—why are you streaking?"

Beth gave her a strange look, then turned back towards the alley entrance.

"Beth!"

"Oh, hi, Kat." Her twin said, giving Kat a forced smile.

"That's all you have to say for yourself?" Why was Beth acting so weird?

Beth shrugged.

"Fine. I'm calling an Uber." Kat pulled out her phone.

Then Beth took off in the direction of the street.

Kat started after her, dropping her phone. "Shit!" She reached down to grab it before running out into the street. She searched the area, trying to find her sister.

Beth was nowhere to be found.

That was when Kat noticed her hoodie crumpled on the ground. She snagged it and brushed it off before putting it back on. Was Beth running around naked again?

What just happened? Was Beth on something? She thought about calling the police or her parents, but she didn't want to get her sister in trouble if she could help it. Narcing went against the twin code.

Besides, their family had been through enough. She didn't want to add to it.

She pulled out her own phone and cursed. The screen was cracked—it must have happened when she dropped it.

She cautiously scrolled to Beth's contact, pricking her finger with a shard of glass. Dialing, she assumed it would go straight to voicemail because—well, where in the world would her sister have stashed a phone, running around town buck naked?

The call was answered on the first ring.

"Oh, hi, Kat—I'm so glad you called!"

Her sister sounded ... well, she sounded artificially chipper, but otherwise normal. Not winded, not crazy, and definitely not high.

Kat's worry faded, and anger reared up in its place. This was not funny.

"Beth, I don't know what you're on, or what sort of prank you're pulling, but this is getting out of hand. I know you're excited to go out and try new things, but doing drugs and," she lowered her voice and hissed, "streaking is just—what would Mom and Dad say if they found out?"

"Um ... Kat? I ... what?" Beth sounded utterly confused.

Kat was right there with her.

She could hear her own voice falter. "I just—I just saw you downtown. You were—you came up to me and told me—" She was rambling, needed to stop talking. None of this made sense.

Beth sounded worried. "Kitty-Kat ... I've been home all morning working on my English paper. You're kinda freaking me out."

How? What was going on? Beth was the world's worst liar, so Kat knew she wasn't lying.

Kat needed to get off the phone, needed to figure out what was happening.

She latched onto the first lame excuse that came to mind and blurted, "Uh, never mind. Bad joke. Hey, I gotta go—good luck with the English paper."

"Yeah ... okay?" Beth's voice was familiar and soothing, like when they were kids. "You sure you're okay, Kitty Kat?"

"Sure thing, Bethy—we'll talk soon, gotta run." She hung up and shoved her phone in her purse.

That thing with Beth—it happened, right? She looked around, trying to find some proof that she wasn't going crazy. Her sweatshirt had a smudge of dirt on it, but that didn't prove anything, not really.

She spun around and spotted a man sitting at the bus stop, scrolling on his phone. Feeling ten shades of stupid, she walked over to him.

"Hey, this may sound strange, but did you see a woman run by, um, naked a couple of minutes ago?"

He looked up and gave her a lop-sided grin. "Um, no. Pretty sure I would have noticed that. But I just got here—guess I missed all the fun, huh?"

"Um, yeah, it was pretty crazy. Thanks, anyway." Kat backed away, almost tripping over a trash bin as she high-tailed it out of there. She stuck her headphones and sunglasses back on, retreating from sensory overload.

She made the trek back to her brother's place on legs that felt like lead. Fire coursed through her veins, a potent mix of fear and exhaustion.

What the actual fuck? Was she losing her mind?

Were hallucinations a symptom of Syndrome Q?

[PART 6]
SECRETS

THE
VALMORAN
CHRONICLES

22

HIDDEN IN PLAIN SIGHT

VALMORAN REPUBLIC, PLANET KRONAI, THE TEMPLE OF
THE SEVEN

MATTHAI VALTRELLIN, FUTURE HIGH PRIEST

~

MATTHAI TOSSED and turned that night, stomach unsettled
from the rich food and wine. His new robes lay folded
nearby, a tangible reminder of his new status.

Any time he managed to sleep, dreams haunted him. Kat-a-
reen showing up in his chambers, bleeding. Finding out that
she was in the Temple holding cells. Falling into a sea of
pilgrims and being torn limb from limb.

But mostly, he dreamed of her.

None of it was rational—dreams seldom were—but he
couldn't remember how often he woke with a start, heart
racing, checking the corner of his room to see if she was there.

As he stared at the stone ceiling, the feast replayed in his mind, a blur of faces and voices. He had smiled, nodded, played his part.

But he couldn't remember who he met during the evening.

Except Callum.

Well, and Vargus Trix, who caused something of a scene. Matthai had an inkling they had Callum to thank for preventing an incident between Vargus and the Threllian Ambassador from escalating.

Everything else was just a stream of faces and pleasantries.

When Callum came through the receiving line, it was obvious the empath could sense Matthai wasn't well. For a moment, Matthai had been sure the man was about to inquire about it, but in the end, Callum was discreet and said nothing.

Matthai shuddered to think what his inner world must have felt like to an empath. It had been like someone else was wearing his skin, smiling with his mouth.

A prisoner inside his own body and mind. He shuddered, trying not to dwell on it.

He engaged his Hix interface, intent on finding a vid to watch. Maybe it would make the world feel less surreal.

He found the other new Legends of the Lost Colony adaptation, the one Talia called 'sappy.'

The room transformed when he flicked his eyes over the 'immersive vid' option.

Actors materialized, their voices crisp and clear, as if they were there in the room with him. The stark stone walls of Matthai's chambers faded away, replaced by the lush, alien landscape of an unexplored world. The sounds of running water, insects, and jungle creatures filled his ears.

This version of the Legends was an adventure vid, with the expedition discovering a secret homeworld. Versions like this were intriguing—the idea of an uncharted paradise world being discovered was almost magical.

And complete fantasy, of course.

Everyone knew the last new Valmoran homeworld was discovered during the Threllian Wars.

Just a few minutes into the film, he gave up. His mind was too distracted, too unsettled.

He shut off the vid and used his Hix to draw a hot bath, making his way to his bath chamber. Maybe it would help him get some rest.

As he soaked in the warm water, he traced the intricate tiles depicting the seven phases of Valmoran life, as he so often did. In some ways, he understood his place in the galaxy even less today than two days prior.

In others, he felt ... secure. He was Kat-a-reen's Amara.

It was truth, fundamental. Essential and permanent.

His fingers brushed over his brand new mate mark, and he thought of the thousand potentials on his mating list, each praying they might become the next High Priestess.

It would be none of them—and it would cause an uproar.

He shuddered, imagining the scandal erupting when the truth came to light. The political fallout, the public outcry ...

Casting it from his mind, he filled his thoughts with Kat-a-reen instead.

He had to locate her. He must.

The Temple bells tolled the approaching dawn. There was no way he was falling asleep again. Better to while away the morning in the garden than to return to bed with his troubled thoughts.

He slipped on his new robes, frowning at their lavish embellishments, then grabbed one of the utility robes he always wore for gardening.

In the hallway, he ran into Janna, stationed outside his door.

"Couldn't sleep?"

Matthai shook his head. "Thought it might be nice to get my hands dirty this morning."

"You and your dirt." Janna teased. "It's a good plan, Scion. Let's go, then."

The cool morning air was a welcome relief as they made their way to the East Garden. As he neared, he saw a familiar figure among the cloria bushes, barely visible in the pre-dawn light.

Miral, the old gardener, straightened as Matthai approached. "Matthai, my boy," she said, her weathered face creasing into a smile. "Plenty of work needs doing this morning." She nodded toward a spot where she'd set out a second set of gardening tools.

His eyes pricked with tears as he realized she'd been expecting him.

Matthai donned the gardening robe to protect his lavish robes and reached for a pair of pruning shears.

They worked in companionable silence, clearing out the last batch of cloria flowers that hadn't blossomed to make room for the new hybrids. The repetitive task, the feel of soil between Matthai's fingers, soothed his nerves, and his anxiety settled.

"So, that new batch of clorias," Miral said, her keen eyes studying the delicate seedlings. "Do you think they'll take this time?"

Matthai paused, considering. "I hope so," he admitted. "But we won't know until they're big enough to transplant."

"Mhm. Well, let me know when you want to move them to your new quarters. I know you won't let anyone else touch them."

Matthai forced a chuckle, grateful for the offer, but not for the unwelcome reminder of his impending move.

"Hmm ... Liyara always did love clorias, didn't she?"

Matthai felt a familiar ache in his chest at the mention of his sister. "Yeah—a magical garden of glowing blue flowers," He couldn't help the smile that tugged at his mouth at the memory of a wild young Liyara, dancing around the East Garden, telling him how amazing it would be.

"And now you're making it a reality."

Matthai scoffed. "Two phases of attempts, and every batch a failure—hardly a reality."

Miral cocked her head to one side, shrugging a shoulder. "I'd call it ... perseverance. And you're getting close. These ones fared much better than the ones before."

They were getting closer. Every generation.

"But Scion," Miral continued. "I have to wonder ..." She set down her shears and caught his gaze. "Make sure you know why you're still doing this. Don't just do it for Liyara."

His heart clenched at the sound of his sister's name, as it always did, but perhaps ... less. Was that because of time, or Kat-a-reen?

He considered Miral's words. As much as he missed his sister and wanted to honor her memory, the cloria weren't only about her anymore.

Somewhere along the way, they had become his passion, something tangible, enchanting, and impermanent he could create.

Beauty and purpose amid grief and duty.

As they continued to work, the familiar scents and sensations of the garden were an anchor, pulling him back to himself.

Tension drained from his body as the sun rose, bathing the garden in golden light. The Temple grounds began to stir, the sounds of distant activity picking up.

"Scion?"

Matthai turned to see Talia approaching, a gentle smile on her lips. "I thought I might find you here."

"Just needed some fresh air," he said, brushing the soil from his hands.

Talia nodded, her expression understanding. "Better?"

Matthai gave a curt nod. He wasn't feeling terrific, but better.

She shook her head, chuckling. "You should have seen Janna last night with Vargus Trix. For a minute there, I was sure she was gonna throttle him with his own wings."

Matthai couldn't help but laugh at the image. "I'm surprised she didn't."

"Oh, she wanted to," Talia said, her eyes twinkling. "But then she'd get demoted, and that wouldn't do. You're stuck with us."

A smile curved his lips. He had people here, people who— even if he couldn't be fully himself around them—did care for him. Maybe he wasn't quite as alone as he'd thought.

"Well—" Miral wiped her hands on her apron and stood, stretching her back. "I think it's about time for some breakfast. Care to join me?"

"That sounds perfect," Talia replied before Matthai could respond. "We should all eat before the day gets too busy."

They both looked at him for permission. Talia, of course, couldn't go without him, as she was serving as his guard. "Sure." He had nothing planned this morning, a definite novelty in his overbooked life.

As they entered the familiar cafeteria, Matthai felt a pang of nostalgia. The simple space, with its long tables and benches, held memories of countless meals shared with his fellow adepts.

Feeling alone, most of the time.

After grabbing food, Miral and Talia discussed the logistics of moving Matthai's belongings, their voices fading into background chatter. Matthai stirred his porridge, his mind wandering.

Talia paused mid-sentence, her sharp eyes catching his lack of enthusiasm. "Scion, you've barely touched your food."

Matthai shrugged. "I'm still full from last night's feast."

Talia's frown deepened, but she didn't press the issue.

Matthai's thoughts drifted back to the cloria blooms, the generations of varieties that couldn't blossom in the wild, that never met their full potential.

Cloria that were never meant to flower in their climate.

Sometimes, he felt like he was in the wrong climate, unable to bloom.

Like the flowers he was hybridizing, Valtrellins had been bred for 217 generations—to ensure they were all God-touched.

But the image of the unflowering bushes would not leave his mind. Generations of cloria.

Generations of Valtrellins.

And himself, the newest generation.

An urge rose in his mind, insistent and demanding. "Talia," he said, interrupting their conversation, "I'd like to visit the Museum of Valtrellin History."

Talia nodded, scooping up the last of her breakfast. "Of course, Scion. Now?"

"Yes," Matthai said. "Now feels like the right time."

～

THE VALTRELLIN HISTORY Museum transformed as Matthai entered.

Static exhibits came to life with vivid imagery and informative displays. An AI guide began speaking to him in flawless Standard, offering insights into each exhibit they passed.

No matter who visited, the overlay adjusted its language, cultural references, and even visual style to allow pilgrims throughout the Temple to connect with their faith and history.

It was a marvel of inclusivity.

They moved through the chronological exhibits, starting with sparse information about the First Epoch, in the savage age before Valmorans knew the Gods.

Matthai strode forward toward the Second Epoch and paused before the exhibit on the First Priestess. It depicted a dramatization of his ancestor, the first of the Valtrellin Priestesses, during her momentous encounter with the Obelisk.

Matthai wondered about that part of the scripture. When the Obelisk spoke to him during his ordination, it had been terrifying, but not like in this story. He certainly hadn't felt an influx of knowledge, or been incapacitated for seven days and seven nights.

'Words, once spoken, cannot be unspoken.'

The Obelisk's message to Matthai could have referred to his vows, which he couldn't rescind. Or perhaps it was a warning about confiding in Callum about Kat-a-reen. Or maybe it had been foolish to promise to help her when he had no idea where to start.

The Obelisk's words *were* meaningful, but Matthai had expected something ... more.

To be overcome with knowledge.

Awestruck.

Weren't the Obelisks supposed to share profound knowledge? At the start of the Third Epoch, they had given the command of spaceflight to his ancestors, had shown them the gates above each planet, how to navigate the network between worlds. The Obelisks had taught them advanced mathematics.

And he, the future High Priest, meant to guide a civilization of trillions, merely got an ambiguous warning about minding his tongue.

Perhaps one needed to ask questions to get answers. Matthai hadn't thought to during his first visit—he'd been too focused on trying not to jump away.

He should schedule another audience with the Obelisk.

The Gods should be able to help him find Kat-a-reen. He pulled up the Temple program to request an appointment.

Given the influx of pilgrims, they'd probably need to open it for him outside of regular hours, but they would do it for their Ordained Scion.

The Gods would be able to help. They would know what to do.

He should have thought of it sooner.

After marking his request as urgent and sending it off, he glanced up at Talia. She, who claimed to hate museums, was engrossed in a nearby exhibit documenting the ancient weaponry from the Second Epoch.

A question formed in his mind, one he'd never thought to ask before.

"Have *you* been to see the Obelisk?" Matthai asked, glancing at Talia.

She shrugged. "Sure."

"Did you," he furrowed his brow, "Did you feel any different, you know ... after?"

Talia cocked her head to the side. "No, not really. Mostly, it was a pain to get an appointment. And the cleansing rituals, the security checks ..."

She shook her head as if remembering something unpleasant.

Strange. Matthai hadn't had to go through all that. "Security checks?"

Talia nodded. "Oh, yeah—they want to make sure you're as pure as the day you were born, going in there. I mean, it makes sense—gotta protect the Obelisks, right?"

"Why? From ... who?" Matthai frowned.

Talia sighed. "Who knows? But when you've worked in security as long as I have, nothing surprises you anymore. And as for the Obelisks ... I haven't been back. I get my wisdom from the scriptures—that's good enough for me."

They rounded a corner, entering the Third Epoch.

The Technological Revelation. The Obelisks rewarded Valmoran obedience with the knowledge of spaceflight and advanced mathematics. The rapid expansion and discovery that followed—all guided by the wisdom of the High Priests.

He wondered again why the Obelisk hadn't shared something more meaningful with him. Was he ... somehow deficient?

The discovery of countless Valmoran homeworlds, each new planet a testament to their expanding civilization. The establishment of Temples to honor the Obelisk on each world created a vast network of faith, unifying their people across the stars.

As they continued towards the end of the Third Epoch, the mood shifted dramatically. The darker chapters of Valmoran history.

These exhibits were a cautionary tale.

A heaviness settled in Matthai's chest as they approached the time of the Great Threllian Wars. The displays were sobering, showcasing generations of religious and cultural misunderstandings.

The escalation of hostilities had spanned generations and ended catastrophically in the near-genocide of the Threllian species.

"This exhibit is always so ... harrowing," Matthai said.

"The Threllian Wars ..." Talia shook her head. "We went from exploring every corner of the galaxy to being terrified of our own shadow."

Exploration beyond known Valmoran space was still strictly regulated, almost taboo. "Yeah ... that's kind of sad, too. But I meant the Threllians." His heart clenched, looking at a display showing one of the Threllian-occupied homeworlds, littered with dead and dying Threllians, and sobbing native Valmorans tending to them.

Talia pressed her mouth into a thin line. "It was a long time ago, though. Now we've got the Peacekeepers and the treaty to make sure nothing like that happens again.

Matthai's jaw clenched even as his heart ached. "I just ... I can't believe our ancestors went that far. I'm glad everyone is paying reparations, but it just ... doesn't feel like enough, you know?"

"For nearly wiping out their entire species?" Talia scoffed. "No amount of money could make that okay."

Matthai looked over at Talia, whose nostrils had flared with anger. Her subspecies had historically been categorized as a 'brute species', acceptable for enslavement, and their population still hadn't recovered.

"Hey," he said, "Let's move on, okay?"

Her gaze lingered on the exhibit a few moments longer, before she jerked her head and started walking again.

Though they were leaving behind the shame of cultural atrocities, these exhibits always filled Matthai with familial shame.

The Era of Exclusionism.

Matthai's stomach twisted as they paused before a display showing ornate robes and the first zanchion crafted during the Era of Exclusionism.

Seventeen generations ago, Matthai's ancestors decided to hide the Obelisks away.

For eleven long, dark generations, the High Priests proclaimed that only those of God-touched Valtrellin blood were worthy to commune with the Gods.

They built extravagant new Temples to replace the ancient ones, wore lavish clothing and jewelry, and invited the wealthy and powerful to dine with them.

Ceremonial robes, zanchions, medallions—all introduced during this era of indulgence and elitism. That level of depraved privilege seemed at odds with the Temple's current message of inclusivity and service.

"I'm glad I didn't live back then," he murmured. He always wondered, if he had—would he have spoken out against Exclusionism? Or would he have been part of the problem?

He hoped he would have seen the wrongness in the situation, but how could you ever know how you would act in a completely different situation?

The angry man's words from during his procession echoed in his mind. 'Take back the Obelisks! The Obelisks belong to the people!'

The man's words made no sense—he was obviously troubled —but Matthai understood his anger. The Valtrellins during Exclusionism had no right to rule, not with the hubris they showed ... just the thought of stealing the Gods away from the people was unconscionable.

His conversation with Callum about hierarchy and the difference between earned and unearned privilege came to mind.

As did his own words to Callum: 'Blood may have secured my role, but it is mine to earn the right to rule.'

Matthai was destined to become the High Priest, but what had he done to earn it?

Nothing. He had been born a Valtrellin.

He shook his head, trying to dispel those insidious doubts. The Gods must have a plan. Even if he didn't understand it yet, unworthy as he felt, he had to have faith.

Eventually, they reached the exhibit marking the abolishment of Exclusionism. Matthai exhaled, relieved.

His more recent ancestors had reopened the Obelisks to the people, ushering in a new age of inclusivity and spiritual connection.

After generations of Exclusionism, the Valtrellins returned to their true purpose: serving the Gods and guiding the Valmoran people.

Grand ceremonies had marked the occasion, excitement rippling through the galaxy as the Temple once again welcomed all who sought wisdom from the Gods.

When they reached the end of the museum, Matthai slipped behind the curtain that walled off the space reserved for future exhibits.

He sat on the bench facing the empty space where his and Kat-a-reen's exhibit would one day stand.

Whether the galaxy was ready for it or not, Kat-a-reen was their next High Priestess.

The thought both thrilled and terrified him.

He could almost see it: the two of them, side by side, guiding the Valmoran people with wisdom and compassion. Though he barely knew her, Matthai had sensed Kat-a-reen's resolve. He had no doubt she would make a brilliant counterpart.

A half smile played on his lips as he imagined introducing her to the wonders of the Temple.

She would love the clorias—he was sure of it.

But it wasn't just about showing Kat-a-reen his world. Matthai was eager to learn about his future mate. Their bond wasn't love—not yet, but he knew that would come with time.

With Kat-a-reen as his partner, the daunting task of being High Priest seemed ... manageable. *Right*, even.

He remembered the faith that had shone in her eyes. Faith ... in *him*.

If he was destined to become someone worthy of such trust, that meant ... he could do this?

He let out a deep breath, nodding to himself. In a strange way, knowing that in the future his mate had unshakeable faith in him ... made the impossible feel manageable. Predestined.

The path ahead was clear.

Find Kat-a-reen, bring her home, and together, they would shoulder the sacred duty of the High Priesthood. They would make their mark on Valmoran history, not just as names in an exhibit, but as faithful servants of their people and their Gods.

His heart swelled with determination. He would earn his right to rule and prove himself worthy of the trust Kat-a-reen, his parents, his people, and the Gods placed in him.

And they could face anything together. He was sure of it.

First, though, he had to find her.

He needed to contact Callum, to start planning their search. Maybe they could—

A message notification from his parents intruded, flashing on his mindscreen.

Usually, this would be merely irritating, but today ... today it caused a surge of pure dread to flow from his head down to his toes, leaving him lightheaded in its wake.

And then he felt it ... the tingling at the back of his skull.

The world tilted and twisted. Not again.

"I am here. I am now. I will not jump away," Matthai whispered, rocking back and forth to ground himself. Pressing his feet down into the floor.

He struggled to draw a full breath. The weight of impending ... *something* ... pressed down on his chest.

Breathe.

The intensity of his reaction startled him. Why should a simple summons from his parents affect him so strongly?

And yet, his gut told him this was no ordinary meeting.

Nevertheless, he flicked his eyes to open it.

Please report to the High Priests' inner sanctum at
your earliest convenience.

Matthai swallowed, déjà vu making the world seem suddenly surreal.

"What is it?" Talia asked, noticing his sudden stillness.

He looked up at her, hands gripping the insides of his sleeves to hide their shaking. "It's my parents. They want to see me in the inner sanctum. Immediately."

~

THE WALK to the cathedral passed in a blur. Matthai's body felt weak, muscles shaking as they took the inner paths to the old Temple.

The grounds were still busier than usual, but with the festivities over, most of the pilgrims had gone. For everyone else, life was finally returning to normal after months of preparation.

Matthai barely registered his surroundings, too preoccupied with what this meeting might be about.

Secrets.

Somehow, his heart sank and raced at the same time.

They passed through the ancient cathedral where he had taken his vows the night before. Bustling priests worked to clean and pack away the decorations from the ordination, restoring everything to its former state, as if nothing had changed.

But everything had changed.

His muscles tensed as they entered the back of the cathedral, the ancient stone walkways dim and narrow.

The air grew cooler, carrying the musty scent of ages past. Matthai's footsteps echoed off the stone walls, a thundering beat accompanying the rushing of his heartbeat in his ears.

The back passages, only open to caretakers and older priests, felt vaguely tomb-like today.

As they rounded a corner, Talia stopped, her hand briefly touching Matthai's arm. "No one is allowed past this point," she murmured, her voice barely above a whisper.

Matthai nodded, swallowing hard. "None except High Priests and their successors."

Steeling himself, Matthai approached the door to the High Priest's inner sanctum, pulse racing, unsure if it was from anticipation or dread.

He had never been through this door, wasn't sure he really wanted to go inside ... but his parents were waiting for him, so he forced his feet forward.

The modern security panel seemed out of place in this ancient place—it seemed like overkill. Everyone knew this room was forbidden to all but the High Priests.

He scanned his Hix, and a message appeared.

Welcome, Ordained Scion Matthai Valtrellin. Please enter the security booth.

The sleek metal door slid open with a soft hiss, revealing a closet-sized metal room. Matthai hesitated, eyes darting between the booth and the ancient stonework surrounding it.

It looked like the security airlocks used on the Arbiter ansibles. He'd read about them, but would need to ask Callum later. They were necessary to ensure no one impersonated a Representative during voting.

But why would the inner sanctum require that level of security?

When he stepped inside, the door slid closed behind him. It whirred and clicked into place, setting him even more on edge. He was locked inside.

The sudden silence was oppressive, punctuated only by his ragged breathing.

Please perform retinal scan and handprint verification, then stand still for a technology scan.

His heart pounded, blood thrumming in his ears as he stood still for the scanner.

Verification complete. You may now enter the inner sanctum.

Matthai's mind spun. What would he find there? What secrets did the room hold? The door slid open, revealing a—

—disappointingly mundane chamber.

The scent of polished wood wafted his way as he stepped inside.

Thick blue curtains draped the walls, and a sturdy stone desk sat in each corner of the room. Bookshelves lined most walls, except one contained an altar with a cleansing bowl. A low table sat in the center of the room, surrounded by plush couches.

A small but ornate box was the only item on the table.

Matthai wasn't sure what he had been expecting, but this was underwhelming after the process he'd just gone through to enter.

His parents rose as he entered, their faces a mixture of relief and apprehension. His father gestured to the couch. "Matthai, please, sit."

"Did you sleep well, son?" his mother asked. She attempted a smile, but it didn't reach her eyes. Dark circles ringed her eyes, as if she hadn't slept. His father didn't look much better.

Matthai's throat felt dry as he answered, "Fitfully." he said, then rushed to add, "But I'm awake and ready."

Though he wasn't as confident as he tried to sound. He wasn't sure he would ever be ready for this meeting.

His father nodded, face somber. He reached for the box on the table, sliding it in front of Matthai. "This is yours now."

The box was ornately carved of rich brown wood and inlaid with blue gems in the shape of the Valtrellin crest. He suspected he wouldn't like what was inside, and his fears were confirmed when he opened the lid.

Inside, on a bed of plush blue fabric, was a High Priest's medallion: etched silver and blue gems elegantly crafted in the shape of the Valtrellin crest.

Commissioned during the height of Exclusionism when the priests were at their most proud and extravagant.

He wasn't sure why his family kept the cursed things. They symbolized the most shameful period in the Valtrellin family's history. A symbol of self-important indulgence and greed.

He pulled it out. Heavy, robust. It must be worth a fortune.

"Go ahead—put it on," his mother urged. Once he had, she added, "That medallion is precious—you must never take it off and guard it with your life."

Matthai's brow furrowed, his fingers tracing the intricate design. They were expensive, sure, and had sentimental value, but 'guard it with your life' seemed extreme. It was just a piece of jewelry.

"It's a key," his father added, answering his unspoken question.

Matthai's eyes widened. That ... was about the last thing he expected to hear. "To what?"

His father leaned forward, his voice low and urgent. "We'll get to that. But first ..." Soren closed his eyes, then looked over and met Phina's gaze. "I suppose we should get this over with."

His mother took a deep breath, her hands twisting in her lap. "Today, we will share many truths with you. Secrets guarded by the Valtrellin family for seventeen generations." She covered her face with her hands briefly, a gesture Matthai had rarely seen in his regal mother. "Gods, this is difficult. I still remember the day your grandparents brought me here."

"And I remember you bringing me here after our mating ceremony," Soren said.

Phina gave him a sad little smile. "Yeah, not exactly the mating gift I would have liked to give you, darling."

Soren grasped her hand tight. "We got through it."

Then Soren caught Matthai's gaze and inclined his head.

Matthai's stomach churned at the thought of burdening Kat-a-reen with whatever this was. Maybe he could shoulder it alone. But it didn't sound like that was how it worked.

Phina leaned forward, her gaze intense. "First, understand there is an explanation for everything we're about to tell you. The Valtrellins have served the Valmoran people for 217 generations."

"The people?" Matthai's said. "I thought we served the Gods."

His parents shared a look that made him wish he hadn't asked.

Phina reached for his hand. "Oh, Matthai. We still have much to explain."

Something dark and ominous settled in Matthai's gut, making him glad he'd mostly skipped breakfast. He had a feeling that whatever he was about to hear was going to be heart-rending and horrific.

His father sighed—a deep, weary sound. "Matthai, what we're about to tell you ... it's not easy to hear. But you must understand, it's crucial. Seventeen generations ago, the Obelisks ... changed. By the accounts of our ancestors, it was sudden, and the results were devastating."

Matthai felt the blood drain from his face, his fingers digging into the plush fabric of the couch. Seventeen generations ago ... that was the start of Exclusionism. When the Valtrellins declared only the High Priests were holy enough to commune with the Obelisks.

But there was nothing in the histories about something being wrong with them.

It couldn't be true. There were over three hundred Obelisks in the galaxy, and before Exclusionism, pilgrims and scholars had free access to them. If they changed, surely someone would have written about it.

Everyone would have written about it.

"No," Matthai said, shaking his head, "If the Obelisks changed, it would be all over the histories." But even as he spoke, his voice faltered.

"You're right to question this, son," his father said. "But the truth is complicated. By the time our ancestors learned what was happening, the danger had already begun to spread. It would have been impossible to remove all traces of what happened."

"There was no alternative but to hide the truth in plain sight," his mother said. "Now, it is so mundane as to go unnoticed."

Mundane? Hidden in plain sight? None of this was making sense.

Phina placed her hands in her lap, running her fingertips over the filigreed pattern on her robes. "You have to understand— our ancestors made a tremendous sacrifice, inciting the people to hate them, enduring endless threats against their lives, and guarding the Temple against the constant threat of war."

"They had to—everything depended on the people believing our motivation for hiding the Obelisks was inflated self-importance."

"You're saying Exclusionism was all an act?" Matthai asked, his voice rising in disbelief.

His father nodded. "They bore those dangers, all that hatred —to protect the Valmoran people.

Matthai's mind reeled. Protect them from what? *The Obelisks?*

That made no sense.

The Obelisks were the source of knowledge and truth. Of things great and small. Seen and unseen.

The Valtrellins from the Era of Exclusionism were almost universally reviled. Now his parents claimed their heinous behavior had somehow been ... heroic. But how? Why?

"This isn't making any sense—"

"—Matthai," his father interjected, his voice firm but understanding, "Perhaps the rest of this story will be easier to explain once we go down below."

Matthai's eyes darted around the room, searching for any sign of a hidden passage. Down below? He glanced around, seeing no doors, no stairways.

His mother stood, her face a mask of resolve. "I wish we didn't have to share this burden with you, Matthai. But we must."

His parents moved in the direction of the back wall.

"Come," she said.

They approached one of the many bookshelves, and she removed a book from the second shelf. Reaching through the gap, it looked like she was searching for something, then she tugged her arm down.

A hidden lever?

Matthai's breath caught as he took a step backward. The bookshelf slid out of the way, revealing the stone wall.

And a depression in the stone with the exact contours of the Valtrellin medallion.

"This is it, son."

Matthai's hands trembled as he removed the medallion from his neck. He wasn't sure he wanted to know what was down there. If it was terrible enough that his ancestors would rather lie, allow the people to hate them ...

Perhaps it was better not to know.

But, no. Matthai was the Ordained Scion now, and whatever was down there was now his responsibility.

But beyond that, now that he was aware of the existence of secrets—and the extremes his family took to obscure them—a desire to *know* stirred within him. Temptation and perverse fascination.

Knowing that terrible secrets lurked, but never learning what they were ... over time, that would drive him insane.

He only hoped that the truth was less devastating than he feared.

Placing the medallion into the depression in the stone wall, he heard the faint sounds of machinery working, clicking, whirring. Whatever was happening was mechanical, unusual in this modern age.

A rush of cool, musty air hit Matthai's face as the wall receded. A crack appeared down the center, becoming two stone doors that swung backward.

Into darkness.

His head spun. This was too surreal ... secret passages in the ancient Temple? It was like something out of an adventure vid.

Or a horror vid. Suddenly, Matthai remembered every character who had ever ventured into the dark unknown ... only to meet some dreadful fate.

A shiver ran down his spine, even as sweat beaded on the back of his neck.

The light from the room only extended a few feet into the corridor—no, it was a stairway. It gaped open like the gullet of a creature of nightmares.

Matthai stood, transfixed, at the precipice.

Down there rested secrets so terrible that generations of Valtrellins invited shame and hatred on themselves—had nearly incited a war against the Temple—just to keep them hidden.

THE VALMORAN CHRONICLES

23

LEGENDS AND LIES

VALMORAN REPUBLIC, PLANET KRONAI, THE TEMPLE OF THE SEVEN

MATTHAI VALTRELLIN, FUTURE HIGH PRIEST

~

MATTHAI SQUINTED into the gaping maw of the dark stairwell.

"There is no electricity in the archive, and no fire is permitted," Phina said. "So always remember to bring a light source with you."

The word "archive" reverberated in his mind, sending a chill down his spine.

A flicker of unease stirred in Matthai's gut. What secrets could require such elaborate precautions?

"Also, your Hix signal will be blocked once we enter."

A hint of forced amusement entered Soren's tone as he added, "I hope your Standard isn't too rusty, son."

"I'll manage." He accepted the Safelight with trembling hands, then followed his father.

He imagined it was what venturing into the void felt like.

Once inside, his mother returned to the doorway to press her medallion into a depression in the wall.

The doors swung shut behind them, drowning them in oppressive silence. Darkness pressed in, suffocating and palpable. The stairway extended so far in front of them that the light cast by their lanterns tapered off into nothing.

As they descended, the temperature plummeted, the chill seeping into Matthai's bones. With a shaking hand, he reached out to steady himself against the wall.

In the flickering light of the lanterns, Matthai realized with a shock that the tunnel was bored straight through solid rock. And to think ... this had been inside—no, beneath—the cathedral he visited daily. He shivered.

Generations of dark legacy seemed to press down on him with each step. How long had his family guarded these secrets?

And at what cost?

Finally, their light shone on a door up ahead. This one, unlike the one above, didn't require a key. But it was bolted shut.

His mother released the bolt and then pushed the door open. "Come." She stepped through and beckoned for him to follow.

Matthai held his light up, shining it into the room. The vast chamber was almost cave-like, except it was obviously well-maintained. The air chilled his nostrils, but wasn't musty or damp. It smelled ... like old paper and ancient secrets.

Books.

Wall-to-wall, the space was crammed with shelves of actual physical books. Thousands of them.

Matthai's heart raced, foreboding blending with awe at the sight. The lure of secrets was compelling, enticing him to explore—but it was nearly smothered by his apprehension of what he might uncover. Nearly, but not quite.

Curiosity got the better of him, and he stepped forward before he realized it, walking into the narrow gap between the nearest rows of shelves.

"What is all this?"

His mother answered, "Every version of the Legends of the Lost Colonies. And every shred of evidence surrounding them that could be gathered."

"The Legends? Why?" Matthai whirled to face her, heart pounding. A terrible suspicion rose, but he pushed it back. "But those are just stories, right?"

"No, son." His father frowned, shaking his head. "Our ancestors spread most of the original Legends.

His mother caught his eyes. "But you're right—they're mostly just stories. Before long, they became so popular we no longer needed to create them."

Mostly? Matthai's world tilted, his mind swirling with questions.

There wasn't a Valmoran alive who didn't know about the Legends of the Lost Colony—but why would the Temple have created them?

If the Legends were true ... but they obviously couldn't *all* be true.

The Legends were adventure stories—or horror stories—depending on the adaptation. But no matter what, several things remained constant.

A secret colony ship, built during the height of Anti-Expansionism. A roguish captain and a zealous priest, leading over a thousand Valmorans on a clandestine journey to find a lost homeworld.

And in the end ... they never returned.

A lost homeworld.

His mind spun with the implications, some too terrible to bear.

Matthai's legs trembled, threatening to give out. He gripped the nearest shelf for support.

If there was a lost homeworld out there, then the Temple lied to the people. No—*his ancestors lied.* They announced that the Gods told them all homeworlds had been discovered.

He swallowed through the lump forming in his throat and found his mouth had gone dry.

Maybe ... there had been a mission, but no secret homeworld?

Because if there had been another homeworld, one that hadn't been returned to the fold ... then his family had been acting in direct defiance of the will of the Gods for seventeen generations.

Matthai's mind vacillated between outrage at the deception and a desperate need to believe in his family's integrity.

"You're not saying ..." Matthai's voice was barely a whisper, the words sticking in his throat.

His father closed his eyes, nodding. "Our ancestors were able to overwhelm the true version of events with more compelling Legends." He gestured at the shelves of books. "Every false account of the Legends is in this archive. And hidden among them, the only copy of the truth."

A chill ran through Matthai, his skin prickling with dread. He glanced back towards the door. Part of him wanted to run, to pretend he'd never heard any of this.

He could never un-know what they were about to tell him.

"Come, son," his mother said, "Let us show you to your desk. We have it all set up for you."

Desk? He trailed after her, feeling dazed. Each step felt like a monumental effort, his body heavy with the weight of the revelations.

He had to be dreaming.

Security booths, medallions that acted as secret keys, secret passages under the cathedral, the Legends being true ... this had to be a dream.

It had to.

But the numbness in his fingers, the heaviness in his legs—felt all too real.

As they walked deeper into the archive, a part of Matthai clung to his knowledge of his parents. They were honorable people, great High Priests. If they were willing to perpetuate whatever this was, there had to be a good reason, right?

The rows of bookshelves opened into a work area in the back. In the center, a large stone table sat surrounded by chairs. Along the back wall, four desks were in a neat row.

Enough for the current High Priestess and Priest, the heir, and the heir's mate.

One for each person bound to these cursed secrets.

Kat-a-reen's face flashed in his mind, but he pushed it away. He couldn't bear to think of her, not now. Not when his entire world was crumbling around him.

Instead, he surveyed the room.

His parents must occupy the desks on the right since they were clearly in use. The far one was undoubtedly his father's —neat and tidy. The other overflowed with books, some sitting open to different pages. That one had to be his mother's.

The far desk on the left was bare, but the one his mother approached had something on top.

A book? He stepped closer.

"This will be your workspace when you're down in the archives. We never work electronically here, and you won't have your Hix to assist you, so I hope you paid attention in your ancient language courses."

He bristled, but held his tongue. Was that why he had been required to take so many of those classes? They told him it was so he could study the ancient religious texts and impart wisdom to the people.

Another deception. The realization cut deep, a blade to the chest.

Anger flared in Matthai's chest, warring with a lifetime of trust and respect for his parents.

"This is your first journal. In it, you will record everything you study and observe here. Everything that future High Priests may need to know. It must never leave this room, except for when you are on a tour of the temples. The journals are bio-coded. No one but you can open this one, and we will teach you to read and write in the code we use for record-keeping."

Record what? And bio-locked journals, written in code? They still hadn't explained ... any of this.

His cheeks heated, jaw clenching. Matthai wasn't prone to anger, but right now, he might explode if they didn't start making sense. His jaw clenched, teeth grinding together.

Matthai took a deep breath, counting to seven, trying to calm his body and mind.

There had to be an explanation. His parents were *good* people.

They toiled day and night to inspire and guide the people of the Valmoran homeworlds. He had seen the love shining in their eyes when they worked with visitors to the Temple.

He had *seen* it.

With deliberate patience, he took a step backward to look them both in the eyes.

"Why don't we sit down, and you can explain this to me?" Then he moved to the table in the center of the room, nearly falling into his seat; his legs were so weak.

Once they joined him, they sat for a moment in painful silence. His parents stared at one another as if in silent conversation.

For all the Gods' sake—why wouldn't they just come out with it already?

With a calm he didn't feel, Matthai said, "I need to know the truth. Explain this to me, please."

They shared another glance, and then his father reached over to squeeze his mate's hand. Then he nodded, almost to himself, and began.

"Seventeen generations ago, a priest named Helia arrived at the First Temple in a panic. She demanded to speak to the High Priests, in private. She told them she'd been on a holy mission granted to her by the Obelisk of her Temple. Helia claimed to have been given knowledge of a secret gate that led to the final Valmoran homeworld."

"But when she went to the High Priests of her own temple to request that they form an expedition, they thought she'd gone mad and put her in seclusion."

"Helia escaped, feeling what she described as a relentless compulsion to complete the Gods' mission. Feeling she couldn't rely on the Temple to help, she convinced an explorer that she knew the way to an undiscovered homeworld."

"However, in those days, because of the Anti-Expansionist policies in the Old Valmoran Empire, they had to construct the ship in deep space, and did everything they could to cover up all records of their activities."

"They found the gate, exactly where the Obelisk told Helia it would be. But when they went through it, into the Black Swirl—"

Matthai's eyes widened. "—the Black Swirl is real, too?" It was another myth—one told to scare people on space voyages. A fabled galaxy that made ships disappear.

He gripped the sleeves of his robes to calm his shaking hands.

His father nodded.

"What happened to them?" The words poured out, even though he wasn't sure he wanted to know the answer.

His father's face darkened. "According to Helia, they located the homeworld and established a base of operations from which to initiate first contact."

That answered one of his questions, and he didn't like the explanation.

Matthai's stomach churned.

His ancestors had told the people all homeworlds were discovered.

These weren't just secrets ... they were lies. And if they lied about this ...

But, no. There must be a reasonable explanation. There *must.*

"Before they could make contact, a creature Helia called 'The Nightmare' visited them. It appeared to all of them, first as a dark cloud, then morphing into 'the visage of each person's self' before commanding them in their own voices."

The hair on the back of Matthai's neck rose. "What did it say to them?"

"It told them the galaxy was claimed, then gave them a time limit to leave or be eliminated."

A chill ran down Matthai's spine as the implications hit him. If this Nightmare was real, maybe that was the reason for the lies?

Matthai leaned forward, gripping the edge of his seat, the stone digging into his palms. "But the ship never returned.

That's how the story always goes—why didn't they return after the warning?"

"According to Helia, their compulsion to complete the mission was too strong. She saw the danger and fought through her own madness, but couldn't convince anyone to leave with her. That was when she returned to the First Temple to warn the High Priests."

Matthai's mind raced, trying to make sense of the impossible. A lost homeworld, a mysterious creature, a doomed mission ... it was almost too fantastic to be believed.

"So what happened? Did the Temple send help?"

His father shook his head. "Unfortunately, they believed she was insane. She'd been reported missing by her home Temple, and her strange ideas had also been reported. They ... detained her."

Detained her? "What, they threw her in a holding cell?" Matthai's voice rose, disbelief and anger coloring his tone.

Soren grimaced. "Yes, but out of caution, they also sent a scout to the location she had given and ordered a thorough investigation to see if these ideas had spread throughout the Valmoran people."

"And it was fortunate they did," his mother said gravely.

"Because?"

"The High Priests realized dangerous ideas were spreading, threatening to plunge the Valmoran people into civil war during a time of fragile recovery."

Matthai's head spun, the implications whirling through his mind. The Great Threllian War, Anti-Expansionism, the threat of civil war ...

"But ... why were they so worried? It was just ideas, right?"

They shared a glance, then both shook their heads. Phina took Matthai's hand in hers. "Not just ideas, Matthai—though you should never discount how insidious ideas can be. No—the Obelisks were spreading the *compulsion* to go. A compulsion so intense that people had to be imprisoned to prevent them from trying to fulfill the Obelisk's mandate."

His shoulders felt heavy, the situation threatening to crush him. His ancestors' impossible choice was alarmingly clear: risk the destruction of their civilization through war or alien threat ... or take drastic measures.

It didn't make the deception about the lost homeworld any easier to stomach.

"So what happened to the scout ship?"

Phina shook her head. "When they found the base of operations in the Black Swirl, it was deserted. Everyone was just ... gone. The Temple scouts were too late."

He clutched the insides of his sleeves. He'd heard countless versions of the Legends, and some were horror stories. But this version was by far the most chilling.

"What do you mean, 'gone'?" he asked. "Like, they evacuated?"

His father shook his head. "No, son—the base was intact. No ships had left. The base reported life signs one second, and the next, no Valmoran life was detected." He took a deep breath, as if it physically pained him to continue.

Matthai shook his head in horrified disbelief. An entire expedition vanished without a trace? The mere thought of a monster that powerful ... it was the stuff of nightmares.

"When the scout returned, the High Priests freed Helia. They assembled the High Priests' Council for a secret emergency session. After reviewing all evidence—and after careful deliberation—they resolved that the only way to guarantee the safety of the Valmoran people and prevent civil war within the Old Empire was to destroy all traces of what happened."

Matthai shook his head vehemently, his voice rising with each word. "But that doesn't make sense—there had to be other options!"

His father scrubbed a hand across his jaw, then let out a soft groan. "You have to understand—by that point, it had become clear that ..." He again made eye contact with the High Priestess, who nodded, resignation written across her features. "... that something was wrong with the Obelisks."

Matthai felt a cold sweat creep over his skin. "What do you mean? The Obelisks are fine. I was just there, last night ..." His voice trailed off, uncertainty and dread settling in the pit of his stomach.

His mind reeled as the puzzle pieces began falling into place.

If something had been wrong with the Obelisks for generations, it could explain the extreme measures his ancestors had taken.

But the implications for their faith, their entire way of life, were staggering.

His parents exchanged a long, heavy look, the burden they carried etched into every line of their faces.

Frustration surged, fueled by Matthai's apprehension about where the conversation was headed.

"Matthai ..." His mother closed her eyes, seeming to work up the courage to continue. When she opened them, they glistened with unshed tears. "I wish I didn't have to tell you this."

His heart drummed, his chest rising and falling with his too-quick breaths. The anticipation was unbearable, the dread all-consuming.

Forcing gentleness into his tone, Mathai reached across the table to take her hand. "Mother, just tell me ... you have to, right?"

She sighed. "You were in the Museum of Valmoran History this morning. It's ... nice, the immersive experience."

Matthai furrowed his brow at the non sequitur. Why was she talking to him about the museum? "Well, sure, but I turned off the sound partway through so I could think."

"Matthai ... what if I told you there are parts of the Temple's Hix program that cannot be deactivated? Areas where we don't even tell people that a Hix overlay exists?"

His blood ran cold, heart skipping a beat. He shook his head violently.

"Do you remember when the Hix device was invented?"

"Six generations ago..." The words caught in his throat, mouth dry.

Six generations.

No, it couldn't be ... they wouldn't ... not that.

Never *that.*

His ancestors had reopened the Obelisks to the public six generations ago, after eleven generations of Exclusionism.

With great fanfare and a celebration of the new state-of-the-art Temple Hix program ...

The foundations under his feet crumbled, reality rending into disconnected pieces.

"No. That can't be. We wouldn't do that to the people." The volume of his voice rose alongside his panic. "We wouldn't do that to the *Gods.*"

She swallowed audibly, then gave a weak nod.

Denial, hot and fierce, surged through Matthai.

It was a lie—it had to be.

His family, his faith ... everything he had ever known and believed in ...

He could accept that his family had lied about Exclusionism, and maybe even that they concealed the existence of the lost homeworld.

But this? *No.*

His family would never lie to the people about something so ...

Sacred.

Holy.

Fundamental to the Valmoran way of life.

He had just been there last night. The Obelisk had spoken to him. Spoken into his mind, imparted wisdom from the Gods.

'Words, once spoken, cannot be unspoken.'

Those words had been a message to Matthai. From the Obelisk. From the Gods.

Except, no—they had been just part of an elaborate simulation. A ruse.

A hoax.

A lie.

The world began to distort. If Matthai didn't calm himself, he would jump away.

His breath came in quick, sharp gasps, chest heaving with the effort to draw air. Panic clawed at his throat, threatening to consume him.

He had to calm down, to regain control ... but how could he, when everything he had ever known was a lie?

Breathe. In through the nose—one, two, three, four.

If his suspicions were true, then the Valtrellin family no longer served the Gods—and hadn't for the last seventeen generations.

Out through the mouth—five, six, seven. Just breathe.

If they were true, then six generations ago, his family conspired to commit sacrilege.

I am here. I am now. I will not jump away.

He didn't want to believe it …

The Hix device could project images into people's minds and sounds into their thoughts.

Valmorans used it to augment reality every day. To seamlessly translate spoken and written language.

Every person who set foot on Temple grounds was required to enable the Temple Hix program.

It was so mundane that it went unnoticed—just part of the process of identifying pilgrims before they entered. It was required, so they could interact with the Temple exhibits in their native language.

And also … those security measures Talia mentioned …

Pilgrims bathed, dressed in Temple robes, scanned for unapproved technology …

For the protection of the Obelisks …

Except that was a lie, too.

They prohibited unapproved technology because *they couldn't allow anyone to discover the truth about the Obelisks.*

Matthai's stomach soured, and he swallowed, tasting bile. This couldn't be true.

He had sacrificed everything for the Temple, for his duty.

His dreams, his life, his future ...

And for what? Liyara had died fleeing from this duty.

He could be searching for Kat-a-reen right now, if not for this duty.

All to fulfill his sacred role.

To honor the Obelisks and act as a servant to the Gods.

Except that his family no longer served the Gods. He wasn't sure what they served anymore.

And yet ... if the Obelisks had truly gone wrong, if they had been compelling Valmorans to take a voyage that led to annihilation ...

Anger at the lies warred with a creeping, miserable understanding of the impossible dilemma his ancestors had faced.

Though he hated it, it made sense that they felt they had no other option.

Maybe it *had* been the only option.

His hands shook as he spoke his next words—from fear, from anger, from dread. Matthai didn't want their confirmation, but he needed it.

He closed his eyes, steeling himself. Preparing to be devastated.

Then he spoke, his voice resigned.

"We never reopened the Obelisks to the people, did we?"

His father shook his head, expression weary. "No, son—we did not."

And with those words, Matthai Valtrellin's world crumbled for the second time.

He had never imagined anything could be more heart-wrenching than losing Liyara.

But how was he supposed to reconcile a lifetime spent revering the Obelisks, of sacrifice in the name of duty, with the knowledge that the Obelisks in the Temples were mere technological idols?

As he scrutinized his parents' expectant faces, his gut lurched. They appeared unfamiliar, as if they were not who they claimed to be.

As if he'd never known them.

Was there anything he could trust at this point? There was a lost homeworld out there. The Legends were based on fact. The Obelisks were a hoax.

If his family was willing to spread false information, cover up the truth, and conspire for generations to keep the real Obelisks from the people, what else were they capable of?

"So—the Obelisks in the cathedral above are ... fakes."

His father closed his eyes and gave a sad nod.

"Please tell me that's everything," Matthai said, though he feared the answer.

"I'm afraid not, son. The depths of the secrets we bear go much, much deeper."

AFTERWORD

Thank you so much for reading Emergence. This is my debut novel, the fulfillment of a lifelong dream, and the begining of a long journey into the universe of TVC. I hope it exceeded your expectations and brought you delight.

If you loved this book, please leave a review—on Amazon, Goodreads, Bookbub. As an indie author, reviews are the lifeblood of my business, and word of mouth is gold.

If you adored this book, please share it with a friend or two (or ten ... or all your social media followers—that would work, too).

TVC is a labor of love, and I dream of it finding its way to everyone who will enjoy it. As an indie, I don't have a marketing department (it's just me, wearing all the hats), so it's impossible to compete with large publishing houses in the traditional way.

I largely rely on perseverence, groundswell, and luck. Perhaps you can be part of that luck.

Thank you for your readership, and your help in spreading the word.

Stay awesome!

ALSO BY POPPY ORION

REVELATION: THE VALMORAN CHRONICLES, VOLUME 2

Release Date: 9-17-2024

CONVERGENCE: THE VALMORAN CHRONICLES, VOLUME 3

Release Date: 11-17-2024

MAELSTROM: THE VALMORAN CHRONICLES, VOLUME 4

Release Date: 2025

EXPEDITION: THE VALMORAN CHRONICLES, VOLUME 5

Release Date: 2025

At the time of publication, each book in The Valmoran Chronicles is first published as a season on Kindle Vella, before being revised and extended for the novel format.

I know that readers are often concerned about the progress on books in their favorite series (I'm the same), and this is a way I can provide transparency as well as an opportunity for a sneak peek to those readers who are eager to learn what's next.

Find TVC news, exclusive content, and the TVC reader community here: https://www.readTVC.com

Printed in Great Britain
by Amazon

47536075R00235